DEER SEASON

FLYOVER FICTION • Series editor: Ron Hansen

Deer
Season

Erin Flanagan

University of Nebraska Press • Lincoln

© 2021 by the Board of Regents of
the University of Nebraska

All rights reserved. ♾

Library of Congress Cataloging-in-Publication Data
Names: Flanagan, Erin, author.
Title: Deer season / Erin Flanagan.
Description: Lincoln: University of Nebraska
Press, [2021] | Series: Flyover fiction
Identifiers: LCCN 2021007573
ISBN 9781496226815 (paperback)
ISBN 9781496228345 (epub)
ISBN 9781496228352 (pdf)
Subjects: LCSH: Farm life—Fiction. | People
with mental disabilities—Fiction. | Teenage
girls—Fiction. | Missing persons—Fiction.
Classification: LCC PS3606.L356 D44 2021
DDC 813/.6—dc23
LC record available at https://lccn.loc.gov/2021007573

Set in Whitman by Laura Buis.
Designed by L. Auten.

For Judy and Ken Flanagan

ACKNOWLEDGMENTS

Thanks to the Ohio Arts Council for its continued support; the Antioch Writers' Workshop for welcoming me into its community; and Wright State University for providing me with a professional home, wonderful colleagues, and the funny, brilliant students I'm honored to teach.

Thanks to the good people at the Wayne County Sheriff's Department and the Nebraska Game and Parks Commission who helped me piece together procedures in the 1980s; Michael Dunekacke for his Nebraska and hunting expertise; Chris Garland for his Nintendo knowledge; and librarians Kayla Hennis and Holly Jackson for their research assistance (and also to Holly for reading a copy of the novel and providing her sensitive insights). Any inaccuracies or mistakes are on me.

Huge thanks to the entire staff of the University of Nebraska Press for their continued support of my work, with a special shout-out to Elizabeth Gratch and to Courtney Ochsner for her counsel on this book.

Thanks to writer friends Sharon Short and Christina Consolino and to Tiffany Yates Martin at FoxPrint Editorial for your wise advise in early and late drafts; Carol Loranger, for regular writing meetups, both virtually and in person; Charlotte Hogg, my writing partner and personal Oprah for twenty years; family members and pupu winners Doug Hansen, Andrew Hansen, Alicia Warbitton, Nat Henry, and Katie

Smith; and all in the Milligan contingent, especially Gene, Lynda, and Melinda Shea. A special thanks to my folks, Judy and Ken Flanagan, and my sister, Kelly Hansen, for their accurate memories and an adventure-filled childhood on the farm (yes, even Kelly, who made me spit toothpaste into the toilet, although she swears only once).

So many thanks to Barry Milligan, the best problem solver I know.

And finally, teary-eyed thank-yous to my kids, Ellen Milligan, Neil Milligan, and Cora Dunekacke. I love you guys a crazy, stupid amount.

DEER SEASON

1

Alma held the four-week-old pig against her left hip and pinned him to her side with an elbow. With her right hand she held his ear across his eye as Clyle positioned the syringe perpendicular to the flesh and injected the antibiotics into the piglet's neck. The pig squealed and Alma's grip wobbled as Clyle caught the pig by his two back legs, swooped him into the air, and streaked his back with a green Paintstik. On the ground the pig scuttered his hooves against the cement before gaining traction and taking off across the small pen to the rest of the litter.

This wasn't how Alma wanted to spend a Saturday afternoon. This wasn't how anyone wanted to spend a Saturday afternoon, but Hal had left Friday with some yahoos to go hunting the first weekend of deer season. She secured another pig across her knee as Clyle gave the shot, marked the piglet with the Paintstik, then moved her to the floor. There were two left unmarked, congregated by the far slatted wall. Clyle grabbed the plywood panel he used to divert the pigs, moving it right to left until one of the piglets was trapped, then reached down and picked him up by the back legs.

Hard to believe Clyle did this every week—the physical labor of it, the monotony and noise—but Alma had long accepted her husband was a better and more patient human being than she was. A year ago she'd started menopause, and her doctor had told her it could go on for up to a decade, a

1

grin on his bland face as if to say, "How about that?" She didn't remember how long the change had lasted for her mother, but a year in, she and Clyle were already tested by the changes. He had told her early in their marriage that she was a woman who could ill afford a bad mood, given her natural disposition.

Clyle passed the next pig to Alma—a big one at sixteen pounds—and she got him into position, covered his eye with his ear, and rubbed the tip of his snout to calm him down. It could always be worse, she tried to remind herself. It could be not just four-week shots but castration day, a job she swore she'd never do again after they hired Hal.

Hal had worked on the farm for nearly a decade now, but this was the first time he'd gotten his deer permit, and Alma was nervous as a long-tailed cat about him going off with his buddies. Thursday, when he told Alma about the hunting invitation, unease had set in. She hadn't understood why Larry Burke and Sam Gary wanted Hal with them on the hunting trip to Valentine in the first place. She enjoyed Hal's company, sure enough, but she wasn't twenty-eight and pumped up on firearms and testosterone. Thursday night she'd called Larry's wife to get the scoop. It turned out Larry's cousin had to make an emergency trip out of town and couldn't stand the thought of his deer stand sitting empty the first weekend of the season, so he invited Larry down. "You tell them to keep it in line with Hal there," Alma said, and she'd imagined Cheryl and Larry having a good laugh about that later, about Alma Costagan calling to keep tabs on the retard. Oh, she definitely did not see the best in people. Clyle was right.

Clyle wiped his forehead. "One left," he said, as if she couldn't count. "You ready?"

"I'm standing here, aren't I?" she snapped. She had to shout over the hogs squealing, the metal-on-metal clang as the older pigs knocked up the feed bins with their snouts. When she moved from Chicago to Nebraska, Alma had thought the silence would be deafening, but that was hard to remember in a pen of squealing livestock.

She picked up the last unmarked piglet and held down his ear. Clyle stuck the tough skin and pushed the plunger home as the animal let out a bloodcurdling squeal. He marked the back, and Alma dropped the wiggling animal to the ground, where he bucked his tiny body twice before blending in with the rest of the litter. She shook out her sore arms. She'd be covered in bruises by morning.

Clyle stuck the Paintstik in the pocket of his Carhartt jacket and gathered the empty syringes. "Bet you'll be glad to get Hal back on Monday."

Alma snorted. "He's going to get an earful." The last thing she'd said before he drove away was "You call me collect every day, Hal, you hear? I don't care about the charges." She'd written down their phone number for him, knowing he didn't have it memorized, and tucked it in his hand. Yet here it was Saturday, and she hadn't heard word one. Surely there was a pay phone nearby in Valentine, so why hadn't he called?

"I'm sure he just got busy," Clyle said, as if she'd asked the question out loud. "Too much beer last night and an early morning in the stand."

Alma supposed he was right, but still, it needled her.

She took another look around the pen and counted the green lines on the pigs' backs, double-checking they'd vaccinated them all. Already these pigs were growing out of their cuteness: the jowls filling in, the nostrils in the snouts widening, the teacup cuteness of piglets fading by week four. Earlier in the week Hal had docked two tails because their littermates had tried to bit them off. The older they got, the uglier, she thought. The smarter and meaner as well.

3

Clyle bent over and scratched one of the pigs behind the ear, and the rest came running, nosing at his hand like a pack of dogs, hoping for his affection.

"Still cuter than the devil," he said, and she wondered how it was two people could see things so differently.

"Maybe," she conceded. "But just you wait."

2

The familiar scraping noise of his mother pulling the roasting pan out from the lower pantry shelf rang through the house as Milo Ahern came down the stairs. She always made roast on Sunday morning for them to eat when they got home from church, complete with cloth napkins at the dining room table. Milo hated roast and fingerling potatoes and carrot chunks, the desiccated onion skins always left in the garbage, stinking up the whole house until his father had him empty it at the end of the meal. Maybe it wasn't so much that he hated roast but hated what it meant: same recap of the sermon, his family at the table, the same damn dinner every week. What was the saying—"Familiarity breeds contempt"? His English teacher had told them last week that Aesop said that and that Mark Twain had added "and children." That seemed about right. They were reading *The Adventures of Tom Sawyer* in class. Milo was already through *The Adventures of Huckleberry Finn*, which he thought was a better book, but Mrs. Toner would have had a coronary in class trying to talk about Black people.

In the kitchen his mom was at the butcher block, wearing an apron over her blouse and skirt, Aunt Sally at the kitchen table. "Morning, sunshine," Sally said, and toasted him with a cup of coffee. "You drinking this stuff yet?"

"Not yet," he said, and she nodded.

"George started about six months ago. Puts hair on his chest. He tried to drink it black, like his father, but couldn't hack it so I add three scoops of sugar rather than cream so his dad can't tell." George was his fourteen-year-old cousin and a pain in Milo's butt. He'd had to share his room with him last night. George made him sleep on the lower trundle bed, then leaned over the edge with a trail of spit oozing from his mouth to Milo's forehead, seeing how close he could get before slurping it back up. One time he was too late and it landed in Milo's ear, and Milo dreamed all night about spiders.

Milo's aunt and uncle and cousin had driven to Gunthrum for his confirmation at the Lutheran church, his "lifelong pledge of fidelity to Christ." Milo's best friend, Scott, had whispered to him during one of the first classes, "I'm not pledging lifelong fidelity to anyone, much less a guy." They'd started after-school classes at ten years old and now, at twelve, were ready for the big show. The classes were supposed to help them lead as Christians in the community, but what it had really done was prove that it was just as easy to cheat in church as it was in school. At least that's what it proved to Scott; Milo studied on the sly, too embarrassed to admit this to his friend.

Those were his big secrets—that he liked to learn and follow the rules—which were a lot lamer than his sister's. The night before, he'd heard the slow and steady whisk of Peggy's window rising, the familiar scrape of the drainpipe. His father stood outside last summer, his feed cap pushed back, trying to figure out what had happened to the house. "Scraped clean off," he said of the paint, pulling the drain-pipe away from the wood siding. Did he think there were bears loose in Iowa now? That the deer had grown opposable thumbs? His dad had Milo out there later that weekend on a ladder painting behind the drainpipe as part of his chores. No wonder he didn't like Tom Sawyer.

Pastor Barnes had told them that today would be a lot like the baptism for infants—the dour baptismal font, the pouring of the water—only they'd be able to answer questions for themselves instead of their parents responding. Lisa Rasmussen, a girl in his class, drove with her mother and brother forty-five minutes to Sioux City, where she went to a Holy Roller church at the YMCA and they baptized people in their swimming suits at the pool. He'd dreamed last night, along with the spiders, that he'd show up at the Lutheran church, and this was the plan, but he didn't have a bathing suit. Instead, they made him do it naked, and everyone laughed at him. He didn't know why this God business needed to be so stressful.

"Milo?" Aunt Sally said again.

"Sorry, what?"

"Are you excited about today?"

Before he could answer—and what could he say? yes, as long as he didn't have to be naked?—the door opened and his father came in along with Uncle Randall and George, bringing in the fresh, crisp smell of snow. The storm had started around ten the night before, an oddity this early in November.

"Cold out there," his dad said, and leaned over to kiss his wife on the cheek, what Milo knew was a show. His parents were more affectionate when his aunt and uncle were in town. When he was little, Peggy had told him that Randall and their mom used to be an item. For a long time this had confused him—how two relatives could date—but the logistics of it had finally added up when he was eight and understood the family tree. His parents hadn't kissed for eons other than the obligatory peck after his father woke up in his recliner during *Cagney and Lacey* and before he went to bed. His dad liked the blonde woman on the show who wore soft, fluffy sweaters in pastel colors.

"Randall didn't think to bring a jacket to feed the hogs," his dad continued. "Had to wear an old windbreaker." His mom had a separate washing machine for the clothes they wore in the pens, an old washer she had replaced last year with a new Whirlpool. Joe poured himself a cup of coffee and took a sip, then poured a second cup and handed it to his brother.

"You could have given him your coat," Milo's mom said as she cranked a pepper grinder over the meat in the roasting pan.

"Wasn't that bad," Randall said, but his hands were stiff, the skin reddened with white creases at the knuckles. Uncle Randall loosened his grip on the warm coffee cup.

"There was a dead pig," George interjected, distending his belly. "Bloated with veins on its guts."

"Oh, for the love of Pete," Aunt Sally said.

"It was awesome," George continued. "I got to pick it up by the foot and haul it to the tree where they come and pick up the dead animals."

"Wash your hands," Sally said, but George just stood there. If Milo didn't do what his mother said—well, he didn't even know what would happen. Peggy was the one who rebelled, not him, as evidenced by the fact he was downstairs with his hair wet from a shower and an uncomfortable oxford tucked into his corduroys and she hadn't even made it out of bed.

Sally handed George a cup of his sugared coffee, then took the coffeepot and refilled Randall and Joe's cups. "You boys better get ready. We don't want to be late for Milo's big day."

They had three bathrooms in the house—the one he and Peggy used, the one off his parents' room, and the one in the basement where his dad showered after chores—but you could only use one shower at a time because of the water pressure.

8

His dad said he'd take the one in the basement and George could go upstairs, and Randall could take the one off his room. "Be sure not to track anything on the carpet, Ran," his father said. "I know you're not used to getting your boots muddy." He said this even though Randall had left his boots on the porch, a size-too-big pair he'd borrowed from his brother.

"You've always got to make a crack, don't you, Joe?" Randall said.

Joe laughed. "It's what big brothers are for."

His mom stood at the butcher block peeling carrots, then dicing them into chunks. "Milo," she said. "Why don't you go upstairs and see if Peggy's up yet."

"She's not."

She pointed the peeler at him. "Then get her up." So much for his special day. Wasn't it enough he was entering into a contract with Christ? Now he had to get his sister up too?

"And you," Aunt Sally said pointing to George. "You stink."

Milo followed George up the stairs, where George went into his room, already lifting his shirt over his head, his back thickening now that he was fourteen and a good three inches taller than he'd been a year ago. Milo still had the chest he had when he was a nine-year-old, just with longer, more gangly arms. Milo was going to knock on Peggy's door but then thought better of it and just barged in, hoping he'd startle her and piss her off.

He opened his mouth to shout "Get up!" but the bed was empty—sloppy-made like it was most days, a corner of the sheet hanging down eight inches below the rumpled quilt, the pillow mashed into the headboard. "Peg?" He waited for her to answer then went to check the bathroom. George came out of Milo's room with his Dopp kit, a shiny gold zipper running down the middle of the black leather.

"You seen Peggy?" Milo asked.

George shook his head as he fumbled for his razor, making a big show of it. "Why?"

"Never mind." Milo didn't want to envy that Dopp kit, but he did. He liked things to be organized and methodical, and he liked the idea that he would have somewhere to go, like a hotel with room service or summer music camp. Milo thought about the window scraping open the night before, the telltale sound of Peggy's shimmy down the drainpipe. She must have snuck out, probably to meet Laura, and there was enough snow after she went that no tracks would be left. It was a bold move with visiting family in the house. Aunt Sally and Uncle Randall were on a hide-a-bed in the living room right next to the pipe, and everyone knew Uncle Randall didn't sleep well on it because of his back. Milo thought of her coming home sheepishly later in the day, maybe blisters on her feet from some kind of stupid girl shoe. He'd be the golden boy, recently confirmed and beginning his life as a pious servant. Milo didn't want to be a gleeful jerk about this, but man, was she going to be in a world of trouble.

He headed back down the stairs and found his mom in the kitchen. "Can I talk to you for a second?" He had the sense this wasn't something he should say in front of Aunt Sally, who was still at the table, flipping through an issue of *Good Housekeeping* with a pair of scissors in her hand.

"What is it, Milo? I'm busy." His mother held up her wet hands, a potato in one and a knife in the other.

"Um. I need to tell you something."

"Can't you tell me here?"

"It's Peggy. She's not there."

Aunt Sally looked up, and his mother paused. "What do you mean she's not there?"

"I mean, she's not in her room. I don't think she slept in her bed."

Aunt Sally shook her head and turned the page. "They always say girls are easier in the beginning but harder later on." She pointed at the magazine. "Read it right here a few issues ago."

His mom bonked herself lightly on the head with the back of her hand holding the potato. "Silly me. I must have forgotten she was staying over with Laura last night. Those two hardly spend a night apart." She set the potato down and wiped her hands on her apron. "I'll give her mother a call." There was a phone on the kitchen wall, but she turned down the hallway toward their bedroom.

He supposed that could be it. She'd just fallen asleep at Laura's instead of coming home, but more likely, Peggy had planned it knowing their mom wouldn't make a stink with relatives in the house. Both he and his sister seemed to be insomniacs, a condition Milo had read about at the library in the *A–Z Health Guide* from the Mayo Clinic. Peggy begged to stay up and watch Letterman on weeknights, and most weekends she could be found prowling the house until at least two in the morning or standing in front of the glow of the fridge, her slack hand on the door as she bent at the waist to peer in. "What're you looking for?" Milo had said to her one night from behind, and Peggy about jumped out of her skin, then swatted at his head and called him a little creep for startling her.

Sometimes during those nights, when neither of them could sleep, they'd play Uno or gin rummy. Somewhere between slapping down the Wild Draw 4 and claiming victory, he and Peggy would talk like actual people. For a twelve-year-old nerd and a volleyball-playing cheerleader, they had more in common than others might expect, and a lot of their time was spent talking about the days they'd leave for college, their Podunk years in Gunthrum behind them. He stopped on his way up the stairs, a hand gripping the railing.

She hadn't left, had she? Left him behind?

It had probably been two weeks since they'd had a real conversation, Peggy sneaking back into the house after one o'clock on a Tuesday, clothes rumpled and whiskey breath. She'd poked her head into Milo's room and asked if he was still awake. "What else would I be when you make that much noise sneaking into the house?"

She'd sat on the corner of his bed—weird!—and asked how school was going.

"What are you even talking about?" he'd asked. School questions at one in the morning? She was drunk for sure. There was a red-and-purple mark on her neck just above the collarbone. "Is that a hickey?"

She giggled and put a hand over her mouth. "Maybe."

"Real sexy, Pegs. Way to burst some topical blood vessels in the name of love."

"I never said it was love," she'd said, and tickled a hand toward his feet. "But I never said it wasn't," she continued in a singsongy voice.

Milo grabbed his loafers from his closet, sat on the bed, and slipped them on. Over hands of Uno they talked about how she'd go to UNL and join a sorority and meet a fraternity brother who planned to move to a real city, one with malls and a seafood restaurant and cultural stuff like a museum with art she didn't understand. Milo wanted to head straight to a coast and a top liberal arts college, where he'd learn a foreign language and try to pull off a monocle. She told him he'd look like Charlie McCarthy, but her idea of fashion was neon feather earrings, so what did she know. Both agreed they didn't want to end up anything like their parents, although

Peggy thought some of the younger parents were cool. "Not cool-cool," she'd said. "Just like. Adult. That's what I want," she'd said. "To be an adult."

She swore as soon as she got settled in Lincoln she'd have him come visit for the weekend. Take him to the campus bookstore and let him get a bottomless bucket of popcorn at the movies. She said she'd take him to a frat party even though he knew he'd spend all of it hiding in a bathroom. Milo shook his head. No, she wouldn't have left him behind.

His mother clicked her heels up the stairs to check Peggy's room, then downstairs to the basement, where his father was showering. Milo hurried after her, an old hand at eaves-dropping. Peggy had her friends over most weekends, and they'd talk about the most ridiculous stuff, but no matter how dumb it was, Milo didn't want to miss a word. That crap about a glass against the door and one end against your ear? It didn't work at all, but a cracked door could elicit all kinds of information.

His parents' voices were whispers now, but Milo strained until they separated, like individual notes in a song. "Last I knew she went to bed," his mother said.

"And what time was that?"

"Nine thirty? Ten?" Milo rolled his eyes. Peggy never went to bed for real before midnight. "I assumed she just wanted to get away from George." Her voice went lower, and Milo couldn't make it out.

"Well, we've got to go," his father said in response. "Milo's got his goddamn confirmation."

A moment later his mother's heels crossed the cement floor, and Milo scrambled up to his room to grab his tie. George was standing in the bathroom with a towel wrapped around his waist, his beefy chest naked. The beginning lump of a bicep flexed as he shaved through the inch-thick foam on his cheeks and neck, a wet washcloth left haphazardly on the gold, tree-shaped jewelry hanger that sat on the corner of the counter. Peggy's bracelets and necklaces dangled from the branches, and in between the leaves were sets of earrings, the backs hidden behind. The silver charm bracelet with a football, helmet, and cleat hung on the top branch, the bracelet she always wore for cheerleading.

"What're you looking at?" George asked, a smirk still visible under the foam.

"Not much." Milo looked pointedly at his cousin's flabby trunk then scurried into his room before George could retaliate.

Twenty minutes later the two families loaded into their respective vehicles, stomped their snowy shoes against the car doors' edges, and steered their cars toward town—Milo in his mom's LeSabre, with his dad behind the wheel, and Uncle Randall and his brood in their new Cadillac. When they'd driven up last night in the shiny white car, his father had come out with a beer in his hand and said, "How the hell you afford that?" before he'd even said hello.

At the end of the lane Milo saw the tiny dead pig, probably no more than eight weeks old, its mouth stiff with rigor mortis. In the other car George pointing enthusiastically at the corpse.

On the way into Gunthrum his father steered with his wrist as he normally did, his pointer finger rising in a one-finger wave as they passed the sparse oncoming traffic of Highway 57. "Where'd he get that damn much money?" he asked, turning toward Milo's mom. "Man's barely ever had a pot to piss in."

"Well, now he's got a Cadillac," Milo's mom said matter-of-factly. Did she mean he could piss in his Cadillac?

In the church lobby Pastor Barnes asked about Peggy, and Milo's mother lied, saying she was home with a headache. Aunt Sally and Uncle Joe were already seated in the pew. "Another one?" Pastor Barnes said, shaking his head. "Poor girl."

But Milo knew what her "headaches" really were: hangovers. Peggy was a good liar, or maybe their parents were just dumb, but they believed her every time. One more of these mysterious headaches and she'd have a medical team flying her to Clarkson Hospital in Omaha. Though this wasn't a lie on Peggy's part, he had to remind himself; it was a lie on his parents', which was much more interesting.

Milo took his spot between his mom and George, Scott Ross three pews ahead of them. Scott kept turning around and moving his ears up and down, a stupid trick Milo had tried in the mirror a hundred times, but no matter how hard he concentrated, he couldn't will it to happen. He grinned at his friend, and Scott stuck out his tongue, slowly, slowly, until it was aimed at the ear next to him, a woman with no sense of humor in a green-and-navy plaid jumper. She reached up and snatched Scott's tongue in her fist, and he gagged, surprised, catching the attention of his mother to his right. Milo snorted with a hand over his mouth, trying not to laugh out loud, and his own mother shot him a withering look. *This is not the morning to misbehave*, that look said. This was not the morning to draw attention to the Ahern clan.

The woman let go of Scott's tongue, and he snuck one more look over his shoulder at Milo to say *Can you freaking believe that?* but Milo was facing front now and could only see his friend in the periphery. When his mother glanced at him a second time, he kept his eyes locked on Pastor Barnes, who was talking about something boring. Milo's mother patted his hand and then kept her own hand over his. Maybe I should be embarrassed by this, Milo thought, but he was too busy concentrating on the fact that he was winning, the favorite child for once in his life.

Pastor Barnes paused in his long-winded way, the silence bringing back the attention of those who had drifted. "And now," he said, "our catechism class of 1985, please rise." Milo and Scott stood up in tandem, along with a smattering of other twelve-year-olds across the church. "Please join me at the front," Pastor Barnes said, and Milo shimmied out against the knees of his parents, aunt, uncle, and George, almost missing the burning pinch Peggy would have delivered on the tender underside of his arm.

Pastor Barnes ladled the water over Milo's head, and a trickle rolled toward his mouth. Milo instinctually pressed his lips together. Did that screw up the baptism? Maybe he'd just rejected Jesus? It was hard to tell, but whether he had or not, it felt like a ruse. He looked at his hands, embarrassed to think he was expecting stigmata, but other than nails chewed to the quick, they were hands just like anyone else's.

Twenty minutes later the congregation filed into the foyer. His father slapped Milo's back, and his mother kissed his cheek; then there was a lot of their nervous parent whispering back and forth, deciding if they could skip the coffee and cake altogether or if that would draw more attention. Milo thought he'd feel different after the baptism, purer, maybe even lighter, but other than a damp spot on the back of the head, he felt exactly the same. Peggy, even in absentia, concerned them more.

"We can't just sneak out, Joe," his mother whispered, and eventually Tonya Gary came over and hugged Milo congratulations, then told his mother she'd made a new recipe, a blueberry coffeecake with a lemon glaze that his mother "absolutely had to try." Mrs. Gary was one of his parents' friends, even though she was much younger, a phenomenon in small towns. People grouped by interests, not age—mainly those who liked to drink and those who didn't. While his mother wasn't a big drinker, his father was, and most Friday and Saturday nights found his parents in someone's basement with the kids sacked in front of the TV in the den. Because Aunt Sally and Uncle Lou were in town, they'd forgone the usual party the night before, although his dad and uncle still went to the OK for rounds of drinks.

"I'm just going to get a bite," his mother said, and Joe warned, "Not long," but his mother was already halfway to the kitchen.

Milo made his way to Laura, Peggy's friend, who was eating at least her second doughnut.

"Why'd your mom really call me?" Laura asked, her mouth full of cake. When she had asked Mrs. Ahern after the service, his mother had said something about looking for Peggy's church shoes.

"Peggy didn't come home."

Laura's eyes widened, a crumb of doughnut at the corner of her mouth. "Like, at all?"

"I don't think so."

"Holy shit," she whispered. An old woman—like, old-old— stared at them with ghostly eyes.

"Was she with you last night?" he asked, and Laura gave him a look like, *What kind of idiot do you think I am?* "I'm not going to tell anyone," he said. "I'm just asking. Trust me, if I wanted to spill dirt on you two, I'd have plenty already."

"She was for a while. At Castle Farm." It was what everyone called the abandoned farm north of town because of how run-down the farmhouse was. "The name's ironic," Peggy had told

17

Milo once, as if anyone needed to explain irony to him. He was working his way through a book on literary terms that the librarian had special-ordered from Wayne State. She'd thunked it on her desk and scooted it across. "Okay, smarty-pants. Quiz in a week," but she'd winked when she said it and didn't make him sign an oath in blood like she normally did when students got books from the college.

"You think she's all right?" For the first time he felt a tickle of dread. He'd been giddy earlier at the trouble she'd find herself in and then angry thinking maybe she had left without him, but now?

"Trust me," Laura said, sneaking a doughnut hole from his plate. "That girl can take care of herself." Milo supposed it was true. His sister had evaded a shoplifting charge at Ben Franklin when she scooped a pack of Lip Smackers, and once she'd come home drunk and eaten chips with their father without him figuring it out. Milo had been in the car with her one time when she had blown through a stop sign and then sweet-talked her way out a ticket. The cop knew their dad, but still.

When Milo thought about it—really thought about it—what kind of trouble had Peggy gotten into?

"Besides," Laura continued, "she's probably home by now. I bet she crept into her room and is going to manage to convince your mom she was there all along. She's so skinny your mom just didn't see her tucked under the covers."

"What time did you last see her Saturday night?" Milo hoped he sounded like Captain Furillo on *Hill Street Blues*, or even better, Mick Belker; he wished he had a notebook he could write her answer in.

"Last night?" Laura tapped a hot chocolate stirrer against her bottom lip. This was why she was Milo's favorite of Peggy's friends: she'd stand and talk to a twelve-year-old in a public place. "I guess a little before midnight? I ended up leaving with Kerry, who's in the doghouse with my folks for keeping me out too late last weekend. When I left, Peggy was feeling no pain."

Kerry and Peggy had been an item the year before, but like with most guys, Peggy had moved on. Milo knew from his eavesdropping that there had been extensive conversations about Laura's inevitable interest in Kerry (he was Gunthrum's quarterback and starting center, with hair like Tom Wopat), but Peggy had assured Laura she had her blessing. In a class of twenty-three there were bound to be some repeats on the spit swapping.

"Did she have a ride home?"

Laura blew a burst of air into her bangs and knocked into his shoulder with hers. "She said it was fine. At least two of the football players weren't blotto because they had weights in the morning, so there were people to drive her." She squinted at Milo. "Do you think it's bad I left her?"

"No, it's bad she never came home, but that's on her."

Laura laughed. "Knowing Peggy, that just means she's got a great story to tell."

Across the room his mother held up her hand, the fingers spread wide: five minutes until it was time to go. "I should go get our coats," Milo said as George sauntered up, leering at Laura with his chest puffed out.

"In your dreams," Laura said, and George deflated. She stopped Milo with a hand on his arm. "Have her call me, will you?"

"Yeah, as soon as she's done getting chewed out." There'd be no need for subtle eavesdropping the way his dad screamed.

In the entryway Milo found his father's black coat that he wore only on Sundays. It was heavy wool and nearly indistinguishable from every other dad's except it shared a hook with

Milo's own babyish car coat, the same one he'd had since fifth grade, now an inch too short at the wrists. Normally when his mother gave the five-minute warning, Milo knew he had at least fifteen minutes to try to sneak some extra doughnuts and cranberry juice, and he'd still be tucked in the back of the Buick with a book for a good long while before his parents finally extricated themselves from the crowd. He put on his coat and carried his dad's to the communal room, his mother already wearing hers with her purse over her shoulder.

"Come on," she said to Milo, and then for the benefit of the woman next to her, "We'd better get home and see how Peggy's doing."

"Poor dear," the woman said, and his mother smiled.

They met up with Aunt Sally and Uncle Randall, who were talking to Pastor Barnes, a man who had been in Randall's grade from kindergarten through senior year. It was weird to think that Pastor Barnes—the man who taught him the apostles but had also tried to have a very embarrassing talk with the boys in the class about the birds and the bees in a respectable Christian marriage—had gone to high school like anyone else. It was weird to think his father had, too, and that Uncle Randall, four years younger than his brother, had once lived in this town on their very farm. Pastor Barnes clapped Randall on the back and said it was good to see him.

"Always good to see you, Harry," Randall said. Milo couldn't believe someone would call the pastor by his first name. Even his folks, older but used to the pastor's role in the town, called him Pastor Barnes.

Outside, the snow was thick and wet. Aunt Sally and his mother ran in their heels in short pecks to their respective passenger seats, his mother holding the church service program over her head against the snow, the ink of Milo's name running on the backside along with those of all the other

Lutheran kids from his class. They'd framed Peggy's communion program; it hung in the hallway.

Milo could imagine arriving home, his father parking the Buick in his mother's side of the garage, Randall a mile or two behind because he was no longer used to country roads. The three of them would slam shut their doors, the cranking sound of the garage door rolling down louder from the cold. They'd get to the front door and open it, most likely with Milo in the lead, and the assaulting smell of the roast in the oven would hit them, almost done by now. It would be a smell that at first would make his mouth water with anticipation until he remembered how little he liked it anymore, how sick he was of that dried-out beef.

"Peggy?" their mother would yell up the stairs, and there, in the church parking lot, it made Milo's breath catch in his throat, the anticipation of whether she'd answer.

3

Clyle glanced at his watch as Hal's truck bumped down the snowy ruts of the lane. It was almost eight thirty. Clyle could count on both hands the number of times Hal had arrived past eight in the morning, usually at the farm by a quarter to, hoping if he made it before Alma got home from her school bus route and onto the next thing on the to-do list, he could talk her into some ham and eggs. Usually he could.

"Run into some trouble this morning?" Clyle asked, as Hal jumped from the driver's seat.

"Sorry. Forgot to set my clock." Hal had the look Clyle had come to expect most Monday mornings—puffy eyes, ashen skin—the result of a two- or three-night bender. Clyle was sure it was worse after two days in a deer stand with Larry and Sam. He would have drunk his share too.

"How was the hunting trip?"

Hal's face widened into a smug smile, but he didn't meet Clyle's eyes. "I got a deer. A doe, but she was a big one."

Clyle tried to hide his surprise. He'd been teaching Hal to shoot for about nine months now but hadn't figured when it came down to it that he'd have the wherewithal to really fire the gun and hit anything. "Good for you."

"Really big. Almost a buck." Hal reached back toward his truck and grabbed his slippers from the cab so he could set them next to Clyle's on the kitchen rug.

Alma's Ford Vega turned from the gravel road down the lane, bouncing where Hal's truck had been moments before. She turned off the car, then climbed out and pointed a gloved finger at Hal. "I've got a bone to pick with you."

He raised a hand to his chest. "Me?"

"Yeah, you. I told you to call me from the cabin and let me know you got there okay, and I didn't hear a peep. Not word one."

Hal raised his chin and gave Alma a defiant look. "I don't have to check in with you. I'm not a child."

"No, you're not," she agreed. "You're an adult. And as an adult, you have certain responsibilities to keep your word to people. Do you understand, Hal?" She was using what Clyle referred to as her bus driver voice, the one she used to shush kids and keep them in line, no-nonsense enough she could get a senior boy to take his seat. She tried it on him every now and again—why haven't you taken this garbage out yet, Clyle Costagan? You think I'm your maid?—and while he never liked it, by God he did what she asked.

"Let's get inside and have some breakfast," Clyle said.

Alma nodded once. "Okay, then. But only because I'm hungry." She turned to Hal. "Scrambled or fried?"

"I'm *not* hungry."

"Oh, don't be ornery. I've just delivered a bus full of whiners complaining the snowstorm came on a weekend and didn't cancel any school. I don't need to hear it from you as well, Hal Bullard." Hal pursed his lips. "All righty then," she said and went in the house, letting the screen door slam behind her.

Inside, Clyle put two pieces of toast in the toaster and got the butter and peanut butter out from the cupboard. He poured himself and Hal cups of coffee, Hal's with plenty of cream and sugar. They sat in their respective seats, and Clyle flipped on the AM radio for the morning hog reports. "So, tell me about this trip," Clyle said. "You have fun?" He knew Alma had been worried about it all weekend even if she didn't say so. He could tell by the irritated way she kept pulling out the errors in her crochet and talking about how Remington Steele should just keep it in his pants and give that poor Laura Holt a break. This was Alma at her most communicative.

"No one could believe it, that I got such a big doe, but I did." Hal held his hands in the position of a rifle and squinted an eye.

"'Course you did," Clyle said, but he had his doubts. "Say, didn't you have a buck-only permit?"

"No," Hal said defensively. "It was for all deer," and with that, tears flooded Hal's eyes. It was something Clyle still wasn't used to after the near decade Hal had worked for him: how quickly he teared up. Glancing at Hal, you wouldn't know anything was wrong with him. He'd been in a swimming accident when he was two years old—that's why he didn't look like the other slow kids. Oxygen deprivation. He was handsome by most people's standards. Just over six feet tall, broad shoulders, tan and rugged skin, a head full of mahogany hair. Not stopping any traffic in Hollywood, but for this neck of the woods, a man who caught a lot of women's eyes. Until they talked to him for a spell.

Clyle had seen it more than once. They'd be running an errand a town or two over, and they'd stop at a little diner for lunch or the post office to mail a package for Alma. A woman behind the counter would get to jawing with Hal, her bosom pointed forward or maybe a playful hand on his arm, and then Hal would say something that didn't quite compute. Maybe he'd be too enthusiastic talking about a program on TV or laugh at something she said, but more like a little brother laughs, with a big guffaw, his upper gums exposed as he tried not to get caught sneaking a peak at the woman's breasts. There'd be a shift in her stance, a quick succession of blinks as she backed up, realizing something wasn't quite how it seemed.

In these moments Clyle always felt helpless, but fact was, Hal was interested in these women. In conversations Clyle forced himself to have, he and Hal had talked about what happened to his body when he saw a pretty girl or what it might be like to go on a date, and God help him, Clyle told Hal what he could do to relieve some of the physical pressure, preferably in the shower so he wouldn't mess the sheets. It was like raising a twelve-year-old boy day in, day out, one who never grew up, but with a man's needs.

"I must have been mistaken," Clyle said, but he knew he wasn't. Hal had only been authorized to shoot bucks and he knew it, but he wasn't sure what the point was of pushing it now. Dead was dead. Clyle buttered a piece of toast and followed it with a gob of peanut butter, then set it on a paper towel in front of Hal and repeated the process for himself, Hal sniffing across the table. "You want to tell me about it?" He assumed Hal was upset he'd shot the wrong deer and probably got an earful about it at the check station and a healthy fine to boot. Already he'd be in a world of fines for hunting out of his unit.

"They didn't think I could do it," Hal said, his voice barely a whisper.

Alma came back from the bathroom, grabbed a carton of eggs from the fridge, and clattered a pan on the stove. "Who didn't think you could do what, Hal?"

"Larry and Sam. They didn't think I could shoot a deer. They thought they'd get to shoot my limit too."

It angered Clyle that those boys had used Hal like that, although it did answer the question of why they'd invited him. They weren't boys who did a thing just for the goodness of doing it. A few years ago Hal had called him from the OK Corral, his words slurred with drink, telling him his friends had abandoned him there.

Clyle had gone to pick Hal up at one in the morning, Hal sitting on the curb as Clyle drove up, his head bent between his knees with a line of drool to the splattered mess at his feet and a black eye. It was his fifth-year high school reunion. What a ridiculous time to even have a reunion when no one had changed a whit since high school, as proved by that night. People had bought Hal shots and gotten him good and sick like a carnival sideshow, then left him without a ride. Clyle found out later they'd made a game of getting Hal to try and kiss a girl too, one of the cheerleaders now married with a psychology degree, and she'd run around the bar shrieking. Everyone had laughed at Hal as he trailed behind, his arms out like Frankenstein's monster. When her husband showed up after the street dance, he'd taken a swing at Hal, who clocked him good back, and when Peck Randolph arrived, no one said a word in Hal's defense.

That reunion certainly wasn't the first time Hal had gotten drunk or the last. He liked the sweet drinks— Southern Comfort or vodka with orange juice—not beer or straight whiskey, and he drank it like a child in greedy gulps, certain someone would find out how good it was and take it away.

Hal had slept on their couch that night, and then the next morning his body capitulated as he stood up, a hand over his mouth as he ran toward the bathroom, only making it halfway. Alma had given him hell but then cleaned up after him on her hands and knees. About once a month Hal would stay overnight, either drunk after the bar or too many drinks here with Clyle or even just tired after staying for dinner and a made-for-TV movie. At some point they'd started referring to the guest room upstairs as Hal's room, as if he'd grown up in the house all along. Clyle and Alma had agreed the hunting trip wasn't a good idea, but fact was, Hal was a grown man, and he couldn't spend all his time with two old birds like them. He needed some friends because Hal, like any twenty-eight-year-old, liked to blow off some steam.

Alma cracked eggs in the pan.

"I left them there," Hal said.

Alma turned around, wiping her hands on the towel tucked into the waist of her jeans. "Left who where?"

"Larry and Sam."

"In Valentine?" Clyle asked.

Hal nodded, and Clyle smiled behind his mug. "I bet they were none too happy about that."

"I bet not!" Hal agreed. "But Saturday I get up, and they're gone. No note, nothing. They came back for lunch, and we ate those ham sandwiches you packed"—he nodded at Alma, a shaky smile on his face—"thank you, and they told me I couldn't come. It wasn't safe. They'd already been out and got a deer each and said they were thick as ticks." His eyes glistened. "I just left them there when they said I couldn't go back out that night and came home."

"You got home Saturday night?" Alma asked, as Clyle said, "So, when'd you get the doe then, Hal?"

"There was a deer just a little ways from the cabin. So I raised my gun and shot her." He held a hand to his heart. "Right here."

"Right outside the cabin?" Clyle asked. That didn't make much sense. Deer weren't as smart as pigs, but they were no dummies and learned fast. It would be odd for a deer to be that close to a cabin during hunting season, even if the deer were plentiful.

"Not *right* there. A little ways from the cabin, I guess. Not close enough to the cabin anyone's going to see blood."

Clyle glanced at Alma and back. "They wouldn't see blood?" That didn't make much sense either.

"No, there wasn't any blood right by the *cabin*."

"So, you shot it a ways from the cabin?"

"I guess so. Yes"

"You get a fine at the check station for the doe not matching your permit?"

Hal shifted his eyes. "The station was closed."

Clyle glanced at Alma, then back at Hal. He'd been afraid this was going to happen. Hal had sworn up and down that Larry had a limited permit to hunt his cousin's land and that it was all on the up and up, but that station was no more closed than on the moon. Hal's limit must have been a backup plan in case they couldn't get past the check; they'd let him take the fall for anything that didn't match the permits.

Clyle let out a tired breath. "You can't just hunt illegally, Hal. I didn't teach you to shoot so you could break the rules."

"I didn't break the rules! I shot that doe fair and square and put it in the back of my pickup. Then when I got it home, I tried to finish it myself, but it was a big mess, so I left it and went to the OK instead."

Understanding dawned on Clyle: he'd tried to dress the deer. "Where'd you do this, Hal?" Clyle asked, as he calmly folded the corners on his napkin.

"In my kitchen. I figured if I was going to eat it that would make the most sense."

Clyle put a finger on the pulse near his eye, imagining the mess. There'd be blood everywhere. Even now, in early winter, with two days of snow, the kitchen would have begun to smell.

"Where's the carcass now?"

Hal looked at Clyle beseechingly. "You told me not to waste any meat, that the deer would give its life so I could eat, but I didn't eat one bite of it. Not one."

Clyle would deal with the permit issue later. He had a friend at Nebraska Game he could call to straighten things out, even though it would likely cost a few hundred dollars and get Hal a misdemeanor. "We should head back to your place. See about cleaning up your kitchen."

"I already cleaned," Hal answered, but Clyle knew what that would look like. Hal did very well with routine and jobs he understood—washing his dishes after dinner at night, making his bed, tucking in his shirts—but if it was something new, Clyle had to walk him through in painstaking detail. He remembered almost a year ago when he'd first started teaching Hal about guns, how slowly, methodically, Hal would load the muzzle. And if something didn't go as planned or if Hal was emotional, all bets were off. Clyle had witnessed it too many times—Hal unhinged by a change in plan or from coming face-to-face with his own limitations.

Alma scooped up three plates of eggs and set two on the table, then pulled a gallon of bleach from under the sink. "Here," she said. "I'd go myself, but I've got to get the bus serviced before the afternoon route, and I have errands in town."

"I can do it myself," Hal said, already scooping the eggs in his mouth, the ones he insisted he didn't want to eat.

"I'll help you get the house cleaned up," Clyle said.

"What about vaccines? Don't we got those today?"

"They'll have to wait."

"But we—" Hal started, but Clyle held up his hand. "Fine." Hal took the napkin from his lap and wiped his mouth.

After they put their dishes in the sink, Clyle and Alma followed Hal out to his truck, parked over by the wire silo.

When Clyle had first driven Alma down the lane fourteen years ago, she'd asked if that was where they kept the animals. Clyle peered in Hal's truck bed; there was a smeary drag of blood six inches wide that went from the cab through the bed and trailed up the hatch. Clyle felt a trickle of apprehension, remembering the last time he'd seen a smear of blood in a truck, this one in his own cab after Hal had put a boy in the hospital in high school.

"Good Lord," Alma said, handing the bleach to Clyle. "Have fun, boys. I'm heading to town."

She walked back toward the house, and Clyle pointed to the truck bed. "You've got to wash that out, son."

"I know." Hal said defensively. "I was going to, I was."

Clyle sighed. Sometimes he wondered how Hal managed on his own. What must he have thought dragging that deer in the front door, through the foyer, and into the kitchen, all of it luckily covered in linoleum? Hal had a small acreage a few miles north of the Costagans' farm, rent $125 a month and Clyle's signature cosigned on the lease. Hal had grown up in apartment after apartment with his mother, and now behind his house he had two sheep he'd named Peanut Butter and Jelly that Alma and Clyle had gotten him earlier that summer for his twenty-eighth birthday. Clyle and Hal had built a small three-quarter shed for them. It'd been about the time he had that crush on Peggy Ahern and learned she loved lambs.

Dragging in that carcass yesterday must have felt like quite an accomplishment until he'd stood in front of it with a knife in his hand and no idea where to start. Would he have known to slice at the sternum, starting at the heart, or would he have hacked away at the head? The very thought of it made Clyle weary. He loved Hal, he did, but if it had been up to him, they'd have hired a regular high school boy for the weekends and called it good.

He placed the bleach gallon in the back of Hal's truck as Hal climbed in the driver's side of the old Dodge. This was Clyle's favorite time of year—sunny and cold with snow on the ground—and he took a moment to appreciate it. Looking back in the weeks to come, he'd remember that moment and how simple it had seemed, even with the headache of the carcass to clean, the chores stacking up for the day, the call he'd have to make about the illegal harvest. Clyle gave the passenger door a good yank, and it screeched open with a grinding metal sound. The door was bent in on its frame.

"Hal?" he said, walking to the truck's front. The red paint had scuffed off around a significant dent, and the right headlight was shattered. "What happened?"

"It's nothing," Hal said.

"You get in an accident?"

Hal glanced at the sky, a cool and piercing blue. "I don't know."

"What did you hit?"

"Nothing."

"Hal, is that—"

"What?"

Clyle looked closer at the scrape. The front of the truck had been washed recently, maybe even that morning, the paint glistening unevenly at the dent. "Did you wash your grill? Is that why you're late?"

"I just—" Hal stopped.

"You hit your garage again? Is that it?"

"I guess. Saturday night after the OK."

Clyle and Alma had been encouraging Hal for years to leave that bar alone, but he loved it—shots of Southern Comfort for a dollar and a popcorn machine where you could eat for free. They even let him run a tab every month and pay it after Clyle paid him so he didn't need to worry about remembering the bill. Clyle wasn't happy to know Hal was at the bar again or happy to know Hal had been driving drunk again. Hal's rental house had one of those narrow one-stall garages from the 1920s. It was big enough for a small car like Alma's Vega but barely fit Hal's Dodge, especially when Hal had a belly full of liquor. He'd hit it probably a dozen times already but had never fessed up so easily. Lying was the rote course for Hal, part of his compromised mind.

"All right," Clyle conceded with some hesitation. "But you've got to be more careful. Park in the drive if you've been drinking."

"Okay."

"All right." Clyle climbed into the cab and gave the door a mighty yank, locking it just in case.

At the house, as expected, a ghastly pink stain marred the floor. Clyle put his hands on his hips. "Where is it?"

"What?"

"The deer."

Hal bit his lower lip. "I took it to the dump." He meant the hole of garbage on his landlord's farm across the road. Clyle would be getting a call from Mick Langdon later that day; he was surprised he hadn't already. That man was nosy as they came and hardly seemed to sleep. He'd bet Hal did it when Mick was at church, the only time the man didn't seem to have one eye cocked on his gravel road, an average of two cars tooling by per hour. If that man lived in town, he'd have a nervous breakdown.

"How'd you get it there?"

"Wheelbarrow."

Clyle sighed. "Got to clean that too."

"I already did."

"I'm sure you did, Hal," Clyle said and held up the bottle of bleach. "But we've got to do it again."

Already the day was barreling down: snow removal, vaccines, three more hogs sequestered with the scours since last night, and who knew how many more there'd be by now. Maybe a quick bleach rinse in the kitchen would be okay, and who really cleaned out a wheelbarrow anyway? His father had told Clyle when he was a child that farming was the best and worst job in the world. "You're never done," he'd said. "Just depends on how you see that."

"Here," Clyle said and handed Hal the bleach. "Start running a bucket. We've got lots to do."

4

Alma turned into the parking lot behind Gunthrum Foods. It was the one thing she loved about small towns—you never parked more than thirty feet away from the front door you wanted. Inside, she grabbed a cart from the corral by the manager's desk and started toward the produce aisle—two slim shelves with only the most common vegetables: tomatoes (woeful this time of year), carrots, onions, potatoes, maybe radishes. In Chicago she'd been able to get leeks and turnips. One time back in Chicago she'd made tempura for a dinner party, but if she wanted anything like that now, it meant an hour drive to Sioux City.

She grabbed a head of iceberg lettuce and a bottle of Dorothy Lynch, then steered through the aisles, where she threw cans of chicken broth, a bag of hamburger buns, and a box of spaghetti into the cart. She passed an endcap of Oreo cookies, Hal's favorite, on her way to the canned peas. No matter how many batches of homemade cookies she made him and no matter how many recipes she tried, all he wanted were Oreos. Good Lord, sometimes that man didn't have a lick of sense, but in the way that no men do. Done up as he was about the deer, she tossed a bag into her cart. Later she'd put four on a plate for him along with his afternoon sweet coffee, his face lighting up the way it did. "I don't know why you'd like these better than my oatmeal chocolate chip, but there you go," she'd say, and he'd grab her arm in a hug as she pretended to shake him off.

Back by the butcher's counter she saw two women, one of whom was Larry's wife, Cheryl, the woman Alma had talked to on the phone before Hal took that blasted trip. It didn't matter if Alma lived here or Chicago—no matter what, the place was overrun with assholes. It took everything she had not to ram her cart into Cheryl's, but she'd learned in her fourteen years on the farm to bite her tongue when need be. She would drive Cheryl and Larry's daughter on the bus for sports when she got older; she knew Larry's mother through the library board. Alma was still considered an outsider, Clyle's city wife.

Cheryl glanced over, but her friend kept chatting, her hands moving like frenetic birds. "In church Linda was saying she was home, but I guess that's not the case. Word is Joe called Peck that afternoon because Saturday night's the last anyone saw her." The woman put a hand to her face. "Going on Monday afternoon, can you imagine? What would you do if Hattie was gone that long?"

Cheryl whipped her attention back to her friend. "What about Hattie?"

"I'm just saying, you're a mother yourself. Imagine your little girl gone all that time."

"Hattie's only two. It's not the same."

"You think that now," the woman insisted.

The woman with the bird hands turned around, and Alma recognized her as Tonya Gary, the wife of the other yahoo that took Hal out of town. Alma rolled her cart toward the two women, parking an inch or two in front of theirs at the butcher counter and ready to give them a piece of her mind. "I heard about that stunt your husbands pulled this weekend."

"What stunt?" Cheryl said, her face switching to greedy and alert. She had bags under her eyes. Tired, Alma guessed, from putting up with Larry's shit.

"You know, trick a compromised man into trusting them so they could get his game. You two ought to be ashamed of yourselves being married to those men. I'm surprised they let Hal sleep inside."

"I don't think—" Tonya began, but Cheryl cut her off.

"Hal's the one who left them there, so don't be telling us about 'poor Hal.'"

Alma waved a hand to dismiss her. "Best thing he could have done."

Cheryl put her hands on her meaty hips. "They had to walk five miles to Larry's cousin's house," she continued. "You know that? They stopped at one farmhouse and no one was home, so they had to keep walking. Five miles on Sunday just to get to a phone and call me so I could go pick them up."

"You should have let them walk home," Alma said, and turned her cart away.

"Oh." Cheryl stomped her foot. "Wouldn't it be nice to always be right? To be so self-righteous?"

"It is," Alma agreed. She headed toward the checkout to pay and put another bag of Oreos in her cart for Hal to take home, knowing he'd eat too many the first night, no matter how many times she warned him he'd make himself sick.

The cashier, Lana Boswell, took each item in her hand and with her preposterously long nails clacked the prices into the cash register's keys. Why anyone would pay good money to make themselves look ridiculous and make their job more difficult was a question Alma didn't know the answer to. "You hear?" Lana asked, which was how most conversations with her started. She was one of those women who knew everything coming and going in Gunthrum, the pointer on the compass that stayed put while all the information circled around her.

"I don't need to know," Alma said, sure it would be about Hal and how he'd left those idiots at a cabin to fend for themselves. Poor babies. How many hours had it taken Hal to drive the two hundred miles home? She'd highlighted the trip on the atlas, but still. That was when she'd assumed he'd have Larry and Sam in the truck to help him read the map.

"Gone since Saturday night," Lana said, clicking away.

Alma paused with the bottle of dressing suspended above the conveyor, assuming she was talking about Larry and Sam. "I thought they were home."

"They who?" Lana asked, a hound sniffing out new blood.

"Who were you talking about?"

"The Ahern girl." Lana stopped her clacking to tell the story again. Good Lord, Peggy Ahern. That girl lived a half-mile down the road. She ran away, and don't we all know what certain girls can be like. That or she was taken in the night, they were saying. Stolen from her bed by a madman. Alma had read *In Cold Blood* the year it came out; that book had circled in the back of her brain when she and Clyle had weighed all the options after his mother was diagnosed with lymphoma and they'd decided to temporarily move back to the farm where he grew up. Temporarily, her foot.

"Linda said at church on Sunday that Peggy was home with the flu, which we all know means hungover, but then turns out that wasn't the case. Cheryl said she saw Peggy out at Castle Farm Saturday night drunk as a skunk, but who knows what happened after that."

When Alma was seventeen, she'd gotten ahold of a friend's father's whiskey and come home drunk. Her parents were still up, and she had tried to appear sober as she ate cold soup, unable to find her mouth with a spoon. The worst part was she'd convinced herself she'd pulled it off until the next morning, when her mother had set up an obstacle course of chores to get through as penance, her brother horizontal on the couch watching *Gillette Calvacade of Sports* as she vacuumed the rug.

She thought of Hal drunk on her sofa after his high school reunion, how she'd cleaned up after him. She would have been that kind of mother, not the cold brand she'd been raised by.

Alma shook her head. "She's a teenager. She'll wise up in a day or two and come back home."

"I don't know." Lana clicked in the price of Oreos. "Sure she's the runaway type?"

"Teenagers are teenagers," Alma said. "Hormones and all that." Her years in social work had taught her that people, especially teenagers, did all kinds of stupid things, consequences be damned. The bigger the consequences, the more fun it was apt to be.

"Not to mention her dad and the drinking." Lana took the coupons Alma held out. "Speaking of which, I heard Hal was out at Castle Farm, too, in his usual Saturday night state. Cheryl said he could barely string a set of words together."

Alma looked at her sharply. "What's Hal got to do with anything?"

"I'm just saying. He was out on a hunting trip, but then he's home unexpectedly. And I think we all know he was sweet on that Ahern girl."

Alma stiffened her mouth. The damn picnic last summer. "If having a crush were a crime, you'd be in for two life sentences the way you flirt with any man who comes in here." Lana laughed, but all the same, Alma flashed to the blood in the pickup bed that morning.

"Either way," Lana continued. "I'm not saying anything, just trying to piece together the facts. Joe Ahern called Peck on Sunday afternoon after church and asked him to look into it, so he is. He was here this morning to see if I knew anything about it," Lana said self-importantly, as if this were about her, not Peggy. She hit a final button on the cash register. "Fourteen eighty-five."

Alma dug in her wallet for the correct change. "Highway robbery."

"Supply and demand." Lana took the bills and change from Alma's palm, scratching her with those ludicrous nails as she did so. A shiver shot down Alma's back.

In the parking lot Tonya stopped Alma at her car, a bag of groceries in each arm. "Sorry about that," she said, and nodded toward Gunthrum Foods. "Cheryl's still grouchy over having to get the guys. Sam said she was in a real mood about it when she showed up. Said he almost called me to come get him so he wouldn't have to ride with her and Larry, she was being such a nasty."

Alma stared at her blankly, and Tonya shook her head and hefted the left bag with her knee. "No mind. Just sorry she was a bit of a pill. I didn't know that's why they asked Hal. I thought they were being nice."

"And that didn't raise any red flags?"

Tonya looked at her; she had the open, honest face of a doughnut. "What do you mean?"

"Never mind." Alma clicked the driver's seat forward with her foot and set the groceries in the back. "You just tell your husband to stay away from Hal."

Tonya laughed. "In a town this size? Good luck with that."

Alma parked at the school and walked the few blocks to the service station, where she'd pick up the school bus for the afternoon route. She'd quit social work when they decided to move, although not really, as she shepherded her mother-in-law through hospice. All she'd quit was getting paid for it. She'd started driving the bus shortly after they'd moved to the farm as a way to make ends meet while Clyle got into the swing of a farmer's budget cycle, but she'd kept the job because she missed working. Irv Johnston, the school principal, didn't keep it a secret he wasn't all that fond of Alma and would just as soon have her off the payroll. She kept those kids in line, that was for sure, but what was that weird business of her taking in Hal? That's what he asked people, but really, it was because back in their drinking days she'd eviscerated him in front of his friends, calling him a glorified babysitter and stooge. He'd been gunning for her ever since, and who could blame him? She actually admired that he had a little gumption.

Alma was still grousing to herself about Lana bringing up Hal when she arrived at the station. That was Gunthrum to a tee: everyone trying to turn everything into World War III. In Chicago she'd known their neighbors to the left enough to wave and ask after their two boys, but those were the only people on the block she could identify by name. Here she assumed everyone knew her social security number and her bra size. But that business of connecting Hal to Peggy. Alma had to admit, that had her more than irritated. It had her worried.

She'd first met Hal on the school bus, a boy who was always sweet by nature if not by action. He used to get swept up into the mess of peer pressure as easily as anyone else, but once a week, after she dropped off the regular kids, she'd take him and another boy, a deaf mute, on what the kids called the "short bus" to the special school a town over. Hal used to regularly bring her gifts—usually something homemade, like a drawing of his neighbor's dog or an elbow macaroni necklace. Once he'd tried to give her a five-dollar bill, and she had to explain that wasn't appropriate. "But I like you," he'd said. "We're friends." She thanked him and folded it into her wallet, where it was to this day.

In the station she saw a pair of boots pointing out from underneath a Plymouth Horizon. "Lonnie? That you?"

41

Lonnie McGee had hit on her years ago at a party welcoming them to town. He'd run a pinkie finger up the length of her arm, and Alma'd spilled her drink down the front of her blouse. She supposed she'd been attractive enough if you liked a big rump and the natural look, but Clyle was two steps away and an old friend of Lonnie's from high school. She eventually began to realize that in Gunthrum there wasn't much to do, so everyone killed the hours and days sniffing around someone they shouldn't. At the party, still new to the town, she'd concentrated on blotting at her blouse with a napkin, and then Lonnie had leaned closer asking if he could help. When she'd slapped his hand away, he'd laughed! She guessed when you threw that many lines in the water, you couldn't have ego attached to all of them. Word spread soon enough, though, that she was loyal to Clyle, and the come-ons stopped—that or men got to know her and quit wanting to make them.

Earlier that day of the party, Alma had driven all the way to Sioux City to buy Gruyère and Emmentaler cheeses for fondue. She'd cut three baguettes into neat one-inch squares. A woman at the party—she didn't know names yet—had stared into the fondue pot perplexed. "So you dip it? In the cheese?" she asked, and Alma said yes, handing her a skewer. The woman had taken a bite and grimaced. "Well, that's sure not cheddar."

Lonnie rolled out from underneath the car and stood up, sticking an oily rag in the back pocket of his service overalls. He held up a hand in greeting, a genuine smile on his face. That party had been fourteen years ago, water under the bridge. Behind the cash register he found her keys among the collection mounted on the back wall and handed them over. "Need you back in five thousand," he said, and reached for the clipboard he used to bill the school, pressing down hard on the white sheet so it would show clearly on the pink and yellow copies. Window washer fluid: check. Brake fluid: check.

"Where's your sidekick?" she asked, referring to Larry Burke, who worked for Lonnie at the service station and body shop. When she made the appointment for the oil change on Friday, it was so she could come in and see Larry after the hunting trip and thank him or berate him, depending on how Hal was when he got home. She'd been right to lean toward berating.

"Called in sick. Said his legs hurt from all that walking. He and Sam had to hoof it nearly half-dozen miles to a farmhouse."

"Five," she corrected. "It was five miles."

"Near six, I said."

"Well, that's only half the story. You know they only took Hal so they could get his limit? Wanted him to spend the whole hunting trip in the cabin like a dolt."

Lonnie shook his head. "I don't know. Seemed pretty happy with the way things turned out when I saw him at the OK on Saturday night. Said he bagged his first deer." Alma pursed her lips. "Holding no grudges, by the looks of it."

"He's got a right to celebrate," Alma said. "Much as the next guy."

"Oh, he was." Lonnie tore the check sheet at the perforated line and handed Alma the pink copy. "Found him in his truck with his eyes closed when I left, snoring to beat the band."

"It ever occur to you *you* could have helped him?"

"I told him to go home," Lonnie said. "I said, 'You go straight home, Hal, you hear?'"

"And what'd he say?"

"'I promise.' And then he started the truck and headed home." Only now Alma knew he hadn't gone home, not directly anyway. What had he been doing at Castle Farm?

"You hear about Peggy Ahern?" Lonnie asked, and Alma repeated what Lana had told her. She guessed she wasn't much better than the rest of them.

"I doubt it's much to worry about yet," Lonnie said. "Girls like Peggy do crazy things."

"What do you mean by 'girls like Peggy'?"

"Nothing, I suppose, other than girls that age. Girls in general. You know, the hysterical sex."

"Oh, for Pete's sake."

Lonnie laughed. "If it was anything to worry about, Peck would rally the troops." He pointed at the receipt. "I put your snow tires on too. Figured you'll need them sooner rather than later given this past weekend."

Alma folded the paper and stuck it in her purse. "A little bit like shutting the barn door after the pigs got out, don't you think?"

"You say so, Alma." Lonnie winked at her. "No one wants to argue with a pretty lady."

5

Milo stood in front of the school with the rest of the losers. He hated riding the bus. Normally he'd sit in the gym bleachers reading a book and waiting for Peggy to finish basketball or volleyball practice so he could catch a ride with her. That wasn't an option today, and his parents sure weren't going to come to town to get him either. Scott stood next to him in a short-sleeved shirt with goose pimples visible on his arms. He held his winter coat loosely against the books slung on his hip.

"Why don't you just put your coat back on?" Milo asked.

Scott shook his head. "Don't need it."

Milo didn't understand this kind of grandstanding. If he was cold, he put on a coat—it was as simple as that. But he knew Scott would rather look like the big man on campus, indifferent to the weather. It was much warmer than it had been over the weekend, when snow had fallen for eighteen straight hours. Sunday afternoon, while Sheriff Randolph talked to his parents in the living room, he'd eavesdropped from the hall as fresh flakes continued to accumulate. He wondered if for the rest of his life he'd think about the time his sister went missing while he watched it snow.

Mrs. Costagan rounded the corner in the yellow bus, sliding the door open as she came to a stop. Kids piled on like hogs to the slaughter, a look Milo knew all too well. He'd been helping his folks on the farm since he was three years old, picking cucumbers and tomatoes in the garden. At ten he'd started on the real chores, leading pigs up the chute, slapping the back door of the trailer two times when it was locked and loaded, just like his father did.

He heaved himself up the first large step, and from the driver's seat Mrs. Costagan raised her eyebrows at him. "Milo," she said, and nodded an inch.

"Hi, Mrs. Costagan." She always went by her last name even though the other two drivers went by Miss Deedee and Mr. Mike. Last year, when Milo had checked out *Wuthering Heights* at the Gunthrum library after the librarian had assured him everyone in the book was bananas and knew how to hold a grudge, he was shocked to see the only other name, written in a beautiful cursive on the due date card, was Alma Costagan. His mother said Mrs. Costagan was a weird one, but he'd always liked her, at least what he knew about her, which was this: she'd lived in Chicago.

He'd always wanted to ask whether women wore Reeboks with their business suits like they did on TV and if everyone really ate pizza two inches thick as they dropped the big bills on the Magnificent Mile. He wanted to grow a mustache when he was a grown-up. He'd stroll to his job in the big city, briefcase swinging, all those years in Nebraska in the rearview mirror. He'd tell people at cocktail parties that he used to live on a farm, and they'd widen their eyes, dressed in their tuxes and sequin dresses, and laugh as they all ate caviar. *You? On a farm! Why, I rawther can't imagine!*

Scott slammed into the seat next to him, purposely knocking Milo against the window. "You're like a celebrity," Scott said, and Milo rolled his eyes. "No, really. I just saw Lisa Rasmussen give you the stink eye for like the eighth time today." Scott clutched at his heart. "What I wouldn't give to have Lisa Rasmussen check me out."

"I suppose," Milo said, and then, "She's good-looking, all right." He knew Scott thought so because he'd said it about a million times, although what he said was a lot more crude than "good-looking." And she was, but geez, was that all Scott wanted to talk about now? He would come over to play Atari and spend half the night yakking about whether or not Peggy was going to come downstairs in her shortie sleep shirt. It had only happened one time, but Scott hadn't been able to forget it. It was like the time Scott's dog had found popcorn in Scott's parents' bedroom, where Milo and Scott had snuck to watch a movie, and after that, every time the dog came inside, he ran to Scott's dad's side of the bed.

It wasn't that Milo didn't like girls; it was just, couldn't they talk about other things as well? "Maybe if you weren't such a gomer," he said to Scott, "the girls would like you too."

Scott nodded appreciatively. "Always playing the cool angle." They both knew that wasn't the case. In the last year Scott was the one all the girls were interested in. He'd shot up over the summer—two inches in three months—and spent most of it working on his folks' farm, muscles beginning to pop and define like an adult's. None of his old clothes fit, so his mother took him to the Southern Hills Mall in Sioux City, and now his wardrobe was mainly Dire Straits and Glenn Frey T-shirts and the kind of tight jeans guys wore on TV. That a girl was paying any attention to Milo was a new turn of events. But what did it say that girls were only paying attention to him because his sister was missing?

Eventually it would return to normal, right? His parents were acting like maybe things were fine, but that was just because they didn't want the town to know. On Sunday his aunt Sally and uncle Randall finally left, after his folks said they'd call Sheriff Randolph.

"You sure we can't stay?" Sally had asked.

Milo's mother told her no, thank you, insisting still it was nothing. "I'm sure we'll have this all resolved by that evening, and we'll give you a call."

"Well, buckle down on her when she gets home," Sally said, leaning in to kiss Milo's mom on the cheek. "It's the only way they learn." Like anyone who'd raised George should be giving parenting advice. George had lain down on Milo's bed after church and tossed a ball of socks in the air while his mother packed his duffel bag and put his toothbrush in his Dopp kit next to the shampoo bottle she'd dried with a towel. When he'd told her he couldn't find his tennies, she'd said, "Well, George, you've got to learn to keep better track of your things," but then left him on the bed so she could go look for them. Aunt Sally had wrapped the entire roast in tinfoil so they could eat sandwiches the next day when all of this was behind them. A few minutes later George came in complaining he was hungry, and she tore off a hunk of meat, pulled it apart with a fork, and put it between two Miracle Whip–laden pieces of white bread and told him that would have to do. Milo doubted his mother had eaten since Sunday morning.

"We can just as easily stay here," Aunt Sally had said at the door, all their bags packed in the Cadillac's trunk. "It won't hurt George to miss a day of school tomorrow, no matter what his math teacher says."

"No, no," his mother said, and Milo could tell the effort was beginning to wear. He and his mother were a lot alike and, given their druthers, would rather tuck their feet up with a good book than have to talk to people.

"We'll keep you in our prayers," Randall had said to Milo's father, and Joe snorted.

"I don't think we need the prayer circle starting up just yet. She'll be home by nightfall."

Milo didn't understand why his parents were being so non-chalant. Peggy had never been gone this long before. Sure, she'd spent the night at Laura's and forgot to tell his folks, and one time she ended up stranded during a snowstorm at the Sapp Bros. truck stop in Fremont, but both those times she'd called to let them know she was all right. It made him shudder to think they'd put the town's good opinion ahead of his sister's well-being.

"I just meant—" Randall started.

Joe sat down and opened the Sunday paper in front of him. "I know what you meant."

Randall had stood by the front door a moment, his cap in his hand, before nodding his head and hugging Milo's mom goodbye.

"We'll call when we know anything," his mom whispered in Uncle Randall's ear.

Milo himself alternated between anger at Peggy for once again getting all the attention and a heart-pounding fear that overtook him to the point where he couldn't breathe. What if something really *had* happened to her? Each hour that ticked by, it seemed less and less like a prank, and he felt stomach-sick he'd been mad at her.

Scott slammed Milo's shoulder again so he knocked into the window. "See you, moron."

They'd never ridden the bus all the way to Scott's house in such silence before. Scott was a good friend to sit next to him, a brooding lump, when he could have been at the back of the bus trying to get into Lisa's pants.

"See you," he said, but Scott was halfway down the steps by then. As the bus pulled away, Scott stuck his tongue out between a peace sign he'd made with his left hand and wag-gled it. Good cripes. It was embarrassing being a boy sometimes, but Milo laughed and appreciated it for what it was: Scott acting normal.

A few stops later, at the Rasmussen farm, Lisa dropped a note in Milo's lap as she made her way down the aisle. He unfolded it a mile later, her handwriting loopy and sweet. *I hope you're sister is okay!* An irrational anger spiked over the misspelling of *your*, and he crumpled the note in his fist. Peggy was out there somewhere, and whether his mom wanted to hear it or not, she might be in trouble. He'd watched enough police dramas on TV to know that after forty-eight hours all investigations were knocking at the door of hopeless. But, Milo reminded himself, we're only at forty. Plus, there was the niggling question of whether she'd just up and left in the night. But wouldn't she have taken her favorite clothes or at least her cassette tapes and Walkman? He'd been so angry on Sunday to think she's abandoned him, but now he hoped it was the case. His mind skittered toward the worst-case scenario, but he pulled it back, his jaw clenched.

The bus door opened and closed again with a sucking sound, and only he and Mrs. Costagan were left. She caught his eye in the rearview mirror. "You want to move up? Helps balance the bus."

He picked up his backpack and moved toward the front. "That really helps?"

"No." She shifted into first gear. "It was joke." She pulled to the middle of the gravel road as the Langdon children, Jill and Shelly, walked toward their house, with two feet of air between them but side by side. "You doing okay?" she asked, and there was no need to elaborate. Mrs. Langdon greeted her girls at the front door, an arm wrapping a cardigan against her chest to ward off the cold.

"I guess."

"It's an awful thing," Mrs. Costagan said, and tears sprang to his eyes.

"I'm worried. I'm worried something bad happened."

"Of course you are," she confirmed, and he wanted to hug her. Last night, when his mother was absently cleaning the kitchen counter with a sponge even though she hadn't remembered to make dinner, Milo had asked her if she thought maybe Peggy was gone for good.

His mother had whipped around, a strand of lank hair caught in her mouth, she'd moved her head so fast. "Don't you say that." She grabbed him by the shoulders, leaving a wet rectangle of soap on one side. "Your sister's coming home." He'd bottomed out to his feet when she did it, sure that if had he eaten dinner, he would have thrown it up. The only reason he'd even asked was so she would laugh at the possibility, but her denial left him worse off than he'd been before.

"I prayed about it," Milo said, catching Mrs. Costagan's eye in the rearview mirror, and he had. He'd caught his mind sliding toward panic last night and today during school—*let her be okay, let her be okay*—then lassoed those thoughts and sent them to God. Please God, he prayed, let my sister be okay. He didn't know if such direct requests were usually answered, but it was worth a shot. "I prayed a ton."

"I know that helps a lot of people," Alma said neutrally, which caught Milo up short. Most people he knew would tell him that was the best thing he could do.

They drove the next few miles in silence, but it wasn't like the silence he had at home right now, where he moved through the kitchen without lifting his feet, sure any sound would shatter all of them. The grind of the gears, the crotchety noises of a cranky bus, the battery-powered radio Mrs. Costagan kept Velcroed to the dash so she could listen to AM radio—it wasn't like silence at all.

They passed the Costagan farm, and then Mrs. Costagan slowed toward his lane and did something she never did: she turned down the drive. Normally she dropped kids at the end and stayed on the road; it was up to them to walk. This kind of babying from Mrs. Costagan—a woman who had confiscated cigarettes from a senior on the bus and made him eat one—felt like both a kindness and a coffin nail.

A white police cruiser sat in front of the house, and even without the lights and sirens going, it was enough to send Milo into a panic. He'd been raised with a healthy respect for authority, and the very sight of the gold-and-brown star on the driver's door made him feel guilty for something he hadn't done.

"You know one time I had a girl on the route get on the bus stinking of urine." Mrs. Costagan broke to a stop in front of his house. "I asked her what happened, and she said her dog peed on her leg while she was waiting and she didn't know what to do except get on the bus." She opened the door. "Do you understand what I'm saying?"

Milo shook his head. "Not at all."

She nodded. "I suppose not. It's just, sometimes all you can do is get on the bus."

He hopped off at the last step with both feet together, thinking as he often did of Mary Lou Retton nailing her dismount at the Olympics last year. "Thanks for the ride, Mrs. Costagan."

"Just doing my job." He waited for the sucking *sloop* sound of the bus door closing, and when it didn't come, he turned around. Mrs. Costagan was staring at him, her hand around the door lever. "Keep your chin up," she said, and pulled the door shut.

Inside, his parents and Sheriff Randolph sat in the living room, coffee cups on coasters in front of each of them. The sheriff nodded at Milo, but his parents didn't turn around. "Any other kids gone from church that morning?" he asked. "Any behavior out of the ordinary the last few weeks? Any trouble at school?"

The sheriff sat in the rocking chair Milo's mom had bought at an auction years ago and had always meant to reupholster. The seat was covered in a shiny vinyl, and as Sheriff Randolph leaned forward to ask questions of his parents, the chair made a sound like a wet fart. Milo bit his lip to keep from laughing. He felt like a crazy person, his mood spiking and dropping like an out-of-control airplane. He and Scott had spent an afternoon drinking Mountain Dew and making that fart noise in the chair just a few months ago, and Peggy had come in and told them to stop acting like babies. Scott had let loose with the loudest, wettest belch in the history of belches, and they all had dissolved in a fit of giggles—even Peggy, despite trying to fight it.

Sheriff Randolph shifted his hat from hand to hand but didn't say anything. What could he say? "That wasn't my butt"?

His father got up and stood at the window in what Milo considered his basketball coach stance, from when he coached Milo's peewee league—feet shoulder-width apart and arms crossed tightly on his broad chest. "My daughter isn't just going to up and leave," he said firmly. Milo wondered at that. Did his father really not see how much he and Peggy despised Gunthrum? He wondered sometimes if his father saw them at all or just the version of kids that his mom polished and put in front of him.

"I understand that, Joe." Sheriff Randolph's voice was even. "But she's been gone two days. Yesterday, when you called, you insisted you didn't want a manhunt, that it was all a misunderstanding and you were calling as a courtesy, but you see we're past that, don't you?"

"Don't patronize me, Peck," Joe said, and stormed from the room. Mr. Randolph continued the questions with his mother—what was Peggy wearing Saturday night? Who was she with?—and his mother admitted she didn't know.

She leaned forward. "Despite what Joe thinks, it wasn't that unusual for Peggy to sneak out on the weekends. You know teenagers." Milo sat there dumbfounded. So his mother *had* known.

Sheriff Randolph asked about any family Peggy might have gone to, and his mother explained their closest relatives were here for Milo's confirmation, Grandma Ahern now retired in South Carolina. "We haven't even told Alice yet. Why get her riled up?"

"And where are Randall and Sally now?" Peck asked, and his mother said they'd just left yesterday afternoon. "Everything all right there?"

"What do you mean?"

"Seems a little odd they'd leave when Peggy's missing. I'd think you'd want the support."

His mother thumbed toward the back hallway. "You can imagine how much Joe wants to admit he needs support. Besides." She lowered her voice. "Joe and his brother have always been a bit contentious."

"Contentious how?"

She waved her hand. "It's nothing, Peck. Brothers being brothers."

"That's fine," he said. "But I have to ask." He softened his voice to match Milo's mother's. "And you're sure she wasn't seeing anyone?" Milo got the sense all these questions had been asked before, in the presence of his father.

His mom glanced down the hallway, where his dad had disappeared. "If so, I don't know who, but Peggy wasn't the type to be . . . alone."

Milo leaned against the entry to the living room, his backpack still on his shoulders, and the movement caught his mom's eye. "Sweetie," she said as she turned around, her voice back to normal and bright. "When did you get home?"

"Just a minute ago."

"Well, let me get you a snack." He'd been getting his own snack—four Oreos and a glass of milk—for a year now. It was nice to have his mom home during the day again. This thought was followed, once again, by the bone-crushing guilt of his own betraying thoughts.

Sheriff Randolph stood and told everyone he'd call later that night with any new information. He picked up his coffee cup and followed Milo's mother to the kitchen, where he set the mug in the sink. Milo walked with him to the car, ignoring his mother's demands to put a coat on.

"Sheriff Randolph?" The sheriff stopped with his hand on the car door and turned around, his eyebrows raised. "You think my sister's okay?"

"I don't know, son, but I'll do everything I can. Anything you think might help me figure out where she is?"

He thought about Peggy sitting cross-legged on his bed flapping down Uno card after Uno card, saying she'd spend her life in Gunthrum over her dead body. "Not really."

"You feel free to call me if anything comes up. Your mother has my number." He paused. "And if for some reason you don't want her to know, you can find it in the phone book, you hear?"

Milo wrinkled his brow and was going to ask just what he meant, but he guessed he already knew. He nodded.

"Okay, then," Sheriff Randolph said, and tipped his hat before climbing in his car.

6

Alma parked the bus in the garage with six inches to spare on either side and closed her coat against the cold as she walked to her car. She'd decided after dropping Milo off at home that she'd get takeout, a rare solution on those nights she just couldn't face cooking. The Pizza Ranch had opened by the highway three years ago, and even though it was run by Catholics, they did a booming business. Other than the Standard, which served Sunday turkey dinners to shut-ins, they were the only game in town.

Before turning onto Main, Alma slapped her blinker on, something no one in Gunthrum really did. Everyone assumed they knew where everyone was going, but she felt like following the rules, like taking every precaution she could.

She could not take her mind off of Peggy Ahern. At the town's centennial picnic last summer—Clyle had insisted they go, saying it was his husbandly right to drag Alma to a town event once every hundred years—Peggy had told Hal she liked his shirt. She had put her hand on his arm and flung her hair back like a horse, nearly whinnying.

Alma would bet her year's salary (not that much of a gamble) the girl was sexually active and a troublemaker to boot by the way she reached up and touched Hal's collar, probably at the very moment she told him she liked it. Hal had touched the strap of her tank top in return, and by that time one of Peggy's friends had come over and asked what was going on. Peggy made a stink, and Joe Ahern came running, his drunk voice escalating, demanding to know what Hal had done. The picnic came to a halt. Peck Randolph stood with a spatula over the grill, others pausing their games of bocce and horseshoes. Alma couldn't imagine how difficult it was for Hal to navigate the waters of male-female relationships. Most of the couples she knew wanted to throttle each other at some point or another.

Hal had worn that shirt the next two weeks, hanging around the schoolyard, where Peggy was practicing wind sprints with the volleyball team, his fingers curled in the chain-link fence as he hung his weight slack, his arms up like a monkey's. Eventually, Alma had gotten a call from Peggy's father saying Hal was being a nuisance and was there anything she could do about it? She sat Hal down that afternoon and explained to him that Peggy wasn't interested in a relationship, citing their age difference, but in many ways she was older than him. It hadn't ended up a big deal. Hal had cried for about a half an hour, eventually sniffling and pulling himself together, a wad of used Kleenex on the kitchen table.

She didn't hear another word from Joe Ahern until she ran into him at the bank a few weeks later. Standing in line, he had slapped his deposit slip against his hip. "I appreciate you taking care of that business a while back. Funny business."

"How so?" she asked, but the teller, Bev Barnes, had smiled and said, "You're up, Joe," and that was that.

It hadn't been the first time Hal had gotten one of these crushes. There'd been a few girls back when he was in high school and a college girl at home one summer who worked at the Dairy Dream a town over and every now and again a stranger at the OK. Alma knew enough about how girls worked to know they'd wonder if maybe it wouldn't be so bad, him being a little on the stupid side. But it wasn't just that he was intellectually challenged; it was that he behaved like a boy as well—chicken-winging his hand in his armpit to produce a fart noise to get their attention, snapping a girl's bra.

Alma parked the car and opened the door to the Pizza Ranch, the smell of pepperoni and grease thick in the air. She hated to admit it, but those Catholics made a good pizza. She'd never cared for the deep-dish Chicago style, although Clyle, originally from Gunthrum, loved it. He ordered it for them every chance he got when they lived in the city, so you couldn't say she never made compromises.

A woman emerged from the kitchen through the swinging saloon doors and worked her way into a smile, her pregnant belly straining against her brown Pizza Ranch sweatshirt. "Alma Costagan, what can I do you for?"

Alma ordered a large deluxe with extra sausage, which would take ten minutes. "You want a pop while you wait?"

"Oh, I don't think so." They'd gouge her for it—fifty cents and no to-go cup.

"All righty then," the woman said, and slipped back through the saloon doors. "The day that woman pays for a soda—" she said, probably to her no-nuts husband. Leave it to the Catholics to not worry about lowering their voices when God heard everything. She could imagine Darla running a self-satisfied hand across that taut belly, three kids already at home.

When Alma found out she was pregnant with the first baby, she and Clyle were a year out of college at UIC and still living in Chicago; she was working at a halfway house, and he'd been recruited by IBM after a college aptitude test. Oh, they'd been nervous about that baby! They'd stayed up late to celebrate the night they found out, champagne for the both of them, as was the norm back then, and her saying she hoped they were ready. Did he think they were ready? What hubris to think they were the ones to decide such a thing. Whoever did decided they weren't. Not with that baby or the four that came after. Five babies lost in a space of seven years.

Alma took a seat near the front to wait for her pizza. In the back two boys huddled around the Ms. Pac-Man. One of them slammed his hip against the game as the other howled with laughter. "You smoked it," his friend said. "You smoked it to hell." Alma didn't recognize the boys from her route, so they probably lived in town.

"Let's see you do better." The first one stepped out of his friend's way with a small bow.

The front door opened, and a teenage girl walked in. Her eyes were ringed with black makeup, and her long, lean body looked like a knife blade in a pair of jeans. Alma knew this one. Her father ran the junkyard three miles out of town, and her mother was known for her alcohol sabbaticals, where she'd be gone for a week at a time. The two boys glanced up and started blustering for her attention, cracking it up, hoping she'd look their way. Teenage boys were like apes in a zoo.

The girl leaned against the counter with her pert rump in the air, the inch of skin below her Grateful Dead T-shirt expanding to four. Clearly, she'd seen the boys as well.

"Teri," one of the boys yelled. "Hey, Ter."

She tucked her head under her elbow and looked at them upside down. Another inch and they'd peek her bra band—if she was wearing a bra, Alma reminded herself. She couldn't imagine being out in public without one. Even making the coffee in the morning in just her nightgown made her self-conscious, and she'd hold her breasts down with one arm while she scooped grounds into the drip coffeemaker with the other.

The door opened, and a haggard Peck Randolph walked through the door. "Hey, Darla, it's Peck," he said loudly to the kitchen. "Pizza to go?"

Darla came out from the back with a large box balanced on her belly, grease already seeping through the bottom of the cardboard. "Here you go," she said, and Peck handed her a twenty. As she rang it into the cash register and handed him back the change, she said, "I don't know how anyone can eat pineapple on a pizza."

"To each his own." He put the bills back in his wallet and the change in a jar by the register.

"God bless," Darla said, and Alma rolled her eyes. The teenage girl had moved to the back now. She sloped against Ms. Pac-Man, a piece of cheese pizza sagging in her hand. She contorted her head to the side to catch the pointed end in her mouth, the cheese thinning in a long string.

"Evening, Alma." Peck leaned his hip against the counter with the pizza box in his hand. She'd always liked and not liked Peck. He was a few years younger than her and Clyle and had never been much for the drinking crowd. She and Clyle had been part of that gang when they'd first moved back, but that had stopped eight years ago. She always felt Peck judged the rest of them—the drinkers—and she assumed that because she did the same. She and Clyle still had beers at home and Lord Calvert with Sprite for him every evening, but "drinkers" were those who got together every weekend, both Friday and Saturday night, the smoke so thick in their rec room basements you could hardly see to the wall across from you.

"Bet you've been busy," she said.

"It's been a full day." He slid his wallet into the back pocket of his tan uniform pants. "Say, you live near the Aherns, don't you?" She confirmed she did. "You or Clyle—you see anything?"

"Not a thing."

Peck nodded. He opened the pizza box and shut it again. "Heard Hal bagged his first deer."

Alma smiled ruefully, thinking of Larry and Sam hoofing it through the fields to call Larry's wife. "He did."

"Why you having pizza instead of venison for dinner?" he asked, and she told him about the mix-up, how the carcass ended up in the landfill, an uneasy feeling in her stomach. Was it that he might ask about Hal's permit or something else?

Peck nodded. "His house must have been a mess. Truck too."

"I guess so," Alma confirmed, and added, "Clyle and he cleaned it up. Spick-and-span." She thought of Peck at the picnic last year with his suspended spatula and at the hospital years ago when Hal had beat up that kid from Wayne. "Carcass is at Mick Langdon's if you want to take a look." It was, wasn't it?

"And Hal was back on Saturday? Not Sunday?"

"Yep, although we didn't see him until Monday."

They locked eyes for what Alma found to be an uncomfortable amount of time, then Peck knocked the pizza box twice against the counter and turned toward the door. "You think of anything."

On his way out Peck swung past the three teenagers and said something, and despite themselves, the boys straightened their backs, and the girl, managing to keep her demeaning slouch, at least stopped eating the pizza. He nodded to Alma as he opened the door, the pizza box balanced on his other palm.

Two days. It was a long time for a girl to be missing. In the arcade one of the boys did a pale imitation of Peck, hitching up his pants as he balanced an invisible pizza box. Peck wasn't a pants hitcher, but Alma knew that was who the boy was imitating by the way the other acne-ridden boy laughed.

The girl took another slice of their pizza. "See ya," she said. Not even a thank-you. Both boys watched as she turned at the door and opened it with her backside, the tip of the pizza in her mouth. What had she even been doing there? She hadn't ordered anything, only ate someone else's food. Alma thought about Peggy and that hand on Hal's collar, how quickly she'd garnered his attention.

What amazed her wasn't that a girl had gone missing but that more weren't going missing every day.

7

When Peggy still wasn't home by Tuesday morning, some of the town wives set up a schedule for meals and chores so the Aherns wouldn't have to do anything but find their daughter. Clyle had hosed his work boots off when he finished his own chores before coming inside for a shower to prevent contamination between the farms, and now he sat at his kitchen table in slippers. "It's a terrible thing," he repeated, something he'd said on autopilot for the last twenty-four hours. He tried to think of other terrible things that had happened in Gunthrum. Once, when he was a teenager, a little girl in town was riding on the back of a bicycle her father was pedaling, and she stuck her fingers through the spokes and had her fingers cut clean off at the tips. A boy a class below him had died of a bee sting, his face swelling up like a muddled balloon while they were all playing baseball. Clyle had been at the park when that happened, and he thought of it still whenever he saw the soft rind of an overripe cantaloupe.

Alma stood in the kitchen frosting a pan of cinnamon rolls; a lasagna cooled on the stove burner, already covered in foil. She turned around, a hand on her hip. "I'm not looking forward to this."

"No one is," Clyle agreed. "But it's the right thing to do."

"Don't tell me about the right thing," Alma grumbled, ripping a sheet of tinfoil from the box to cover the rolls.

Hal, fresh from his shower, came down a few moments later, a clean shirt of Clyle's tucked tight into his work pants, his eyes rimmed red. Clyle had been the one to tell him about Peggy; he'd heard about it from Alma Monday night when she came home with a pizza box in one hand and a mouthful of gossip. He knew she hated how much everyone in this town talked, and it amazed him to this day how quickly word could spread. The only reason he hadn't heard earlier was that he'd been working on the farm all day, cocooned away from the rest of the world.

Clyle knew about Hal's crush on Peggy, knew he had come back from that centennial picnic last summer talking about how he had fallen in love. Loading hogs in the trailer the next afternoon, he'd asked Clyle if it was possible Hal himself might get married someday. "You know, like a regular man?"

As Clyle had predicted, Mick Langdon, Hal's landlord, had called earlier that afternoon with follow-up on the hunting trip. "Found a deer in my dump."

Clyle felt a rush of relief. "That must have been a surprise." He hadn't realized how worried he'd been about that deer and whether or not there was one after he heard about Peggy. He hadn't wanted to admit even to himself that when he heard about her disappearance, he thought about the blood in the truck.

"Hal must have thrown it in there while I was at church because you can damn well bet if I'd been there, I would have heard him." Clyle asked Mick if he wanted him to come get the carcass, but Mick figured it could just as easily rot in his dump as Clyle's. "But I thought you should know at least."

"We need to skedaddle," Alma said. "Sooner we go, the sooner we can leave." They piled into the car, one casserole pan balanced on her knees in the passenger's seat, the other on Hal's in the back, where he sat like their child.

At the Aherns', people had parked their cars and trucks carefully on the side of the gravel drive, not one wheel on the grass. Many were the same vehicles parked here on Friday and Saturday nights although never so neatly on the weekend. "Good Lord," Alma said. "Now they've got a house full of people to entertain. I thought the wives would set it up so we weren't all coming at once."

Cheryl and Larry Burke stood on the porch—a paper grocery sack in his arms—speaking to Lonnie McKee and his wife, Diane. They stopped talking as the Costagans and Hal pulled up and parked. The two couples were part of the Aherns' drinking crowd, Cheryl and Larry the youngest members at twenty-eight. Lonnie had hired Larry at the garage a few years back after Larry completed an auto tech degree at Northeast. Most of the people in the crowd had cheered at the football games when Larry scored the touchdowns, leading the Bulldogs to the conference championship. In the years since, like most of the people in Gunthrum, he'd found a way to transition from child to adult with the people he'd known since he was in short pants. Clyle was a rarity— someone who had left town and made another life for himself, then come back—but all he'd ever really wanted was to live in Gunthrum.

"We didn't know if we should go in or just leave the things on the porch," Diane whispered as they walked up. She'd dyed her hair a darker shade of brown, and Clyle thought it made her look older.

"Terrible thing," Lonnie said. "Just terrible."

"That's what I've been saying all day," Clyle said.

Cheryl put her hand on Larry's arm. "Lare gave up bowling league to come tonight, make sure we could do what we can."

"A real hero's tale," Alma muttered, and Cheryl glared at her.

"Hi, Larry," Hal said, and Larry mumbled a "hi" back but didn't turn to look at Hal. Clyle knew from Alma's run into town the day before that Larry and Sam were telling anyone who would listen that Hal had stranded them near Valentine and they'd had to get a ride from Cheryl the next morning. And now this girl was missing, and they probably felt petty trying to drum up sympathy over something as stupid as a hike. They should, Clyle thought.

"I think we can leave it, don't you?" Diane said to no one in particular about the food they'd brought, so Alma rang the doorbell.

"Figures," Cheryl muttered, and they stood a moment in awkward silence until the door opened.

Linda Ahern peered out, her face white as a wax candle. "Come in," she said, and waved them in. "No need standing out on the porch." Her boy, Milo, was behind her, a cautious look on his face.

Cheryl stepped forward. "We don't want to be a bother."

"It's fine," Linda said, and Clyle explained he and Hal were here to help with chores, that they'd stay on the porch in their boots.

"I assume you know what needs to be done?" Linda asked.

"We do," Clyle said. He'd gotten the call from Randall about what to do on the farm. "One feeder works enough like another." He and Hal headed toward the barn, Alma shooting a look over her shoulder as she heaved herself up the steps. Sometimes he worried as much about leaving Alma in a social situation as he did Hal, especially around Diane, but if she was going to say something, it would have been long ago. Alma always spoke her mind, something many of the women around here didn't understand. They'd been raised to be deferential to their men and social norms, neither of which Alma gave a hoot about. It was one of the things he had loved about her in the beginning.

In the Aherns' barn Clyle found the on-off switch for the feed. His own barn wasn't on an electrical system, but he knew well enough how one worked. He flipped the switch, and the machinery rumbled loudly to life as he and Hal stood next to each other watching the PVC pipe with its coiled snake of cable drop feed into both sides of the pens. At home he used a crank to control the depth of the feed, monitoring that it was high enough for the food to flow out but not enough that the hogs could waste it.

Joe had hung simple tools on the walls, the ones most farmers kept in triplicate in the house, toolshed, and barn: pliers, screwdrivers, hammer. It felt strangely intimate being inside another man's barn. He could tell from the way the straw was stacked and the tools were hung on hooks on the walls that Joe Ahern was a fastidious man who believed hard work would be rewarded. A man who thought he could protect himself and his family through sheer will. Hal leaned against a sorting panel and continued to watch the feeder even though the chute unloaded the grain to each bin in exactly the same way. Clyle understood. This was one of the simple pleasures of farming, the repetitive motions, like lulling a baby to sleep.

Growing up, Clyle had always loved the farm. He started chores with his father when he was just a little tyke and was running the tractor by the age of eight. He'd always loved the soreness at the end of the day, the tightened, sunburned skin in the summer and the chap of cold in the winter. He'd left for a college education—his parents had been adamant that he explore his options—and junior year he'd sat next to a pretty girl in Victorian Literature who leaned over and asked if he believed it was true that the Victorians were so prudish they covered even the table legs. She'd smelled like sawdust and wore a maroon cardigan and a skirt that stopped just above her knee. His first introduction to Alma.

"It feels weird being in here," Hal said over the noise of the feeder, and Clyle told him there was nothing to be afraid of. He thought of the boy with the bee sting, how his face had swollen so fast it was like watching a balloon inflate. He and Alma studied together for at least a month for that class until finally she leaned over and kissed him at the library, her mouth wet and tasting of cherry Sucrets. Good Lord, he was embarrassed to admit it, but she was only the fourth girl he'd ever kissed. If it hadn't been for her, they'd still probably be at a long wooden table near the stacks, Clyle debating if he should hold her hand.

While the feeder continued unloading, Clyle and Hal walked through the rows of hogs in the barn, then went to the three large outbuildings. Joe had one of the bigger operations in the county. They turned on the other mechanized feeders and checked the hogs for irregularities. Two piglets in building three had the scours, and Hal and Clyle could tell which ones by their anuses. They each grabbed one by their back legs and separated them in an empty pen; Clyle would leave a note for the next guy. He found the mini-fridge in the third building, the shelves lined neatly with glass bottles, the syringes on top. He filled two with penicillin and grabbed a blue Paintstik—the color for third-day shots at the Aherns— and gave a litter their shots against pneumonia while Hal held them in the football hold.

The loud rattle of the feeders stopped. Hal switched them off, and they made their way back through the buildings, making sure the feeders had filled and the water was fresh. They ended up back at the barn. It was the oldest building by far on the farm, with wood siding and an uneven cement floor, while the newer buildings were corrugated steel, their floors so smooth you could roll a marble straight. No question the Aherns had some money.

In the barn Hal looked up to the hayloft, his voice echoey. "Maybe she's up there," he said. "Maybe she's hiding."

"She's not hiding," Clyle said evenly.

"You never know. I hid in a hayloft for like three days once." That had been back when Hal was in high school and had just started working for them on the weekends. He still lived with his mother then, and at most he'd hidden an afternoon. Marta had caught Hal smoking dope with some boys at school, and he'd come to the Costagans' to hide. Clyle and Alma hadn't even known Hal was there until he appeared at their doorstep, hay in his hair, claiming he was starving to death. Clyle called Marta to tell her they'd found him, and she'd sighed. "Just send that idiot boy home," she said.

"Maybe I should check," Hal said, and turned toward Clyle with wide eyes. "I could be the one to find her. I'd be the hero!"

"No one's going to be a hero," Clyle responded, and then, even though he didn't believe it, "I'm sure she's fine."

In Linda's kitchen Alma cut one of her cinnamon rolls and placed it on a paper plate, setting it on the table next to half a dozen others. Joe Ahern was in the basement with most of the group, but Linda sat at the kitchen table, a cup of coffee in front of her. "We appreciate your help," she said again.

"It's the least we can do," Alma repeated, catching Clyle's eye: *it's time to go.* He agreed, but Linda had insisted they take off their boots and come in for a bite, manners being what they were no matter the circumstances. Who was he to say no to a woman in Linda's position? He didn't think he had ever been in another person's kitchen in just his stockinged feet. Even at home, he put his slippers on to walk to the bathroom in the middle of the night, something he did more and more as he got older.

Diane scooted out of Alma's way and closer to her husband, Lonnie. Clyle knew all about Lonnie putting the moves on Alma all those years ago. She'd told him that night on the drive home, mad as a hornet but laughing too. He looked Lonnie in the eye but couldn't do the same with Diane.

The boy was at the table as well. Milo held a Rubik's Cube in his hand, and while Clyle knew what it was, he asked him. Milo told him and handed it over, the sides turning in Clyle's hands with a satisfying click.

"Ever get it?" he asked.

The boy admitted no. "I'm not very good at puzzles."

"I am," Hal said, and took the cube from Clyle's hand, twisting this way and that, then handing it back. "I can't do it."

"It's hard," Milo said. "I can't get it at all."

"Do you got a bathroom?" Hal asked, and Milo pointed down the hall.

Larry whispered something to his wife, and she shook her head. "It's not the time," she whispered back.

"Time for what?" Milo asked.

"It's nothing, sweetie," Cheryl said to the boy. "We don't need to talk about it now."

"I wanted to apologize to Hal," Larry said to Clyle, clearing his throat. "It wasn't fair of us to bring him along hunting, then not let him hunt."

Alma threw down the dish towel she'd been ringing in her hand. "You're damn straight."

"I'm apologizing here, Alma," Larry said, and Clyle knew how much that would chap her hide: one of her old bus riders using her first name. "Still, we were worried when we got back to the cabin Saturday night and he wasn't there. We didn't know where Hal had gone. Sunday morning we had to call Cheryl here to come get us, stuck up there at my cousin's."

"What's that?" Linda Ahern asked, her head in a fugue, and Clyle thought about the tools lined neatly in the barn, how hopeful they looked.

"Saturday night," Cheryl clarified. "Hal left Larry and Sam up near Valentine and came home early from their hunting trip. Hal was in town Saturday night. I even saw him at the OK."

"Saturday night?" Linda asked. "I don't understand."

Cheryl opened her mouth, but Alma cut her off. "Don't you worry about anything," Alma said to Linda. "I can clean up."

"You sure?"

"I remember where things go, now scoot." Alma took a cookie sheet from the drying rack and put it in its place under the counter as Linda faded out of the room. Alma turned to Cheryl. "What'd you say all that for? Last thing the Aherns need to worry about is your husband's tantrum over having to walk a couple miles."

Cheryl crossed her arms. "I was saying Hal was back in town on Saturday, the night Peggy went—"

Larry stopped her with a hand on the arm, then leaned in, his elbows on his knees, his voice barely above a whisper. "Cheryl was there. At Castle Farm that night. Left before Peggy but saw her there." Clyle looked at Cheryl, but her eyes were down. He snuck a glance at Diane, who had tears in her eyes. She'd always been a softie.

"How'd she look, Cher?" Larry asked, and Cheryl scowled. "Drunk."

"Thing is," Larry said. "She saw Hal there too, and—"

Alma slapped her hands on the counter. "No. I'm not even going to listen to that." Larry glanced at Cheryl. "And it's Mrs. Costagan, you hear me?"

Suddenly loud voices started upstairs—Hal's and then Linda's.

"No!" Hal yelled.

Clyle stood up and rounded the corner, taking the stairs two at a time, Milo and the rest behind him.

"You put that back," Linda said.

Hal had gone to the upstairs bathroom and was standing in the hallway with his hand clasped high above his head. "I wasn't going to keep it," Hal whined. "I just want to look." Linda jumped to try to get whatever was in that clasped hand but barely reached his elbow. Hal looked at Clyle. "I remember Peggy wearing this. They've got everything," he explained, and held out a bracelet made of silver links— small, silver dangly things on the chain. Clyle thought one might be a football helmet. Linda snatched it from his hands.

"I saw him put it in his pocket," Linda said. "I came up here to check on Hal—he was gone a while—and he put it right in his pocket."

"For Pete's sake, Hal," Alma said. "You know better. It's not yours to take."

Milo stepped forward and took the jewelry from his mother. "I'll put it back."

"What's all this?" Joe Ahern said in his rough voice, ascending the stairs.

"It was a misunderstanding," Alma said.

Joe looked from Alma to his wife.

"It's nothing, really," Linda said. "Hal was just confused."

"I'm not confused," Hal said.

"Please," Clyle said. "He didn't mean anything. He's just. You know . . . ." The word *retarded* hung silently in the air. It was something he didn't like to say in front of the boy but true all the same. He thought about Cheryl's intimation—Hal had been back in town Saturday night—as well as the blood in the truck. It didn't mean anything, Clyle reminded himself. He refused to jump to conclusions but knew others in the town would soon enough. Not just because of tonight but because of that blasted picnic.

Joe pointed a finger at Hal. "We don't need this right now, you hear?" Clyle could smell the cloud of alcohol in the air. "We've got enough problems."

"It was a misunderstanding," Linda reasoned. "Go back to the basement. Hal was just here to help with the chores."

"We should get going," Clyle said. "Leave your family be." At the bottom of the stairs Cheryl and Larry stood looking aghast, their hands clasped—Hal Bullard making a scene again. He calculated how long it would take the two of them to shimmy into their coats, turn on the car, and land at the door of the OK: nine minutes. Nine minutes until everyone in Gunthrum thought Hal was involved.

On the way home Alma turned toward Hal. "You shouldn't have taken that bracelet."

"I didn't know. I didn't know that was wrong."

Alma pointed a finger at Hal. "Hal Bullard, that's a flat-out lie. You know right from wrong the same as any other man. You just don't want to admit it."

Clyle drove the half-mile between their house and the Aherns', and as soon as they arrived, Hal clambered out and said he'd see them tomorrow. Clyle stood with Alma in the driveway as Hal climbed into his truck, the keys already hanging in the ignition.

Alma waved as Hal backed up and pointed his truck down the lane. "Just you wait. Joe's going to contact Peck about Hal just as sure as we're standing here. Say he had something to do with Peggy going missing."

"There's no evidence to support that," Clyle said, because really, what was there?

Alma pursed her lips, sweat popping on her forehead. It was thirty-six degrees, and she unzipped her coat; Clyle guessed it was another hot flash.

"You're damn right," she said, and marched inside.

8

Milo knew he should be thinking only about his sister, but his parents had never let him stay up this late before. Everyone had cleared out of the house around midnight, and his parents had turned in shortly after that, not bothering to check if he was in bed. Before he knew it, it was two in the morning, then three. Even his giddiness at the prospect of being up so late was overshadowed by thoughts of his sister. He wobbled back and forth between worrying she was really missing, like truly *not here*, and the thought that she was in Lincoln, Nebraska, right this minute drinking daiquiris through a straw in some meathead's dorm.

He lay down on Peggy's bed even though he knew she'd have a shit fit that he was in her room. The pillow smelled like hairspray and girl sweat, and he inhaled deeply. There wasn't even a sliver of moon, but light streamed into the house from the farm light outside, reflecting off the snow and glinting off the volleyball trophy she'd gotten last year for most blocks, even though she was one of the shortest on the team.

Downstairs he sat in his father's navy recliner, engulfed by its size, and ran his hands over the smooth velour, the Pepsi he'd filched from the fridge on the coaster where his father's whiskey rocks usually sat. In the kitchen he rifled through the junk drawer filled with old keys, clothespins, the turkey lacers for Thanksgiving that his mother wouldn't be able to find later this month. In the back he found an open roll of Life Savers and threw away the yellow one on top, popping the red one into his mouth and biting down. It was tacky and soft and welded the back of his teeth together in a way that made him temporarily panic, fearing his jaw would be forever shut.

The only other times he was awake downstairs in the middle of the night were when he was sick and had come down to wake his mother. All he had to do was put a light hand on her shoulder, even over the covers, and she'd roll toward him and say, "What is it, sweetie?" Then she'd tuck him back in his own bed with a large mixing bowl on the floor in case he threw up and either a cold washrag or a warm one on his forehead. In the morning he'd get to stay home from school, and it was all worth it until he felt his stomach churn again with the sickening realization he was going to puke. Once he did, it was followed by immediate relief, the nausea gone as if with a wave of a wand. It almost made being sick worth it to feel that much better again.

He felt like he'd spent the last two days in a state of routine and not-routine. He'd gone to school, but his teachers had been nice to him; last night his parents had so many people over, it was like a weekend on a Tuesday. How long was a person expected to go on in this kind of limbo—not eating, not sleeping? Because fact was, he was hungry. Freaked out and worried but hungry.

Back in the kitchen, he pulled back the tinfoil on Mrs. Costagan's cinnamon rolls. One row left. With all that was going on, he doubted anyone would notice if he ate one, but who knew? He swore his mother used to measure any leftover brownies with a ruler. Peggy would come in and sneak just a quarter of an inch from the cut that was already there, the butter knife left in the pan. She'd come back and sneak a quarter inch again and again, finally switching tactics from the short cut where a brownie was missing to the long cut of the row. His mother would peel back the tinfoil after dinner to serve them for dessert and say, "My word, who ate all the brownies?" Peggy would never fess up. In her mind she hadn't eaten a full brownie, just a sliver too small to matter.

That was one of the things that bugged Milo most about his sister: how she could justify anything she did. He held on to this with a ray of hope that she really had just run away temporarily to get a taste of independence, that she had convinced herself it wasn't a big deal that she took off in the middle of the night and could show back up anytime. When she walked through the door and his parents flipped, she'd get a confused look on her face. "What's the big deal? I just needed a break. I told you I was going, didn't I?" Somehow she'd get them all to think it was a mistake on their parts, and he'd never felt so willing to take the blame.

Milo picked up the sticky butter knife and cut out one of the rolls, biting into the gooey frosting. He had no idea how to act right now and, six hours past bedtime, felt stupid-tired. Every time he shut his eyes, his body heavy as a bag of wet sand, they'd pop back open. It felt like the few times his mom had let him have a Coke after 5:00 p.m. He thought about praying. Kneeling in front of his bed earlier that evening had comforted him in the same way the routine of his nightly bath had; it had provided normalcy, but that wasn't really the point.

He quietly got a glass of milk from the fridge and slid the gallon back on the shelf. Peggy was the big milk drinker in the family. Would they start buying half-gallons now? Would they put a picture of her on the side? It was the kind of self-torture he usually found delicious—imagining the worst of the worst. Soon the college brochures would trickle in—Peggy was only a junior but a straight A student—and what would it be like to open the mailbox at the end of the lane one day and find one of those in there? Maybe mixed in with pastel sympathy card envelopes so it would be more dramatic.

He tried to feel that tight, sickening pinch of pain, but it felt too forced, and he gave up; all he wanted was to sleep. It was like watching a movie, the music swelling, and knowing he should feel something but being too exhausted from the buildup. Being so tired, it was like it wasn't happening at all, or it was happening to someone else, or maybe only to his parents. He didn't feel anything as much as he felt tired, and he felt terrible admitting that too.

His parents' bedroom door creaked open, and he nearly choked on the roll in his throat. He'd been sure they were asleep, and maybe they had been, but they were both up now. Their voices hummed from the hallway, followed by the quiet shutting of the bathroom door. His dad's voice spiked, and Milo felt it in his heart, like when they used the defibrillator on *Trapper John, M.D.*

"What was he doing with it?" his father asked, his voice clear, not muddied as it had been earlier in the evening by alcohol. Milo had just figured out a few years ago how much his father drank. His dad had tottered in the hallway one evening, a hand on each wall, and he'd asked his sister if Dad was okay, knowing from the *A–Z Health Guide* this could be a sign of a stroke. "He's drunk, stupid," Peggy said, and Milo had looked that up as well, eventually recognizing the fermented smell, the bloodshot and empty eyes.

From the bathroom his mother answered in a muffled tone, but his father continued. "He's the same one we had to stop from harassing her. I don't think it's a coincidence. What's he doing sniffing around here at a time like this? Jesus Christ, show some respect."

The toilet flushed, and the door opened, and his mother strode down the hall toward the kitchen, Milo's father behind her. "Joe, it's almost four in the morning." His father was wearing his white briefs with the stretched-out leg holes and a matching white T-shirt. It would have been comical if Milo hadn't been so struck with fear. He snuck into the dining room, shoving the roll in his mouth as he went. What if they caught him eating something sweet in the middle of the night when he should be in bed?

"I don't fucking care what time it is," his father said. Milo's stomach zinged again from the f-word.

His dad picked up the phone and began dialing, the clickety-clack of the rotary dial audible a room away.

"Joe?" his mother said, but there was no response.

"Peck? Joe Ahern here. . . . I know, but this can't wait. It's about Hal Bullard, the retard." He kept on, but Milo stopped listening. Hal?

Late last summer, after Peggy turned sixteen, Milo would ride into town with her for volleyball practice in the early afternoons, and she'd drop him off at the community pool while the team trained in the gym, then ran sprints at the track. He'd swim for an hour with one eye on the clock, knowing how mad it made Peggy if he was late; then he would put on a T-shirt and head behind the school to eat the snack he'd packed himself. Hal used to watch the team on the track, standing against the chain-link fence until the metal cut red indentations into his forehead. Milo had felt bad for him—it couldn't be easy being retarded—and he knew Peggy thought he was a weirdo, so eventually Milo asked Hal if he wanted part of his tuna fish sandwich so he'd come sit on the bench and not hover like a goon. Hal left the fence and sat next to Milo in the bleachers. "What else you got?" he'd asked, and Milo showed him a small sandwich bag of Oreos,

Hal's face lighting up. Milo's mother had gone back to work as a nurse two years before, and since then she'd bought them things like Planters Cheez Balls and Oreos, things she'd never bought when she'd been home regularly and had the time to bake cookies or make a potato salad.

"Those are my favorite." Hal sat next to Milo on the bench and shoved an Oreo in his mouth, not saying thank-you until he had his mouth full with a second cookie.

Milo pointed at Peggy. "She's my sister."

"So you get to see her every day? Aren't you lucky." It wasn't like when Scott said it, leering out the side of his mouth.

"I don't know," Milo grumbled. "She's not that great."

"Are you kidding? She's the prettiest one by far. And the nicest."

"Not to me." Every morning Milo was the one Peggy would elbow out of the way of the mirror, and he'd have to bend in front of her so he could see himself, a scowl on her face behind him as she held the curling iron in her hair. One time she'd fumbled the hot iron and left a burn like a pink leech on the back of his neck. Every morning she made him spit in the toilet when he brushed his teeth. Every morning he'd bellow down the stairs—"Mom, Peggy won't get out of the bathroom!"—but it didn't do a lick of good. It was one thing to get along with your little brother in the middle of the night with a handful of cards and another thing entirely in the morning when you had bangs to curl.

"Does she like Oreos too?" Hal asked, and Milo complained she'd eat an entire row, submersed in milk six at a time, then swirled with a spoon and eaten like ice cream. She knew they were his favorite. Why did she have to be such a pig? "They're my favorite too." Hal had been watching Peggy intently as she did girl push-ups, her arms shaking, her kneepads stained with grass. "You're so lucky."

Milo realized she might never make him spit in the toilet again. He leaned against the dining room wall with a twinge of pain so deep he knew it was a heart attack. He came into the kitchen clutching his thin chest. Could twelve-year-olds have heart attacks? He touched his mother's elbow, and she startled, his dad still bellowing on the phone, saying he wanted Peck to look into this now, goddamn it, not in the morning. There was a pause as Peck said something, and his dad cut him off: "Because I had a house full of people! I called as soon as I could." Milo figured it was because his father had been too drunk.

His mom turned around, and Milo twisted his face so the pain in his chest would be apparent. "What is it, sweetie?" she said automatically, then "Why aren't you in bed?"

"I don't feel good." It was hard to say the words for real, his breath so tight no air could get out or in. He remembered how on the way home from practice Peggy's face would be bright red, and a sour smell would emanate from the sweaty kneepads on her calves, and Milo would have to roll down the window.

His father was still on the phone. "I saw him myself at the OK. Drunk as a skunk." There was a pause. "With my brother, Randall. Now you listen up, Peck: I want you to talk to Hal Bullard."

Milo tried to imagine Hal with his blank, happy face and broad shoulders being a threat to anyone and couldn't picture it. Although one time Scott, his best friend, had found a baby bird on the sidewalk and crushed it under his Adidas, the bones crunching like twigs. People did things every day that Milo wouldn't have imagined.

Worse, though, it dawned slowly that this meant his dad believed something had happened to Peggy on purpose. Not an accident or a misunderstanding but a *crime*. He thought of his mother telling Sheriff Randolph she wasn't sure if Peggy was seeing someone, how she'd whispered it once his dad was out of the room.

Milo's mother moved her hand from his back to his forehead, the palm of her hand cool against his skin. It felt so . . . normal he could feel the air come back to his lungs, the expansion of his chest. "You need to go to sleep. Have you been up all night?"

"Do I have to go to school?"

His mother paused. "I guess not. I'll call Irv in the morning." Irv Johnston was the school principal, a man who wore the same five pale, short-sleeved button-downs in a rotation every week. Milo liked to categorize people into two groups: those who were sophisticated enough to live in the city and those who were not. He always believed he and Peggy were in the first, but maybe she didn't think that of him. Mr. Johnston was definitely in the latter group, which in Gunthrum was a pretty crowded one. He wondered whether from now on he'd divide the world a different way: before and after.

9

Alma had been following Peck's cruiser for the last two miles. She figured when he turned onto Highway 57 he was heading to their farm, but when he slowed at their lane, there wasn't the usual thrum of satisfaction that came from being right. Since she'd left for her bus route, the guys from Stevarts had shown up and dumped gravel down the lane. Peck's car absorbed the bumps, his suspension obviously better than hers. It was always so odd after they laid the gravel—like driving up a lane that wasn't yours, so different from what it had been just hours ago. Alma parked next to him in the driveway, both of them getting out and slamming their car doors in tandem. It was not quite eight thirty.

"Peck," she said, and he said her name back. "I have a pretty good idea why you're here. Joe Ahern got a bug up his ass?"

"I'm just here to talk," he said.

She wanted to be madder at Peck then she was, but could she blame him? He was just doing his job. She could work up a head of steam over Joe Ahern, though—putting two and two together to get eight.

"Well, come on in then," she said. "I'll put on a pot of coffee and get Clyle."

She rang the cast-iron dinner bell on the porch that had hung there since Clyle was a boy. When they moved to the farm, she'd assumed such a thing was an antiquated cliché— the farm wife ringing the men into dinner—but it was hard to find Clyle on the farm without walking a quarter-mile from building to building, and she had better things to do. She started the pot of coffee and took a crumb cake from the freezer, the dry pockmarks of freezer burn evident even through the cling wrap. She'd made it for Easter eight months ago and, never one to waste food, put the second half in the freezer.

Peck watched her cut the cake. "You don't have to do that," he said.

"I've got more to feed than you," she said. Oh, sometimes she just couldn't stop herself from being a little rude.

She cut off four big slices and put them in the microwave, a paper towel on top. Alma loved her microwave. When Clyle brought it home from Pickett's a year or so ago, she'd told him he was a tomfool—there was no way she needed a gadget that big to do what happened naturally on the stove, but by God, she found an excuse to use it every day.

She watched Clyle emerge from the barn, a rag in his hand that he tucked in his back pocket. It wasn't snowing now, but they were definitely into winter weather; even so, he had on only a long john undershirt and a flannel. Hal emerged behind him tucking his shirt into his pants, his arm going elbow deep. *Was it possible?* She shook her head. He'd hurt people before, yes, but only when provoked, and only men. Men were the root of all problems, she was convinced, even though she sometimes had to sit on her hands to keep from slapping the silly women in town when she was forced to attend meetings for the library board.

Clyle and Hal left their boots on the porch and came into the kitchen, straightening their slippers with their toes and nudging their feet in. "Peck Randolph," Clyle said, and held out a hand for Peck to shake. "What can we do you for?"

"Came to talk about that awful business up the road." Peck thumbed in the direction of the Aherns' farm.

"Awful business," Clyle repeated. "Just awful."

"Sure is."

Hal stared at Peck. "You're in my chair. I always sit there." Alma winced. Hal just couldn't hear how rude he sounded sometimes, how focused on the wrong thing.

"Sorry, son." Peck stood and moved to the middle as Hal settled in, Peck not even blinking at Hal's concern over something as inane as a chair when they were talking about a missing girl. "You like your routine. I can respect that. I have the same breakfast every morning: two poached eggs and a piece of toast."

"So, let me guess," Clyle said. "You got a call from Joe Ahern."

"I did indeed." Peck thanked Alma as she set the first fresh cup of coffee in front of him. "Said you were all out to his place helping last night. Neighborly of you."

"And?" Alma said.

"And Hal," he said, turning to Hal, and Alma admitted to herself again that she liked Peck; most people talked to her and Clyle, not Hal. "Mr. Ahern said you wanted to take a bracelet?"

"I did. I just wanted something of hers. I loved Peggy."

"Well, not exactly loved," Clyle interjected.

"No," Hal said gravely. "I mean it."

"Well, Peggy's who I want to talk to you about." Peck started with questions about the hunting trip—what time Hal left the cabin outside of Valentine, who he left behind, the exact address, what time he got back to town, when he'd shown up at the OK and who was there, and what he'd done point by point after he left.

Hal was in tears by the second question, confused why he was being asked about hunting. He had a natural distrust of men in police uniforms—another way he was like most men his age—that stemmed from a shoplifting charge at the Pamida a town over. Alma was usually behind him, adding the Snickers bar to her tab, but not the day the store manager stopped him at the door, a firm grip on Hal's arm. Hal had yanked his arm back and shoved the entire candy bar in his mouth, and things had escalated from there. In the end the store hadn't pressed charges, but by God, everyone heard about it.

Peck went on, asking him about the blood in his truck.

"How'd you hear about that?" Clyle asked, and Peck raised his eyebrows at Alma. "You told him?"

"I ran into him at the Pizza Ranch Monday night. We don't have anything to hide." Good Lord, why had she let all that slip?

"I know that." Clyle speared a piece of coffee cake into his mouth. "Hal said that was from a deer."

"It *was*," Alma said, and looked pointedly at Clyle.

Clyle ignored her and went on to explain deer were bleeders depending on where they got hit.

"Don't I know it," Peck said. "I've been hunting my whole life." Alma reluctantly set a piece of coffee cake next to Peck's notebook, and he told her thank you. "She said you cleaned out the truck?"

"We did," Clyle confirmed. "Hal tried to dress the deer himself, but it didn't turn out so well."

"And what'd you do with the carcass?"

"I told you that Monday," Alma said. "Hal brought it to Mick Langdon's dump."

"And did you see it there?"

"No, but—" Alma started, and Peck said calmly, "I'd like to hear this from Hal."

"She's right," Hal confirmed. "It's right there at the dump. But I don't know why you'd need to go looking at my deer."

"It was a doe," Clyle said, "and Hal had a buck-only permit. I'm going to take care of the fine."

"I'm not so concerned with the fine right now," Peck said. He looked up from his notebook. "And I'm assuming any hunting license would have been for the Elkhorn unit, not Sandhills?" Hal's mouth fell open in a panic. "Also not my concern right now. I just want to see that deer for myself. But that won't really prove anything, you see. I wish you hadn't done such a good job cleaning out that truck, Hal. A sample could have cleared some things up."

"What do you mean, a sample?" Hal asked. "A sample of what?"

"The blood."

Hal looked at Clyle, then back to Peck. "There wasn't a lot of blood. I mean there was, but not in the truck."

"Not in the truck?"

"No, but where I got it. On the road."

"You hit it on the road?"

"No, I *shot* it on the road." Hal stood up, distressed, and Peck held up both hands as if at gunpoint. "Sit down, Hal. I never said you didn't." He took a bite of the crumb cake and complimented Alma—a lie; the freezer burn had made it like Styrofoam. "And now, Hal, remind me again who you saw at the OK. You see Joe and Randall Ahern?"

"Maybe."

"Yes or no, Hal?" and Hal reluctantly told him yes. "Who else?" Peck asked, but Hal said it blended together with all the other times he'd been at the OK with a snoot full. "Larry Burke? Sam Gary?"

"No, they were in Valentine, where I left them. I saw Cheryl, though, and boy, was she mad."

"What about?"

"She thought Larry had lied about where he was 'cause he was supposed to be with me, but I was at the OK."

"And you got that straightened out?"

Hal shrugged. "I guess."

Peck wrote something in his notebook. "And after you left the OK?"

Hal shifted his eyes to his plate, touching crumbs with his fingertip and slipping it into his mouth. "I just went straight home."

"No detours?"

"I don't think so."

Alma thought back to Larry's dumb mouth rattling the night before. Hadn't he said Cheryl saw Hal at Castle Farm Saturday night? Panic sluiced through her nerves.

Peck set down his fork on his empty plate and told them search parties were going over Castle Farm with a fine-toothed comb, so if there was anything to be found, they'd find it. "I heard you were there, too, on Saturday night, Hal. That sound right?"

"Not *Saturday* night," he said, and Alma flinched. It was the kind of lie he liked best—one based on a partial truth—and she wondered what the catch was. He couldn't have been there Friday—he was in Valentine—but maybe Sunday? Or Saturday night after midnight? When he used to ride the special ed bus, he'd sit behind her in the morning trying to piece together a.m. and p.m. "It doesn't make sense," he'd say. "How can 12:01 be a.m.? It's still nighttime," and she'd go over it again, the switch from postmeridian to antemeridian. "You've got to be wrong," he'd insist, and then they'd go over it one more time on the way home.

Peck circled back to the beginning of the trip, when he shot the deer, the drive home from Valentine, the night at the OK, Castle Farm, asking again how much Hal had to drink. "Nine drinks? Ten?"

"I guess so," Hal said. Alma knew he kept track of drinks about as well as he kept track of Oreos, shoving them in his mouth by the fistful.

"And that bracelet. Peggy's. What'd you want that for?"

Alma's stomach twisted. It reminded her of when she'd been working as a social worker, lobbing her clients softballs and getting them to admit what she already knew was true. But what was true here, exactly?

"To remember her."

"What do you mean, to remember her? Is she gone?"

Alma snorted. "That's enough. Don't trick him with his own words, Peck. He just means remember her in the general sense, like I want to remember a time you weren't sitting at my kitchen table in my own home, edging toward an accusation."

"I understand," Peck said. "I'm sure there are a lot of people who want to remember a time I wasn't in their home. Especially the Aherns, when I was over there asking questions about their missing girl." Eventually, Peck stood up and took his plate to the sink and told them he'd be in touch.

They all walked him to his cruiser, unsure of the protocol. Peck pulled out his keys and unlocked the door; his was one of the only locked cars in town. "And that's your truck, isn't it, Hal?" He nodded to the red Dodge. "Seems like you got in a bit of a fender bender. There's a dent on the right side, and you've got a headlight out."

"He hit his garage," Clyle said. "You can go see it at his place. The whole thing's beat. Getting a big truck like that into his small garage is like trying to drive a bowling ball through a straw."

"Especially if you've been drinking," Peck added, and Hal nodded vigorously. "Okay with you if I go check out your garage, Hal?"

Hal looked at Clyle.

"Nothing wrong with that," Clyle said. Peck told them there'd be a meeting in town tonight to talk about what they knew about Peggy's disappearance and he'd appreciate their attendance. Clyle said they'd do what they could, and Peck climbed in and drove away.

Hal turned to Clyle and Alma. "Why does he want to look at my garage?"

"To see if it matches the dent in your truck," Clyle said. "Which it will, right, Hal?"

Hal grimaced and said yes and that he had to go in to the bathroom.

Alma followed him inside and washed the few dishes. Even a fool could see that hadn't gone well, and Alma was the first to say she was far from a fool. The toilet upstairs flushed, and she heard Hal open the door, then close the one to his room. She'd made a quilt for his bed a few years ago—a log cabin in scrappy blues—and drapes to match. The night she'd showed him, he'd wrapped himself in that quilt and dragged it downstairs to watch *The Dukes of Hazzard*, a grin on his face for a straight hour. Lord, she loved that boy.

Clyle came in as she set the last coffee cup in the drying rack. "Well?" she said. When he didn't answer, she turned around, his head bent toward the table. She looked at the flyaway mess of his hair that had spent the morning under a stocking cap and felt a spark of love for her husband. He had defended Hal to Peck, but would his loyalty continue if things weren't quite as Hal said?

"I guess we'd better call Herb." Herb was the lawyer they used for any land documents they needed drawn up and notarized, and he'd handled legal proceedings when Clyle's mother passed on.

"What's he know about something like this?"

"Not much, I'm guessing, but he's a place to start."

She wrung out the sponge and put it in the dryer rack next to the cups, glad she hadn't defrosted the good sugar cookies for Peck, stingy in that kindness. "I'm sorry, you're right. It's a place to start." Clyle usually raised his eyebrows at the rarity of her apologies but not this time.

"What about Hal?" she asked.

"What about him?"

"Do you think he understands?"

Clyle paused. "I'm not sure *I* do. Right now there isn't even a crime, so he hasn't been accused, Alma. It's clear as mud."

"I guess," she said, but nothing about the visit sat right with her. She knew Hal was lying about something, and if she did, Clyle and Peck did too, but Hal could be a booger about sticking to the untruth. A few years ago he'd been driving doughnuts in the snow in their yard when they were gone, grinding ruts in the grass four inches deep. A hot-rod trick one of his stupid friends had taught him after hours in the Lutheran church parking lot on a Friday night. It hadn't occurred to Hal that the truck tires would tear up the yard beneath the snow; he wasn't a man to always understand consequences. After some prodding, Hal finally came clean in a wash of tears. "It's not that you did it," Alma had told him calmly. "It's that you lied about it." Sometimes she wished her own mother—a hard-luck woman without an ounce of mercy—could get a look at her now.

As if reading her mind, Clyle said, "Not *Saturday* night?"

"I know. But it doesn't prove anything."

"And not much of a defense that he was too drunk to remember going to Castle Farm." But then Clyle reiterated, "They don't have anything to go on here. Don't worry yet, Alma. You heard Peck. Hal got drunk on Saturday night, and he tried to take a bracelet. That's not evidence of anything."

In the yard a possum moseyed its way across the lane, a rat-faced albino. What was it doing out during the day? Alma knew the habits of nocturnal animals and when one's behavior was suspect. After fourteen years she'd grown to love the farm, if not the town. She liked the purposefulness, that there was always something to do—vegetables to can, weeds to pull, flowers to plant, a chute Clyle needed an extra pair of hands to mend.

Back when she was practicing near Chicago, she spent her days helping other people weigh their options for a problem. People used to say to her that she must have a big heart to be a social worker, and she'd reply, "A big brain. The smaller the heart, the better." It wasn't until she'd lost the first baby, and then the second and the third, that she understood the desperation on her clients' faces, the need for someone to tell them what to do. Here on the farm there was always a list of what needed to be done, one she went over every night when she laid her head on her pillow.

"What I think," Clyle continued, "is that we should try to keep him away from the OK until they find her. Keep him away from alcohol." It had taken Hal days to finally admit who had taught him the doughnuts. Say what you would, Hal was loyal, and the man who had taken advantage of that as far back as high school was Larry Burke.

"Call Herb," she repeated. "See what he has to say."

"What about his mother?"

"Herb's?"

"You know who I mean, Alma."

Marta Bullard, Hal's mother, a woman more useless than the rest. Rumor had it that Hal had been a normal boy until an accident at Fremont Lakes when he was two. He'd gone too deep in the water without knowing how to swim, his father in jail and Marta on the shore with her rum and Cokes.

At the ER they'd told Marta he'd been without oxygen for a significant amount of time—very significant, it turned out. After that she'd dried out, found Jesus, and remarried, all the while imagining her simple son as a sign from God, a penance rather than a child. She'd done everything she could to keep him under her thumb, a constant reminder of her sins, rather than let him live his life. She hadn't wanted him to work for the Costagans or finish high school or get his own place. If it had been up to her, she'd have had him stay by her side so she could remain a martyr. When he turned twenty and graduated high school, Alma had helped him rent his first apartment, a furnished studio above Pickett's Hardware with a hot plate and a plant. Eventually, Marta moved to Kearney, three hours away, and married a third fool.

"We're not calling her. Not yet. Hal's got enough to sort out."

"She has a right to know—"

Alma cut him off. "She gave up that right years ago."

"Do you think there's any chance he—?" She was shaking her head before he even finished. "Me either. I'm just asking."

10

The guy who laid the gravel—Clyle's money was on Steve Stevart, the owner of Stevarts Gravel and Sand—had done a good job distributing the three cubic yards of rock from road to house, and Hal just needed to pull the box scraper to smooth the high edges down and get the gravel into the ruts. The lane was one of those Sisyphean tasks of farming, thanks to the daily beating of the heavy equipment driven back and forth. Clyle hated to admit how much help he needed on the farm these days.

At fifty-six he wasn't as spry as he had been at forty-two, when they moved back to Gunthrum, but that didn't mean he had a foot in the grave, no matter what the aches in his knees told him when he got out of bed in the morning. He had to remind himself his father had died at fifty-eight, his feet and hands twisted from complications with rheumatoid arthritis. His dad used to say, "Living is hard, but it beats the alternative." Clyle had wanted nothing more than to put a grandchild in his father's arms before he died, but it hadn't worked out that way.

He'd been awake a lot in the night cataloging the tragedies in Gunthrum beyond the boy with the bee sting. There'd been a farmer who killed another farmer over a land deal after Clyle moved away to college, and then when Clyle was in his thirties, his mother had called to tell him about a husband shooting another man over an affair with his wife. The husband's name had rung a vague bell in Clyle's head, the last names in Gunthrum spanning many generations.

"Shot him through the heart," his mother had said matter-of-factly. "Just like those gangs do up there in Chicago. You think we don't have enough excitement down here on the farm, but we've got plenty. Worst part was, he meant to shoot him in the leg. They'd been friends growing up. Both dated the girl in high school before one finally won out and married her. It was supposed to be a warning shot, but he looked at his friend's face and choked at the last second, pulling the gun up."

"There's no way you can know all that," Clyle told his mother, but like most speculations in small towns, it had quickly become fact. Growing up, Clyle didn't like how quickly gossip traveled, how everyone was always in everyone else's business, but when he moved to Chicago for college, he was surprised how much he missed it. He was in a biology class freshmen year with nearly a hundred other students and only knew three of their names. Alma had been the bright spot of those four years—a girl who knew the ins and outs of survival in the windy city. She was the antithesis of the women he'd known growing up—outspoken, brash, deferential to no one—and he loved how she sent back an overdone steak or haggled for Cubs tickets or debated him about the rights of vagrants. She stood up for herself and had opinions and was the opposite of the woman who raised him, whom he loved dearly but never once heard raise her voice. Somewhere, though, in the last thirty years everything had turned upside down. Turned out he did want a woman like his mother, and Alma, once outspoken, stopped speaking much at all.

With Hal outside working on the lane, Clyle picked up the kitchen phone and called Herb Visser, his number written in the front of the phone book in Clyle's spider-scrawl.

Jelane—Herb's secretary and wife—answered, and after the pleasantries, Clyle said he had some business for Herb, not land related. "Afraid our hired hand might have found himself in a bit of a predicament."

"How's that?" Jelane asked, and Clyle told her about Peggy's disappearance.

"It's just a terrible business," Jelane said. "I heard it on the news. It doesn't look good now, does it? Can't think of another missing girl we've had around here."

"I'm sure there have been some."

"You get out to the big cities like Sioux City or Omaha," Jelane continued on the phone, "there's going to be girls missing all the time, but we do a better job of keeping an eye on them here."

"You think so?"

"Can't say for everyone, especially those Aherns, but I know where my girls are at any given minute." Was that true or just what Jelane believed? "But what's that all got to do with you?" Clyle told her about his hired hand's fondness for the girl, how some might misinterpret, and she mm-hmmed her way to the end. "Got it. I'll have Herb give you a call. He and his brother are on a hunting trip, along with every other person in Nebraska with a gun, but I'll talk to him tonight and give him the message."

He told Jelane goodbye and hung up as Alma came up from the basement, where she'd been flipping a load of laundry. "What'd he say?" she asked, and Clyle said he'd left a message for Herb with Jelane. "Figures. Probably out lighting cigars with our hundred-dollar bills, thinking about all the money he's making."

"I don't think he makes that much. At least not off of us."

Alma harrumphed and got a pound of ground beef out of the fridge to start Maid-Rites for dinner in the Crock-Pot.

"About Marta—" Clyle said again, but Alma cut him off.

"We don't owe that woman a thing."

"I know we don't, but she's still his mother."

Alma pulled a wooden spoon from the crock and leaned against the counter. "I ever tell you what happened when Hal first tried to rent his own apartment?" She had, about a hundred times, but that never stopped Alma from repeating herself. "Marta called Oliver Pickett and told him Hal wasn't to be trusted, that he wasn't capable of living on his own. She dragged up every reason why he shouldn't, back to when he was seven years old and accidentally cut the tail off their cat." He could almost say it along with her, word for word, and he knew what was coming next. "So who cosigned on that rental agreement, Clyle Costagan? Who?"

"We did."

"That's right. So, if anyone needs to know what Hal's up against so they can help him, it's us, and we already do." She glanced at the clock above the desk; it was two forty, and she had to be at the bus garage by three. "I got to skedaddle. You finish browning that meat, would you?"

She put on her down vest and the hat she'd knitted herself, then came over to the table where Clyle sat with his afternoon peanut butter toast. She picked up the toast and took a bite, then wiped her crumbed fingers on her jeans. "How you can eat the same food both morning and night, I'll never know."

Clyle shrugged. Used to be they kissed each other goodbye when one of them left the house, but Alma just walked out the door. The list of what one person would never understand about another went on and on.

Clyle drove a town north and pulled into Vandershoot Vet Practice with Hal in the passenger seat. He'd been going to this vet since they'd moved back to the farm—the same practice Clyle's father had used—with Dan Vandershoot at the helm now, his own father having passed away. Dan went to Iowa State back in the seventies, and there'd been much speculation about whether he'd return, but like so many who tried to get away, he managed his way back thanks to a sick parent.

The same thing had happened to Clyle fourteen years ago, and people had lined up with the condolences and platitudes about how life never turned out the way you expected. He stepped up as the prodigal son and let everyone believe he was a hero for giving up Chicago, but it wasn't long before he was back in the groove of farm life, up at five o'clock to feed the livestock and afternoons spent solving problems—deer in the garden, a rusted disc harrow, rain on the way. The first week back, he'd gone to the OK with Alma, and seven people addressed him by name and asked how his mom was doing. When she passed, his father already gone, he and Alma agreed to finish out the harvest, then ready the farm through winter, and eventually she agreed to stay. It would be good for them, getting out of the city, but it was really just good for him.

Clyle opened the door and followed Hal into the vet's waiting area. While the Vandershoots specialized in livestock, they had a steady clientele of domestic pets as well that had grown under Dan's hand. He had a dog of his own—a black Lab named Clue—that greeted Clyle and Hal as they came in, ringing the bells on the door.

"Hey there." Hal bent to his knee to scratch Clue behind the ears, the dog responding with kisses. "Hey, buddy."

Coming and going through the practice was a steady stream of women who worked as vet techs and receptionists, many of whom looked the same to Clyle—brunette ponytail, indeterminate age, tennis shoes on their feet. Two women sat at the intake desk—Clyle thought they were new, but who could tell?—and he smiled at them as he approached. One of them had turned back to the filing she was working on, but the other, the one closest to the counter, smiled brightly, a hand futzing her bangs higher as she noticed Hal.

"Hi, there!" she said to Clyle. "How can I help?"

"I'm Clyle Costagan."

"Suzie," she said, then instantly blushed. "Sorry. You were probably telling me your name for your file, right? Not to introduce yourself? I'm new, if you can't tell."

Clyle smiled. "Nice to meet you, Suzie."

"Oh." She buried her face halfheartedly in her hands. "I'm embarrassed I did that."

Hal came to the front, Clue at his heels. "Hi, Suzie."

"Hello there," she said to Hal, her blush brightening. "So, you heard too? Ugh. I feel like a dummy."

"Let it go," the other woman said. "You told them your name, not your bra size."

Suzie leaned across the counter toward the two men. "I don't think she likes me very much," she said in a loud whisper.

"I just don't like listening to you apologize over and over," the woman clarified.

Suzie ignored her. She struck Clyle as being similar to Clue in that way, able to listen to only what she wanted to hear. They'd had a dog like that when Clyle was growing up—Patsy, a springer spaniel—who could discern the rattle of dry food into a dish three hundred yards away but wouldn't so much as flinch if you came into the room and told her to get off the davenport.

"And who are you?" Suzie asked Hal. Hal told her his name—first and last—and the other woman turned around, a file in her hand ready to alphabetize.

"Oh!" The name obviously had an impact.

Clyle started; that was fast even for a town away. He wondered for the first time if others, too, had thought of Hal in connection with Peggy even before the blood in the truck and the bracelet.

The other woman was older than Suzie, and Clyle now recognized her; last time he'd been in here, she'd flirted with Hal herself, asked if he and his wife had any pets at home. Hal had snort-laughed so hard—"I'm not *married!*" he exclaimed—that she'd backed off and busied herself with the order of antibiotics Clyle was picking up. The older woman seemed to have forgotten about that but certainly recognized Hal's name now. Was everyone in the county already talking? Everyone in the state of Nebraska? He could imagine her out for drinks with her girlfriends at their town's version of the OK, leaning in luridly to tell them how Hal Bullard looked her up and down like a side of beef, shuddering her shoulders at the memory she now believed.

"Suze?" the woman said. "Can I see you in the back for a second?"

Suzie smiled at Hal and Clyle and rolled her eyes. "I'll be right back, okay? Just have a seat." They were the only people in the waiting room right now other than another old farmer type.

Suzie followed the other gal to the back as the door swung open with another tinkle of the bells and a boy came in with a dog almost his size—part Lab, part hound, from the looks of it. The dog was so lethargic, the boy barely had to hold the leash, and eventually his mother puttered in behind him in a flannel shirt and jeans, her face free of makeup. "You and Ruff sit down," she said to her son and proceeded to the counter. "Hello?" she said loudly. "Anyone back there?" Clue whined at the new dog.

"Two ladies," Hal said. "They said they'd be back in a second, but it's already been a second. A lot of seconds."

"Sit," she said to her son. Clyle scooted out of her way, and Hal went over to the boy and sat in the seat next to him—just one small ping in the bucket of what he didn't understand: you don't sit that close to a stranger in a nearly empty waiting room.

"What's wrong with your dog?" he asked.

The boy ran his hand over the dog's back, the Lab-hound leaning his head on his lap with his jaw dropped, a steady line of drool cascading to the floor. "He's sick. Got in a fight with a raccoon a few days ago, and now he don't hardly eat nothing except the charcoal in the garage. He seized all up this morning, then pooped on the floor, so now my mom thinks he's got rabies."

"That's no good," Hal said. "They're going to kill him if he does."

The boy sniffed. "That's what my mom said. I'd rather die myself."

Hal nodded sagely. "I understand that. I got two sheep named Peanut Butter and Jelly."

The boy smiled. "Them's good names. This is Ruff."

"Like the bark?"

"Yeah."

Hal laughed. "Smart."

The boy's mother had leaned over the counter by now, her heels elevated from the ground. "Anyone back there?" she asked loudly. The old farmer continued to read his paper as if the room were silent.

"Just a sec," the not-Suzie woman said; then Suzie came out a moment later, her skin pale, hardly like the girl who'd been there before at all. She barely glanced at the woman, her energy all focused on Hal as if she'd had a near-death experience. Clyle clenched his hands. He wondered who might have started the rumors. Joe Ahern? Peck? Larry or Lonnie? He didn't want to believe it was Peck, who struck him as an upstanding and fair man.

"Listen," the boy's mother said. "This dog's not getting any better. Can we get a vet to take a look?"

Suzie gulped. "Dr. Dan's out back. Corrine's going to get him."

"It's an emergency," the woman said. "I'm pretty sure it's rabies."

Suzie glanced at Hal. "We're doing everything we can."

"Seems to me," the woman said, "that what you're doing is making googly eyes at a man while my dog's on death's door."

"Oh no!" Suzie slapped a hand to her chest. "I'm not doing that."

Hal scrunched his face, confused, and Clyle felt a spark of anger. No wonder the world was a mystery to him. No wonder. This woman had been flirting with Hal just a moment ago and now seemed horrified. No concern about how that might make Hal feel. No concern at all. Clyle went over and sat on the other side of the boy—no seats between them either—and said it was a fine-looking dog.

"You should see him when he's not all slobbery and gross," the boy said. "He sleeps with his head on my pillow."

Hal reached over to pet Ruff, and the dog let out a quick, high yelp of pain and nipped at Hal's hand, making contact with the palm.

"Ow!" Hal said, and scurried over a seat. "Your dog bit me!"

"He didn't mean to!"

"A little help!" the mother yelled.

Suzie rounded the counter and wrapped the leash tightly around her wrist, Ruff's jaw snapping back again. "You provoked him," she said to Hal, while Clue, used to other animals and their shenanigans, sat patiently in the corner.

"He did no such thing," Clyle said. "I saw it."

"How's your hand?" the mom asked, taking Hal's in hers. "Doesn't look like he broke the skin. I'm so sorry about this. You have to understand, the dog's sick."

"I saw it," Suzie said, her hand whitening from the tight leash. "My God, we're lucky no one else was hurt."

Dan Vandershoot came in from the back room, his hands wet from washing, and Clue came forward and nudged his crotch. "What do we have here?" he asked, his voice convivial.

Clyle knew as well as he was sitting here that Corrine—the older one—had told him Hal Bullard was here. Hal, the man churning through the rumor mill and tied to the missing girl. Clyle felt his heart swell with gratitude that Dan was going to treat them as he always had, his calm demeanor like a balm over people and animals alike. Dan had told Clyle one time that of all the livestock farmers he knew, he thought Clyle was the most humane. He raised those hogs for meat sure as anyone else, but he gave them a good life while they had it. It was the best compliment Clyle ever received.

Suzie and the mother started talking at once, telling different versions of the same story. One said that Hal had provoked the dog; the other leaned on it not being the dog's fault. Dr. Dan walked over and looked at Hal's hand, Ruff now cowering under the boy's feet. "A sturdy lad like you?" he said to Hal. "Why, I bet that barely hurt."

Hal sniffed. "It hurt a little."

Dan clapped a hand on Hal's shoulder. "You going to be okay, son?" Hal nodded. "All right then." He turned his attention to the boy. "Let's get Ruff back for a look."

Suzie handed the leash to Dan as the mother said, "He's never bit anyone before in his life." Had she recognized Hal as well? Did she really think he had provoked the dog?

Over his shoulder Dan said to the receptionist, "You take care of Mr. Costagan's order, Suzie, and be quick about it. He's one of our best customers. Clyle, I'll call you later today if Ruff has anything serious you need to worry about with that bite, but my suspicion is not. Like all of us, Ruff just got to eating something he shouldn't have."

Suzie shuffled to the back room and came back with their six glass bottles of penicillin, syringes rattling in the bottom of the bag. "Here." She handed the bag across the counter to Clyle. It was pinched between her two hands like he might have cooties.

"Hal? Will you get that?" Hal reached over, and Suzie gulped. "He didn't have anything to do with that dog biting, and you know it."

Suzie leaned in and loud-whispered at Clyle, although Hal was as close as he was. "I don't even know why he's out walking the streets. How is it they don't have him in jail right now?"

"Who?" Hal asked.

"You," she said nastily.

"That's it," Clyle said. There was shit he'd always hated about small towns—he remembered that now. He'd call back later today and try to get this girl fired, see what Dr. Dan thought about his humane ways then. Was this what it was going to be like now? The jury already in? "You tell Dan I'll be calling later today about you. About your rudeness."

Suzie looked surprised but then laughed. "Okay, then. You make that call."

In the pickup on the way home, Hal asked Clyle what Suzie had meant. "It's about Peggy, isn't it?"

"It is." Clyle explained the best he could about the conclusions people had drawn.

"You think I should be arrested?"

"I'm saying that's what other people think. There's absolutely no reason you should be." Hal nodded, but Clyle wasn't sure if he understood. "It's not a good idea for you to go out on your own for a while. Let Alma pick up your groceries and what you need from town."

"But what about my friends? I'll want to see my friends at the OK."

How to get this through his thick skull? "They're not your friends anymore, Hal. Never were."

"Just like that?"

"Just like that."

That afternoon Clyle walked across the expanse of their farm to the back shed and wondered if they should get a dog. How different his days would be with a puppy trailing behind him, barking at the pigs when they charged the gate or sleeping on the top of the well, where the cement retained the most sun rays—the warmest spot to lie in the spring and fall. That had been Patsy's favorite spot. She was a farm dog—a liver-and-white springer they'd had since Clyle was a toddler—and one day, out of the blue, she'd bitten a neighbor.

Old Dr. Vandershoot had said it was rage syndrome, which sounded like a made-up thing but was a sudden onset of aggression the dog couldn't control and hardly seemed to remember. A few minutes after she bit the man, she tried to nudge her nose in his lap for treats. Clyle's father had gone out to the back acreage with a loaded gun in one hand and the dog by the collar in the other. Clyle was in the kitchen at the time with his mother, whose shoulders jerked when the shot came.

His father had come back ten minutes later, the gun in one hand, the other empty. For years Clyle had dreamed about

Patsy, to the point he could feel her weight jump on the mattress in his sleep, circle twice, then flop at his feet, her chin tucked on his ankle. He thought about Dan Vandershoot's comment that he was the most humane farmer he'd known. Had Dan's father said the same about Clyle's father, and if so, because of or in spite of what he'd done to Patsy?

It was almost five o'clock now, the sun nearly set. Clyle hung up the Phillips he'd been using to repair a feeder and headed inside, careful to wipe his shit- and mud-stained boots before taking them off on the porch. "Alm?" he said, but there was no answer, even though her car was in the garage. She must be in the shower.

Down the road at the Ahern house, there was nothing to indicate the tragedy they were in the midst of. He thought there should be scorch marks, but it looked like any other farm on a country road. There were times he'd seen Joe Ahern in town, the rare evenings when Clyle went to the OK. Joe was part of that crowd he and Alma had fallen into when they'd moved back, along with his old buddy Lonnie, and it was obvious Joe was the pack leader type. He was in his early forties, a good-looking guy with a lot of land and money. Clyle knew, too, that he'd stepped out plenty on Linda.

When Clyle moved back to Gunthrum with Alma, he began to understand a culture to the town he hadn't known as a boy, or maybe one that hadn't existed when he was growing up in the early fifties: people in small towns slept around and by the seventies, when he moved back, a lot. His first boys' night out at the OK, Alma stuck at a women's church group before she decided she couldn't stomach that nonsense, Lonnie and the rest of them (was Joe there? Clyle couldn't remember) had regaled him with story after story of this or that local woman. Even if half of them were lies and boasting, it made for a hell of a track record. He'd come home to Alma and counted his blessings, even though she was grousing about how all the women did was eat a gossip sandwich with a prayer at the beginning and end as bread.

"A bunch of hens," she'd said later that night in bed. "Peck, peck, peck, peck, peck." When he put his hand on her hip and petted down to her thigh, she picked it up and dropped it to the mattress. "Uh-uh. You got me into this, Clyle Costagan." He thought of the men at the OK talking about the abundance of women. "A smorgasbord," one of them had said, and at the time it had turned Clyle's stomach.

Maybe Peggy's disappearance had something to do with Joe's affairs, but how would that have involved Peggy? And while Clyle knew having an affair wasn't anything to be proud of, it usually didn't end in a kidnapped child, or God knows, half the town would be missing.

He had hoped the funk that had settled into Alma after the miscarriages would be alleviated by the move, and for a while it was. That first summer she'd made plans for a garden, sketching it out on graph paper down to the last beanpole. She'd bought a used Singer and quilted her first nine-patch with mismatched corners that she ended up storing in the trunk of the car for winter weather. Overall he thought she was happier, but those babies lingered, stillborn in her memory as her great failures. And then all that happened with Diane.

He hadn't set out to be unfaithful, but he doubted anyone ever did. She'd just been so . . . uncomplicated. He had Alma criticizing him at home and all their terrible history, and Diane, who seemed to believe he could rescue her from her doldrums, as if his past in Chicago would be an escape by proxy. It started with flirtations at the bank where she worked, then looks across the bridge table, until one night on impulse they'd kissed in a bedroom at one of the drinking parties—who had pulled in whom? He couldn't remember, but that kiss haunted him all that week until they could do it again the following Saturday.

Eventually, they found ways to meet on the sly, her adoration like a salve over the wounds he thought Alma had inflicted. He realized now she had done no such thing—it was his own selfishness that had led to the affair.

Toward the end of it all, Alma said she wanted her days of cutting teeth and tails behind her and could they hire a soft-headed boy to help with chores on the farm? Of course, he said yes. Hal was seventeen at the time and had started working for them on the weekends. Hal struck a chord with Alma for whatever reason, and eventually Clyle felt the same. There was something about having the third chair filled at the breakfast table on the weekends, a buffer and tie between the two of them. When Hal was set to graduate high school, after three years of summers and weekends at the Costagan farm, Clyle said to Alma, "I could use the extra hand full-time. At least during planting and harvest."

She hooked her yarn around the crochet hook, a blanket taking shape in her lap. "Well, it's sure not work I'm going to do."

He and Alma had talked to Hal about going full-time, and then to Marta, his mother, who had been resistant to his working at the Costagans' all along. "He's dumb," she'd said. "Can barely find his way down the high school hallway from math to English, and you think he's going to be able to follow directions on a farm? He needs more guidance than that. More structure."

"We've got plenty of structure," Alma had said. "Breakfast, lunch, dinner, and peanut butter toast between each. He'll be fine."

As much as Marta had resisted, and as confused as Hal had been, caught in the middle, he was an adult and could do what he wanted. Marta moved away a year later, and the boy she'd hovered over for twenty years virtually disappeared from her life. Last year for Christmas she hadn't even sent a card.

Still, she was his mother. When Clyle lived in Chicago, he and his own mother had a weekly call every Sunday afternoon that he sat through with half an ear as she recounted the Gunthrum gossip. He'd putz around the apartment as long as he could before giving in and making the call, an obligation more than a real relationship. But he'd done it because that was what sons did.

He picked up the phone and called information, and a woman with flat vowels told him the number he needed. A moment later Marta answered on the other end. "It's Clyle," he said. "Costagan. Hal might be in some trouble."

11

Milo stood in the hallway outside Peggy's room, drawn by the afternoon light. She'd made him switch rooms two years ago, saying she hated the morning sun on the weekends, and because he was a sucker and would do just about anything she asked of him and because he was more of a morning person, he'd agreed. Hauling armloads of their stuff between the two rooms, she'd knocked him with her hip and said, "Thanks, Mi." In his now-room there were still bald spots in the wall paint where her poster of the Eiffel Tower had hung, a red glob of dried nail polish in the carpet by the closet. These things had never bothered him. He liked the reminders of his sister, her ghost in the room.

Her now-room looked much as it always had, squares of sunshine outlined by the windowpanes in elongated rectangles on the kelly green carpet. The bed was still made in the haphazard way that had let him know Sunday morning that Peggy hadn't been home. When Milo was younger, he used to love solving the mysteries reprinted in the *Gunthrum Pioneer*. "A man is found dead hanging from the rafter in his home with a puddle of water under him but no chair or ladder. The doors and windows are locked." Two of his favorites had been "The Case of the Red-Handed Vandal" and "The Missing Dimes." Eventually, he'd moved up to Raymond Chandler and Tony Hillerman, but these stories were longer and more confusing. He loved the ease of the one-page mysteries that he could solve halfway through. The man had stood on a block of ice; the out-of-town cousin took the dimes.

The bulletin board on Peggy's wall held the two track medals from last spring that his mother still hadn't sewn onto her letterman's jacket. Next to her window, there was a discarded T-shirt she'd worn around the house Saturday afternoon and a pair of gray sweatpants. He walked closer. Inside the sweats, twisted like a nervous napkin, were a pale, pink pair of underpants, a tiny brown stain on the crotch.

"Milo?" his mother said, and he let out a little scream. "What're you doing in here?"

"Just looking around."

Her face softened. "We didn't mean to startle you. Laura's here with Peggy's homework." Laura held a Trapper Keeper against her chest and gave a little wave.

Laura had driven the seven miles from town on Monday and Tuesday as well, with a folder of assignments for Peggy, although it would have been easier to just hand it to Milo after school when he headed to the bus and she to cheer practice. What if Peggy never came home? At what point would Laura stop coming? This was the problem with hope: at some point it had to run out, and in a way wouldn't that be better than waiting for the other shoe to drop? Last year he'd bombed an Algebra I test on a Friday, really stunk it up, and all weekend he thought, whatever the grade is, it's not as bad as wondering. On Monday, when he got it back with a D+ scrawled at the top, he revised that thought. There were worse things than not knowing, and as much as he wanted to know where Peggy was and what had happened to her, maybe that was just him being unable to really believe the worst. Nabbed? Run away? Yes, there were worse things.

"I've got some cleaning downstairs," his mother said, and left the two alone.

Laura rubbed a finger under her nose, then wiped it on her jeans. "It's gross, I know, but I think I've used up every Kleenex on earth."

It was just the kind of thing Peggy would have said to him. Laura walked in and touched one of the pillows at the top of the double bed where she'd spent hundreds of nights.

"Does anything look out of the ordinary?" Milo asked. Near the closet sat the tennies Peggy wore for volleyball, the left one on its side, and he could imagine his sister stepping on the heel with the other foot to remove it and then her socked toe stepping on the right. People who didn't think girls stank didn't have an older sister who played volleyball. A handful of paperbacks were strewn across the window seat cushion, probably Stephen King books or the *Sweet Valley High* series she'd read since junior high, with two obnoxiously blonde twins on the covers. Even the underwear, curled in his sister's sweatpants, seemed like it could lead to answers.

Laura shrugged. "I don't know. Looks the same to me, I guess." She and Peggy had been best friends almost all their lives.

"Do you really think she's missing?" he asked.

Laura looked at him, confused. "Don't you?"

Milo shrugged. "Seems weird, I guess. Someone just disappearing. That kind of thing doesn't really happen in Gunthrum, you know." He peered at Laura. "Nothing happens in Gunthrum. I wonder if that's the problem."

"You mean you think she just left? Where would she go?"

Milo shrugged again. "I don't know. Lincoln? Paris? Who knows."

Laura started shaking her head before he'd finished. "She wouldn't just do that. She'd tell me."

"Well, she didn't tell *me* either."

"Yeah, but you're her little brother. I'm her *best friend*. We didn't have secrets."

Milo looked at Laura incredulously. "You don't think so?" Peggy had plenty of secrets, and those nights over Uno they talked about more than just blowing this pop stand. He knew Peggy couldn't stand that Laura weighed six pounds less than her, and she'd thrown up her dinner two weeks in a row until their mom made her go to the doctor because her throat was so sore. He knew Peggy better than anyone. He knew Peggy had made out with Kerry after he was with Laura and that Peggy felt so terrible about it, she could never tell. He also knew Peggy had had a hickey a few weeks before she disappeared. Had that been Kerry too?

"Of course not," Laura said. "She would never leave without telling me. As a matter of fact . . . ." Laura closed the door, the bottom jamb rifling the top of the green shag carpet. "I'm the one with a secret. It's about that night." No need to clarify which night. She had already told the story to his parents, the police, her own parents.

Milo held his breath. "What?"

"You know how I said Kerry took me home?"

"Yeah?"

"Well, he did. But I heard he went back. He told me he was going cruising since he didn't have to be home until one o'clock, but then some of the football players said they saw him at Castle Farm partying with the oldsters—Hal Bullard, Cheryl Burke, Tonya Gary—and Peggy was still there. You know how he always had a thing for Peggy."

"What thing?"

She rolled her eyes. "Oh, shut up, Milo. You know. We all knew. He was crazy about her." Laura had been dating Kerry for about four months now, and it had been a year since he had dated Peggy. Peggy was the one who told Milo that Laura was going out with Kerry but that she didn't care. "Let her have him. My gift to her." But then a month or so after that, she'd made out with him when they were drunk at Castle Farm. How word didn't get out about *that* he didn't know, but somehow they kept it a secret. And Milo was the only one she'd trusted to tell.

It was interesting to watch the dynamic between the three of them—how Peggy had kicked Kerry around and then how he'd done the same to Laura. Milo had heard Laura crying about how Kerry was sometimes an hour late for dates or how he had told her they'd go cruising after a game and then he'd gone with his friends instead. What was it Milo's father said? Shit rolls downhill.

Laura's eyes dampened. "He broke up with me, can you believe it? He said this stuff with Peggy just stirred up too much. Said he still had a torch for her. Did he think I didn't know that? Did he think *anybody* didn't know that?"

"Maybe he did like her, but she wouldn't go back to him. She wouldn't do that to you." His sister was a pain in his butt, and maybe she'd slipped and kissed Kerry, but overall, she was loyal. She could make him spit in the toilet every morning of his life, but when he was just a second grader and he got his head stuck in a bike rack after school and all the kids had gathered around to laugh at him while the bus monitor found the janitor, Peggy had stood next to the bike rack and shooed the kids away. He didn't remember how it happened or, for God's sake, what he was trying to do putting his head through in the first place, but he could still feel the claustrophobic swelling of his neck between the metal poles and knew the only thing that had calmed him was his sister's hand on his sweaty back.

"I don't know," she said, "but maybe he did something to her? Like, he tried and she rejected him? I can tell you this: Peggy was seeing *someone*, and I bet that drove Kerry insane." Laura sat on the bed and took one of the throw pillows—

crocheted green and yellow granny squares his mother had made—and placed it in her lap.

Milo thought about his mom telling Peck his sister wasn't the type to be alone. He doubted it was Kerry, who Peggy had once called an overgrown toddler. "I'm done changing diapers," she'd said. Milo's chest tightened. All those nights when he'd thought they were so close, almost friends, maybe they meant nothing to her at all. Maybe she'd just been changing *his* diaper. "But who?"

Laura shrugged. "She wouldn't tell me."

"Well, then, how do you know she was seeing someone?"

"It wasn't that tough to figure out. She was super distracted. She didn't wear a ponytail to cheer. On the weekend nights I didn't have a date with Kerry, Peggy would sometimes say she wanted to just stay home, but who wants to do that? Maybe she was out with him." But Peggy had been home some weekend nights. On a Saturday when she was just hanging around the house, she'd dressed in jeans and a sweater rather than her Gunthrum sweats. His mother had teased that she was putting on airs. Milo thought she was practicing for their more sophisticated future—he doubted anyone in the city wore sweats—but maybe it was more than that and she'd snuck out on nights when he didn't even realize. Maybe he'd missed the clues all along.

"But," Milo started, "didn't she dump Kerry? Why would she want him back?"

"Because I wanted him?" Laura tucked the pillow back in the corner, and Milo had to give her credit that she wasn't as dumb as she acted. "And I don't know that it was Kerry. Adult stuff is complicated. She wouldn't hurt me for the world, but she would, you know?"

"I don't know."

"You don't know-know because you're *twelve.*"

Milo hated when people used that as an excuse. It was like people saying you're a boy or from rural Nebraska. What did that have to do with anything? "Did Kerry tell Sheriff Randolph that he was at Castle Farm?"

"I'm sure he did—I did too—but the question is, did he tell him he was there *after* midnight?"

"Why don't you ask him?"

"I can't just ask him," Laura huffed. "What if he really did something and he tries to do something to me too?"

Milo had a gruesome thought but didn't speak it: if he did something *to* her, then what did he do *with* her? He was dizzy at the prospects and filled with a trembling cold; this wasn't a mystery book. It was his sister.

Laura set the file of assignments she'd brought on Peggy's desk, on top of the ones from Monday and Tuesday. "Listen, I gotta go."

"Yeah, okay," he said, and she bopped him on the nose—what was he, six?—and said he'd see her tonight at the assembly. Sheriff Randolph had arranged a whole-town meeting to discuss Peggy's disappearance, and the detective his dad had hired was going to be there with him.

"How can you think your boyfriend would do something like that?" he asked, and Laura shrugged.

"I was going to break up with him anyway."

12

Alma set her quilting in her lap as Hal came in the front door, his face flushed from the cold.

"There's a meeting tonight," he said. "Whole town's going to be there. People think something bad happened." Peck had put an announcement in the weekly edition of the *Gunthrum Pioneer* saying if Peggy wasn't found by Wednesday night, they'd have a town assembly. There were fliers at the school, in Pickett's Hardware, Gunthrum Foods—hardly anywhere you could go in town and not know, which meant Hal must have headed to town despite their requests not to.

Alma poked her needle up from the back of the fabric and looked at Hal. His face was scrunched and concerned, but what was he worried about, exactly? The meeting? What had happened to Peggy? Information that might come out? She pushed those thoughts away and shook her head. "Only bad thing is a girl ran away. End of story."

"Can I ride with you?" Hal asked.

Alma knotted the thread and broke it off with her teeth. "That's not a good idea, Hal. Why don't you sit this one out?"

He furrowed his brow. "Why?"

"It's just . . . ." He sat on the sofa next to her and leaned his head against her shoulder. "You just sit tight. This will all be over before you know it."

She felt him nod as he pointed at the quilt block in her hands—an Irish Chain in Christmas colors with holly appliqué. "That's pretty."

She smiled and leaned over to kiss the top of Hal's head, which smelled of apricot shampoo and feeder dust. "It's for Clyle for Christmas."

"Ain't he lucky," Hal said, and Alma's heart twisted. How long had it been since Clyle felt lucky to be married to her?

When Alma and Clyle moved to Gunthrum, Lonnie and the rest welcomed Clyle back with open arms and took Alma in the bargain, and yes, even she realized she was the sour half of that sale. Nothing like she was now but still a woman who spoke her mind and didn't suffer fools gladly.

It was the early seventies, and the refinished basement phase hit Gunthrum with a wall paneling vengeance. Many people had carried a pool table piece by piece down the basement stairs, added a card table, and started throwing parties. They said it was better than the OK—cheaper—but the real reason was that most of them had kids now and couldn't leave them at home alone. The parents were willing to give over the living room with the TV as long as they could have a space of their own, drinking until all hours of the night, with the kids sacked out upstairs in sleeping bags the parents kept in their trunks.

Alma and Clyle hadn't been big drinkers in Illinois—not teetotalers by any stretch, but she could count on both hands the number of times since college that she'd been drunk—but here it was the thing to do. The parties were always fun to a point—games of bridge and whist, smoking, raucous talk. Every now and again a kid would wander down the stairs to the finished basement looking for his or her mother to ask what time they were going home or whether they could have another bowl of popcorn, and whichever woman was closest to the stairs or soberest would answer the question. "Yes, more popcorn." "No, just fall asleep in your sleeping bag." Depending on how drunk she was, Alma would answer the kid's question herself even though she didn't really know whether it was okay if they had more popcorn or root beer or if they were allowed to watch *The Dick Cavett Show*.

A few years in, on one of those nights when everyone was well into the drink, half of them with an eye squinted shut so they could read their bridge cards or make a seven in the corner pocket, Alma had gone upstairs to get another whiskey Coke, and a man had come up behind her at the kitchen counter. He'd slid his hands around her waist and toward her crotch, and she'd assumed it was Clyle, even though it wasn't like him to be so forward in public, even if they were alone in the room. She'd turned her head around, and Lance Carpenter—married, two kids—had leaned forward and put his oily mouth on hers, one hand up to grab at her breast. She pushed off from the counter and against his chest as hard as she could with the instincts of a caged animal, the back of her head knocking his chin.

"Hey now," Lance said, a hand at his mouth. "Hey." He stumbled against the counter to steady himself.

Alma hadn't known what to say. It was one thing to have men imply they wanted to sleep with her, or even Lonnie, innocent enough when he touched her arm, but to be groped so vilely crossed into new and threatening territory. She stomped downstairs and told Clyle it was time to go. "Let me just finish my drink, Alm."

She told him, "No. Now," and Clyle slapped down his cards, not even finishing his hand. She thought at the time it was loyalty, but maybe he just knew to avoid a scene.

In the passenger side of the pickup that night, staring at the empty two lanes of Highway 57 through the cylinders of headlights, she said, "I had to get out of there."

"It's fine," Clyle had said. "I'm always ready to go when you are." And even though he was drunk, he put one hand over hers in her lap, the truck steady on the road. She couldn't explain yet what it had felt like—the shock of a strange man's hands on her body—and while she figured she would eventually tell Clyle, she never did.

Later that week, her dander still up, Alma sat in the barber's chair at her friend Phyllis's house; Phyllis's husband, one of the gang, had converted the mudroom into a salon. Her wet hair plastered to her head and a vinyl cape around her shoulders, Alma said, "I have half a mind to storm over to Lance's house and tell his own damn wife what's going on."

Phyllis tapped her comb against Alma's shoulder. "Well, let's think about that for a moment. There's something you should know before you go pointing fingers."

Clyle and Diane—that's how Alma found out.

Over dinner, with a forkful of scalloped potatoes in his hand, Clyle told her he called Marta.

Alma slammed the bottle of Dorothy Lynch on the table, the glass reverberating against the wood. "Clyle Costagan, I told you not to do that," she said in her bus driver voice.

"I know you did," Clyle said and set down the bite of potatoes.

"And you did it anyway?"

"I did." He took a drink of his Lord Calvert and Sprite and wiped his mouth with a napkin. "We disagree on this, Alma. I did what I thought was right. She's his only living family."

"And what are we?" she asked. "If that's what you call family, what are we?"

"We are no less his family," Clyle reasoned, "for me having called her."

Alma stood from the table, swooping Clyle's not-quite-finished plate from between his elbows. "What did she say?"

"She was sorry to hear about it all."

"Well, then, Mother of the Year." She scraped the rest of Clyle's salad and potatoes in the pig bucket, an old ice cream gallon they kept under the sink that Alma emptied most mornings, the pigs clamoring to the edge of the pen on cue when she showed up with the plastic bucket in hand.

"She's coming down this weekend."

Alma whipped around. "Here? What in the devil for?"

"He needs her support, Alm. He needs everyone he can get."

Alma shook her head, scrubbing at a dried speck of potato. "That ninny's going to come down here and get him all riled up. She'll have him convinced by the end he can barely tuck himself into bed at night. She'll probably convince him he had something to do with all this." Clyle sat at the table, his drink in his hand. She was tempted to take that away too.

"You need to remember, he hasn't been charged."

Alma brought the plate hard against the porcelain sink, disappointed when it didn't shatter. "That's because they don't have a body! What's going to happen when they do, huh?"

"Are you saying you think Hal is guilty of something?"

She pointed the plate at him. "Don't you even." She remembered back in high school—the boy Hal beat unconscious and that business with Hal's father and the man he killed. How dared Clyle say those words out loud.

"Well, I'm going to assume the evidence will point to him being innocent, Alm. Did that even occur to you?"

"What's occurred to me is that no matter what way the evidence points, my number one concern is Hal." That was the truth: number one over Clyle, number one over innocent or guilty. Her stomach flipped at the thought.

"She's coming," he repeated. "Saturday for lunch."

"You expect me to cook for this woman too?"

"No, I expect Hal to. We'll show her how well he does on his own." He glanced at the schoolhouse wall clock. "It's six thirty. We should head out soon."

"Fine. As soon as I finish these dishes. But I'm mad at you, Clyle. Don't think I'm not."

"I think I know better than that by now."

When Phyllis told Alma about Clyle's affair—Alma with a vulnerable, wet head in the barber's chair—Alma told her that was asinine, Clyle wouldn't do such a thing, but by the time she got home, hair set, she had racked her brain and tried to remember ever having seen Diane and Clyle together at a social event in the last few months. They never sat at the same card table; they never sat next to each other at a football game. There wasn't a single moment when she'd watched Clyle and Diane interact at a party, which she couldn't say about Clyle and any of the other wives. There was always a time when he had helped carry beers down from the kitchen or shared a smoke with one of the ladies on the walk-out porch or a tournament when he'd partnered with them in bridge. The only time she recalled Clyle and Diane together was six months ago, when, unexpectedly, she'd seen them in town.

Driving away from the bank, she'd found them in their cars pointed opposite directions, their driver's windows lined up in the feedstore lot. Alma had driven over, innocent as pie, and said how odd it was to see her own husband in town unexpectedly. Her face burned with shame at the memory, the laugh they must have had about it later.

The next weekend after her visit to the salon, when Clyle said he'd talked to Lonnie at the service station and people were getting together at the Aherns that Saturday, Alma said, "I don't feel like going this week."

"Everything okay?"

"Why wouldn't it be?"

Clyle held his hands up and backed out of the room, his usual response when Alma was in one of her don't-mess-with-me moods. Who could blame him for taking up with Diane, a woman whose disposition when she drank too much was to laugh even harder at everyone's jokes, who wore buttons supporting individual football players even though she didn't have a boy on the team?

That day Alma had come home from Phyllis's salon and run her head under the tub faucet, the sticky mess of her shellacked hair running clean. All the women in town wore Aqua Net like a helmet, but she was tired of trying to fit in, exhausted by rules in this small-town game that no one had bothered to explain to her. She'd made their recipes and attended their church, and still, at most turns she was excluded.

When they were all together on a Friday or Saturday night, the women would roll their eyes at Alma and tell her how lucky she was that her life didn't revolve around kids—soup-and-pie fundraisers for 4H, honor society luncheons, the fifth grade Christmas show. They'd say she was lucky to skip all that boring stuff but then go on to talk about how cute their kids were dressed up as a donkey and a wise man. Diane had been one of the few who had gone out of her way to contact Alma, extending invitations to both a Bible study and a golf league. Alma didn't believe in the Bible and had never swung a single club, so what was she supposed to do about that?

Over the next few months, when Alma ran into the women in town from the crowd and they asked where she and Clyle had been—"You left us in a pickle with the bridge tournament"—she told the women the hangovers had gotten too bad. The nauseous stomach, a headache like a stake through her eye, the way her skin in the morning seemed one size too small. It just confirmed what people had assumed all along: Alma thought she was better than them. That or everyone knew the real reason: that Clyle had finally wised up and gotten a little sweetness in his life and mean old Alma had figured it out. Either side of that coin had them thinking it was her fault, and Alma, who had marginally drunk her way to being one of the gang, was on the outs again and had pulled Clyle out with her.

When Alma arrived at the school gymnasium that night, everyone seemed like an outsider, greeting each other with solemnity and awkwardness. The Aherns and Peck were onstage, where the high schoolers did their yearly musical, off-key renditions of bland favorites. Another man she didn't know stood in a loose-fitting suit with pleated pants and a T-shirt, of all things. She was glad their boy wasn't on display. Milo sat in the bleachers with his backpack on his lap, and next to him, his numb-nuts friend Scott, a wiseass who always walked down the aisle when the bus was moving. Alma wasn't above tapping the brakes hard to make him stumble, a warning eye to him in the rearview mirror. On the other side of Milo sat another meathead, and next to him, two adults, one of whom looked an awful lot like Joe Ahern.

Most of the bleachers were filled in the hot gymnasium, and Alma guessed 80 percent of the town was here. She recognized most of the people, but there were still a few she'd swear she was seeing for the first time. Old women who didn't belong to any of the churches or the few young people who had married Gunthrumites and moved here from a town or two over. Halfway up the bleachers sat Lonnie and Diane. Diane waved discreetly, and Alma nodded back. What else was there to do? She and Clyle walked toward the far end, passing Hal's landlord and neighbor, Mick Langdon, in the first row, and Larry Burke and Sam Gary with their wives two rows up. Cheryl Burke leaned back to talk to the row behind her—a bunch of gossipy lookie-loos just like her. Alma did not like that woman and gave her the stink eye. Even if Larry had apologized at the Aherns that night for taking Hal on the trip, she knew when words were hollow. In her mind this had all become Larry and Sam's fault—not Peggy's disappearance but Hal's alleged involvement. If they hadn't taken him, he wouldn't have shot the deer. Or if they'd taken him and treated him like a real person, he wouldn't have come home early and ended up at the OK with blood in his truck.

Two rows down from them she saw Kerry Saunders, his eyes puffy. He had a Kleenex shoved under his watchband like an old woman and pulled it out to blow his nose. From her perch Alma could see it was damp and ineffective, the snot still slick on his face.

Alma sat down, and a hot flash hit, the gymnasium stuffy with bodies. She unwrapped the itchy scarf from her neck, peeled off her coat like it was full of fire ants, and opened the collar of her shirt as low as she dared.

"Another one?" Clyle asked.

"To beat the band." She took a Gunthrum Foods circular she'd shoved in her purse and waved it back and forth, the cool air a balm on her skin. Clyle turned toward her, pursed his lips, and blew directly in her face, a trace of mint on his breath. He must have brushed his teeth after dinner. He took a breath and blew again, even though they were in the middle of a fight. This was why she'd married Clyle, why she'd stayed with him all these years; he was the kindest man she'd ever known, and yet look at what even he had done.

Peck approached the podium, and the crowd, already quiet, came to attention. "I appreciate you all coming," he began, and there was a screech of feedback from the microphone. Peck jerked his head back, and when the whine died down, he leaned back in but not so close. "I wish it were under better circumstances." He was dressed in his uniform, brown shirt and tan pants, his hands clasped behind his back. "As you all know," he began, and launched into the story of Peggy's disappearance—last seen at Castle Farm shortly after midnight Sunday morning, jeans and a pink sweater. "We've had a lot of you helping us the past few days, and we appreciate it, but with the snow we haven't found as much as we'd hoped. We've got signup sheets at the door for those of you with skid loaders and tractors to help us in the ditches and the fields." Alma shuddered. They were searching for a body now, not a girl.

She caught movement beyond the periphery of her right eye and turned toward the double doors, expecting someone to be waving the signup sheet, but it was Hal waving at Larry and Sam, a smile on his face. Bile rose in her throat. "Good Christ." She nudged Clyle and signaled to the door. "He's not supposed to be here."

"I'll get him," he whispered, and stood up, his town boots beating a hollow echo on the unsteady bleachers.

"Hi, Clyle," Hal said loudly from across the gymnasium, and Alma turned back to the stage, her face burning from the hot flash, her neck tight. She would not give anyone the satisfaction of disapproving of Hal's actions, even though she could feel the crowd turning from Clyle and Hal to her. Let them snicker.

Onstage, Joe Ahern stood up from his seat, then knelt next to the man she didn't recognize—a suit with a T-shirt, for Pete's sake—and pointed toward Hal as he said something to the man.

"All right," Peck said into the microphone a little louder, drawing the attention of the assembly back to him. "Another person I'd like to introduce." He turned toward the man in the suit. "This here's Lee Earl. He's a private investigator out of Omaha who's here to help with the case." Joe Ahern stood up and approached the podium.

Joe nodded to the microphone, and Peck stood back. "I know Peck's doing the best he can with what he's got, but Linda and I agreed bringing in a professional would make the situation run more smoothly. It's Wednesday, for God's sake, and this is the first time we've had a formal meeting to try and find our girl. Lee Earl's been working missing kid cases for most of his career"—Alma chewed on that; he looked no older than thirty—"and Peck here hasn't dealt with one before." Peck took a step forward, but Joe held up his hand. "I don't mean any offense there, Peck. I just know what your days normally look like. I don't care about stepping on anyone's toes right now. I'm here to get my girl back. And if someone has information to share or had a hand in this—" He stopped and swallowed. "I'm talking to you, Hal Bullard—then by God, I'm going to do what I can to get that information."

Hal, hearing his name, smiled until Clyle leaned over and said something to him, then walked him out to the hallway.

131

"Now, Joe, we talked about that," Peck said evenly. "No evidence is pointing in a specific direction right now. Can't say one way or another." Peck turned back to the crowd. "I want you all to know that, but we need your help. Any information you haven't already given about that Saturday night or Sunday morning, or anything else that might be helpful, we need to know." He straightened the tie clip on his uniform and cleared his throat. "Now, Joe has requested that Mr. Earl have a chance to speak, so with that, Lee?" He turned around, and Lee Earl stood up at a leisurely pace and approached the podium, setting both hands on the outer sides, his fingers curled against the wood.

"Much thanks," he began, "to both Sheriff Randolph and the good folks of Gunthrum for coming out tonight." Peck nodded in response, and Alma snorted. Already she didn't like Lee Earl. Too smooth, too confident. She preferred a man who put his head down and got the job done. She wondered what Clyle and Hal were doing out in the hallway or if Clyle had convinced Hal to drive himself home. Maybe Clyle went with him. She checked her purse to make sure he'd given her the car keys before remembering they were resting in the ignition outside, along with every other set of car keys in their respective cars in Gunthrum. City habits died hard.

Lee Earl went on about missing person rates in the state, particularly rural counties, and Alma had to admit the figures were much higher than she would have guessed. How was it children were disappearing that often? And how was it that it hadn't happened in Gunthrum before? Maybe all along they'd been lucky.

Lee finished by saying he was sure Officer Randolph had done the best job he knew how in interviewing anyone related to the case—condescending little shit—but he'd be in touch one by one to hear the story from the horse's mouth.

Alma knew they'd be at the top of the list. She closed her eyes against the panic and tried to imagine what it would feel like outside—the cold air against her skin, the slight freeze to the sweat that had already dried from her hot flash. She imagined Hal as a boy, swimming at Fremont Lakes, his mother on the shore in a one-piece, her mouth slack from sleep and drink. Why did Clyle have to call Marta? What did being a mother have to do with anything? Alma would never have abandoned him like that. She could not.

Peck took the podium one last time to say good night and conclude the meeting. Alma had gathered her coat and was headed to the door before he finished. The crowd filed out of the bleachers slowly around her, row by row, starting at the front, and moved toward the hallway. She kept her eyes faced forward so she wouldn't have to talk to anyone else, sure they, too, had come to conclusions about Hal. Whether they were right or wrong hardly mattered. In the hall she looked for Clyle or Hal, who was usually easy to spot by his height.

"Mrs. Costagan?" someone said, and she turned around to find Milo Ahern. "They went upstairs. Hal and Mr. Costagan."

She started toward the stairs and was surprised when he followed, matching her step for step on the wide staircase to the second floor, where the junior high and high school held their classes. Lockers lined the side walls, and there was a case with a few scant trophies for sports, including regionals in volleyball last year when Peggy was on the team.

Clyle turned at the squeak of her sensible shoes. "Time to go?"

"Yep. Now."

Clyle put a hand on Milo's shoulder. "I'm sorry again you're going through this, son."

He shrugged. "I know."

There were two sets of footsteps on the stairs, and Alma turned as Lee Earl approached with Joe Ahern. She moved closer to Hal and took his arm.

"Milo," Joe said in a rough voice. "Get downstairs. Go help your mother."

"Help her what?"

Joe gave a look like murder to his son. "Now."

"Okay, I'm going." Milo stopped in front of Mr. Earl. "You look like you're on that TV show *Miami Vice*." The man's chest, honest to God, puffed up. "And that's all well and good," Milo continued, "but this is Nebraska." The boy turned on his heel and fled down the stairs as Alma stifled a laugh.

Lee raised a hand. "Kid's upset. I get it. What I'm interested in now is talking to this one." He nodded toward Hal.

"He has a name," Clyle said stiffly.

"I'm sure he does." Lee took a step closer to Hal. "What's your name, boy?"

Confusion blinked on Hal's face.

"Listen," Alma started, but Lee held up a hand.

"That might work on some, boy," he continued, "but not on me. Guilty is guilty and I don't care what kind of handicap you've got. Murder is murder."

Clyle stepped in front of Hal and tears filled Alma's eyes; he would defend Hal, he would, if it all came down to it. In that moment Alma was sure.

"It's not mur—" Joe Ahern started, but Lee held up a hand to that too.

"Not yet, and we're hoping, but I can tell by looking at this one what he's capable of. What do you weigh, boy? Two hundred? What would you do to a little lady like Peggy?"

"That's it." Clyle took Hal by the arm. "We're going home. You want to question him, you come and do it, but it's not happening here tonight. You show us some evidence before

134

you start harassing Hal." Alma's heart surged with love. Clyle could draw a line in the sand better than anyone she knew, and there was nothing she loved more as long as she wasn't on the other side of it.

On the way home Clyle kept one hand on the wheel. When the rare car approached from the other direction, instinctually he lifted one finger off the steering wheel—the farmer wave. She found it endearing he did this even in the dark, with no chance of the other driver seeing him. His first instinct was always kindness. Maybe that was what had bothered her about the affair so much: she hadn't known he was capable of that cruelty, so much like other men.

Back when they knew the Aherns in those days, as part of the drinking crowd, Joe and Linda were barely in their thirties, Peggy in the terrible threes, and Milo not yet born. There was one night when Peggy had fallen down the last few steps into one of the less finished basements, banging her head against the cement floor. She wailed like a banshee, and Linda, in a panic, swooped her daughter into her arms, burying Peggy's red face in her chest. She carried her daughter as if she weighed nothing over to her husband. "Joe," she said. "It's soft. The bump. Isn't that a bad sign?"

Joe ran a hand over Peggy's head. "She's fine, Linny. Kids are resilient." Alma wondered if he regretted that now or if he even remembered.

After Alma's first miscarriage, Clyle had rocked her in his arms, tears on both of their faces. The doctor had estimated she was four months along—all of them had made it beyond the shadowy maybe of just one skipped period—and Clyle had brought her fresh orange juice and crossword books in bed. He'd held her hand for three days, calling in sick to IBM.

But by the fourth baby, he took off an afternoon and went back the next morning. She had told him to do so but was still mad when he did.

She hadn't even told Clyle about the fifth baby—this one in Gunthrum, two years after they moved—yet knew in her heart she held it over him. A year later Hal had tromped up the bus steps on Saint Patrick's Day and asked Alma if she thought he was wearing any green. When she said no, he told her she was wrong, laughing as he pulled the elastic waistband of his green underwear six inches out of his jeans. And a year after that, Clyle started the affair.

That night in bed, she thought about how Lance had cornered her against the counter at that party a decade ago. The alcohol crawling its way back up her throat, the digging, crab-like way his fingers moved toward her crotch. Had Peggy ever felt that panic? Alma turned over in the bed; Clyle was asleep on his side facing her, his lips slightly parted, the comforting stutter of his snore the soundtrack to her nights. She'd always thought the most painful thing in their marriage had been those babies, but maybe she'd been wrong. She touched the side of his face, and his breath caught, the mint overrun now by sour.

His eyes fluttered open. "What is it?"

"Nothing," she said, and he fell back to sleep.

Alma swam up from the syrup of her dream trying to place the sound. The coffeepot? The alarm on the stove? The microwave? It wasn't any of these things, and it wasn't until it was accompanied by a pounding noise—a tight fist against wood—that she realized it was the doorbell. No one had rung their doorbell in years.

"What in the—" Clyle started, and swung his feet out of bed.

Alma's mind was slurry with sleep as she pieced it together. The clock across the room read 1:43. "Someone's at the door."

"Well, I know that," he said, and grabbed the flannel shirt he had hung on the bedpost. She thought of that ridiculous song that had been a hit in the late fifties—*Does your chewing gum lose its flavor on the bedpost overnight?* She'd taken it as a sign that music was heading into the shitter and probably the first sign, too, that she would comprehensively lose her tolerance and humor as she aged, assuming people recognized she'd ever had them.

She grabbed her own flannel shirt and pulled it on over her nightie, a ratty flannel itself that she'd worn for the last ten years. She rounded the corner as Clyle opened the door. Joe Ahern stooped in their doorway, a finger pointing at Clyle. "Is he here?" Joe asked. "We've already been to his house, and it's empty." She took heart that Joe hadn't just barged in, knowing no one in Gunthrum locked their doors, although maybe that would change now and become part of the nightly routine for everyone. Certainly for Joe himself—brush his teeth, turn down the thermostat, check the door.

"Let me make you some coffee," Alma said.

"I don't want any goddamn coffee." His bloodshot eyes narrowed further.

"Here." Clyle led him to a chair. "Alma, I'd take some coffee."

Joe sat back in his chair. A few minutes later he nodded as she put the cup of coffee in front of him, taking a too-hot sip. "You know, when Peggy was a little girl, all she wanted was to raise lambs. I kept telling her we were a hog family, not sheep, but didn't matter—she wanted a lamb. Finally, I spend a weekend renovating one of the pens off the barn, sectioning it off so she could have a goddamn lamb. And you know what? Two weeks in she got sick of it." He attempted a laugh.

"Then when I said it was time for slaughter, you'd think we were taking her goddamn little brother." Joe looked at her, then Clyle. "That's what I was prepared for. Those kinds of ups and downs. That lamb was a goddamned mistake." He ran a hand over his face, his bottom lip stretching down, the veins inside his mouth blue. "I'm drunk."

"It's your right," Clyle said.

"You need a ride home?" Alma asked Joe, and he shook his head.

He peered deep into his coffee mug. "It had to be Hal. Lee Earl said there's no motive other than personal. It just doesn't make any other sense."

"Not much does," Alma said, and Joe snorted.

"I hear one more platitude I'm going to punch something."

"He didn't do anything," Alma said. "Joe, you have to see that Peck doesn't have any evidence."

"Not yet, maybe. I put a call into the *Omaha World-Herald* and talked to a reporter gal about it all. They've barely reported a blip."

"Did you mention Hal?" Alma asked, dread pitting in her stomach.

"You're damn right I did."

The picnic where Peggy had flirted with Hal. It was mid-July, and Alma had given up on making it through the summer in just jeans, a fight she ended up losing each year. Standing in front of her closet, she'd think, varicose veins be damned, and reach for a pair of shorts from the back, praying they'd still fit from the summer before. Each year it seemed another two or three pounds crept on until she was standing on the scale, thirty pounds heavier than when she and Clyle married. She struggled into the shorts, sucking in her tummy to get them buttoned, then stood in the hot sun, sweat trickling between her breasts and down from her hairline, her shoulders pinkening. It had been so hot that day that some of the kids had set up a sprinkler near the picnic shelter, and even those not in swimsuits were running through it, the high school girls in shorts so skimpy they might as well have been swimsuits. Everyone in Gunthrum had seen Peggy reject Hal, had seen how she and her friends laughed at him, and how Hal had stomped away in tears.

Standing in the kitchen now, her flannel shirt folded end across end over her stomach, Alma had a hard time believing it had ever been that warm.

That afternoon at the picnic, before he talked to Peggy, Hal played a game of touch football—football in hundred-degree heat!—and had pushed one of his opponents down, laughing. When the boy got up—he was a high schooler, on the Gunthrum team—Hal offered him a hand, but the boy brushed Hal's arm aside, and Hal kept laughing. He didn't understand that the boy was really mad. Was it because he was bested by a simpleton or because Hal had been too rough? Alma didn't know, but what she did know was that Hal couldn't always read the cues. Same with Peggy. She'd watched that girl flirt with any man who crossed her path—Hal, the boys from his class, Sam Gary and Larry Burke, even Clyle in a way. Talking to Alma's husband in front of her, Peggy had tilted her head a flirty forty-five degrees as if to say, *This is what I'm worth. This is what I have to offer you.*

Alma had heard the mother hens a few years older—Cheryl Burke, Tonya Gary—talking about how Peggy and her cohort, the other high school girls, didn't have a lick of sense. Alma had laughed to herself at the time, knowing these women now in their late twenties were just upset that they couldn't compete with the younger model. They were a whole generation of pretty girls taught to value what they looked like and not much else. Alma was glad she'd never been that kind of pretty, that she'd had to work instead to cultivate a personality, although plenty of people thought that wasn't any great shakes either.

There was a knock on the door, and Randall Ahern poked his head into the kitchen. "Joe?" Randall nodded at the Costagans. "Alma, Clyle." Alma knew Randall lived in Grand Island, about two hours away, and managed a feedstore, a job he started after his John Deere dealership went belly up. He ran it into the ground, people said, and big brother Joe came to bail him out, but now Randall drove a Cadillac, so who could predict how things would turn out. He'd grown up in Gunthrum on the farm next door, but when their parents retired to South Carolina, Joe, as the oldest, inherited the land and acreage.

Still, Randall came down to help his brother every year at planting and harvest, working the land he'd never own, and Alma could imagine that was a bitter pill to swallow.

There was something else about that picnic—what was it?

Joe deep in his cups in her kitchen, Randall at the door—it almost came to her, but just as quickly, it flitted away.

"I'm sorry," Randall said to the Costagans. "I tried to get him home, but it was either drive him here or let him walk." Randall overenunciated his words, trying to sound more sober than he was. "It's been a rough night."

"I imagine," Clyle said. "You want some coffee?"

"Nah. It'll just keep me up even later."

"Here." Clyle stood up. "Let me help you boys to the car."

"Come on," Randall said, and put a hand on Joe's arm, but Joe snapped it out of his grasp. Randall put his palms up as if at gunpoint, irritation clear on his face, but then his expression changed with a small laugh. "Been like this all night. A real pain in the ass."

"My daughter," Joe said, "is missing. Nobody wants to hear about your troubles."

"No one ever has." Randall nodded in a courtly manner to Alma and then Clyle and walked toward the door, his brother still at the table. A car started up, backed out of the driveway, and the headlights swung through the kitchen as the Cadillac pointed toward the lane.

"You're going to have to drive him," Alma said, waving toward Joe, his eyes blank and unfocused, the cup of coffee nearly full in front of him.

"I can walk." Joe stood up, wobbly still but upright.

"I'm sure you can," Clyle said, "but let me give you a ride anyway. For my own peace of mind." Clyle turned around at the door. "I'll be back in a flash."

"See you then," Alma said, and his pickup started a minute later. She took the coffee mugs from the table, dumped the remains down the drain, and put them in the sink. She glanced at the clock: 2:16, and she was wide awake. No use going back to bed now when she knew she'd toss and turn. Back when she was drinking, in her late thirties and forties, those nights they'd spend out late at the parties, she'd come back and flop on the mattress, her eyes closed before she hit the pillow, and then, like clockwork, she'd wake up at two and stay awake until four, too tired to read so much as the paper. She set drinking aside as easily as she would a book she didn't like, only having a glass or two of beer now on occasion, but she knew they all had their weaknesses.

Alma was willing to bet she'd been one of the few sober people at that picnic last summer when Hal had taken a shine to Peggy. It was hot that day, and people were drinking beer like water, the slosh of ice still on the aluminum as they took long gulps, half a can at a time. When she quit drinking, she'd been shocked how people behaved, just how impaired they'd become. The dance moves she thought were so smooth, the raucous jokes they all hee-hawed to, were embarrassing to watch as the only sober person in the group.

Before heading to the centennial, they'd swung by and picked Hal up for the picnic, knowing he'd drink a lot too. She worried about him with alcohol. There were too many incidents where he'd get revved up and keep going, no inner barometer telling him he'd had enough, no sense of when he was going to tip the scales from good times to bad. He seemed to understand that alcohol made him feel great but couldn't make the leap to how terrible it made him feel later on, a fritz between the action and the consequence. She wondered often about how Hal's brain was broken, what synapses, or whatever they were, failed to connect to others. She supposed he was like that about a lot of things. He'd lived in the same town as Peggy most of her life, but then, in her shorts and tank top, she'd put her hand on his collar, and it was like he was seeing her for the first time.

That day at the picnic Peggy flirted with Hal, and he responded like a flower blooming in time lapse. Alma had tried to tell him before that girls were fickle idiots and mean to boot. She'd driven buses long enough to know that, and after someone like Diane—who was supposed to be her friend—would sleep with her husband, she had little patience for her own sex.

She'd watched Peggy and Hal with a cruel fascination, not maternal at all, waiting for that moment when Peggy would give him a patronizing smile, then turn away. She'd wanted that moment to happen, and when it did, she felt a cruel blooming of her own. Hal had touched his shirt where Peggy had, on the collar, and reached out and touched her tank top strap in return.

Peggy whipped around. "Don't touch me!"

Joe Ahern arrived almost immediately, alcohol soaked like the rest of them. "What is it? What's this?"

Alma scurried over. "It's nothing. Really."

"Doesn't sound like nothing," Joe said, his drunk voice like a siren. Lonnie and Diane had stopped their game of bocce; Cheryl and Tonya held horseshoes in their hands.

Larry Burke ran over as well, dropping his beer can on a picnic table. "What do you think you're doing there, Hal? Keep your hands to yourself."

"Hal, let's go," Alma said, and waved to Clyle: *Let's scoot.*

"But I—" Hal took a step toward Peggy, and Larry shoved him toward the car.

"Get going," Larry said. "Get, now."

Hal looked back, bewildered. Cheryl threw her horseshoe, and it clattered around the spike, reverberating in the silence.

At the car, even Clyle, who didn't drink like he used to, had pointed her toward the driver's side and slumped into the passenger seat.

Hal talked about Peggy the whole way home, and when they turned into the lane at the Costagans' farm, he'd wrenched his head behind to stare at the Ahern house, probably wondering which room was Peggy's. Sure, she'd hurt his feelings, but her hair was so long, her shorts so short. Hal came in for dinner—Alma made lasagna with French bread in hopes of soaking up the alcohol—and talked nonstop about how Peggy was so pretty and so nice and do you think she has a boyfriend? Alma sat on her hands as long as she could—not very—then said, "Hal, she's not going to be your girlfriend, you see that, right? That she was just teasing with you?"

"Alma," Clyle warned, but she barreled ahead.

"That girl got the hopes up of probably ten boys at that picnic today, and Hal, you're just one of them. And of those ten, I bet you're last on her list."

Hal looked at her, his face open and bruised. "Why are you being so mean?" he asked.

She clanged the hot pan of lasagna on the table. "Because someone needs to be."

Now she stepped out on the porch to watch for Clyle's headlights and rubbed her hands up her arms, crooked at the elbows against the cold. Why? she asked herself again now. Why did someone have to be so mean? Was it because the one man who was supposed to love her had betrayed her? That she was an old woman and Peggy so young? That her body, once vibrant, had betrayed her as well with those babies?

Or was that just who she was destined to be: a petty, mean woman like her mother?

13

Milo's dad was so mad by the time they left the assembly, telling Sonny Crockett to get his ass to the Costagans and talk to them about the retard, that he and Uncle Randall headed to the OK. Milo had to ride next to George in Aunt Sally's back seat with the imminent threat of purple nurples. Sitting on the sofa at eleven that night, he still had welts on his chest, but at least no one had told him to go to bed yet. George was awake, too, hyped up on Dr. Pepper and sitting in the fart noise–making rocking chair, ripping pages from the women's undergarments section of the Sears catalog.

Aunt Sally snatched the magazine away. "That's it, George. Time for bed."

George whined that he didn't have school the next day, and before she said boo again, it was midnight. When Aunt Sally finally walked George upstairs to help him find his pajamas and toothbrush, she said to Milo's mother, "Doesn't Milo need to get to sleep?" and his mother said, "He's fine. He'll go up when he's ready." She never would have said that before, and he thought it had less to do with her not caring that he was up and more with wanting not to agree with Aunt Sally. When Sally left the room, his mother cocked an eyebrow at him—*not much longer, mister*—but eventually she forgot about him and he was in the clear.

Milo drifted to sleep on a corner of the couch, and woke around 2:00 a.m. to raised voices—his dad's and Randall's, both a little slurry after the OK—his Aunt Sally at the other corner of the davenport. "Every goddamn time you make it about you," his dad said. "Just stay out of the way, Randall."

"I came here to help."

"Oh, please. When have I ever needed your help? You've always needed mine." He started ticking the list off on his fingers. "A loan to get the dealership going. Another loan when that went belly up. Jesus, even when we were kids, you needed me to fight your battles for you."

Randall clenched his fists. "You're not a goddamn self-made man here, Joe. Our folks gave you this farm. You had it handed to you."

"And can you blame them? Imagine what it would look like now if you'd gotten ahold. Piecemealed for sale as you got further and further in debt, one dead crop after another."

"I'm doing great right now." Randall pointed to the driveway. "See that car out there? Paid off."

"And how's that, huh? You start at middle management at a goddamn feedstore and now you're driving a Cadillac?" Joe shook his head. "I don't know, Randall."

"You can't stand it, can you? Me making more money. You want nothing but to keep me under your thumb." Randall's face was red, and so was Milo's father's—the burst red capillaries on their noses a matching set. "Maybe she ran away, you think of that? To get away from you?"

"You fucking—" Joe lunged, and Aunt Sally jumped between the two men, a hand on each chest.

"That's it. Let's go to bed," she said. "That's enough."

"You can't go to bed," Joe said. "You're sleeping in my goddamn living room, on my goddamn couch."

Milo's mom wasn't in the room, and he hoped she'd gone to sleep and was missing all this, but more likely she was awake in her room and hearing every word.

"Fine. We came to help, but we'll go home. Sal, you get George up."

"We can't drive back—" she started, at the same time Milo's dad said, "Oh no. I want you where I can keep an eye on you."

Randall turned from the corner, where he'd been gathering their duffel bags. "What's that mean, Joe?" His voice was low, a threat, and Milo bit his tongue—a trick he'd developed to distract himself from pain with another pain when he was getting a shot at the doctor.

Milo's dad stared at his brother and finally rubbed a tired hand over the net of blood vessels on his nose. "Nothing. I don't know. I've had too much to drink."

"You're damn right," Randall said.

"Here," Joe said. "I'll get out of your way." He looked around the room. "Milo? What the hell are you doing up?"

"Nothing," he mumbled, and scurried from the room. It was almost two thirty. Hardly a record.

The next morning George dipped a soup spoon in a jar of Skippy creamy, pulled it out, and stuck it into an open bag of chocolate chips. Milo had watched him do this half a dozen times already, the spoon always ending up with a smear of peanut butter still on it, along with spit, as it went back in the jar. It was seven fifteen, and he was already up—another night of restless sleep. Aunt Sally had woken George at six to help Uncle Randall with chores, and he claimed he was starving after an hour of actual work.

"George," Aunt Sally said. "How many times have I asked you to stop that? I need those chips for the cookies."

"Three?" George guessed. "Four?"

"Well, too many, now here." She took the bag away from him. Milo couldn't count the number of times he'd watched

147

George misbehave or mouth off and get away with it as Aunt Sally said, "Boys will be boys." Milo was a boy, and *he* didn't act like a butthole.

His mom came into the kitchen and floated a hand across his back. "You sleep okay?" she asked, and Milo shrugged.

"Not really."

"I guess not." His mom picked up the phone. "Let me make a call." Milo heard the staticky echo of the ring muffled against his mom's ear. She leaned against the kitchen sink, and Milo thought of all the times she'd stood there over the years, many of them with a cigarette burning in the ashtray next to her before she'd quit, making her daily to-do list. Even when she didn't work, she had a long list of housecleaning, outside chores, grocery shopping, and laundry. At least he thought that's what must have been on it.

When she'd gone back to work, she said to Milo's father, "I don't know how I'm going to put a forty-hour workweek on top of what I'm doing now," but she'd managed. They still had a home-cooked dinner—usually a hunk of meat with a baked potato and a green veggie, his mother skipping the potato— but breakfasts were always cereal, except on the weekends, and Milo bought the school lunch now. His mom swept the stairs once a week now instead of twice, but other than that, things hadn't changed much. At the family meeting they'd had before she started her job, Peggy had said, "We shouldn't have to take on more just because Mom wants to go back to work," and their mother had promised they wouldn't have to shoulder the majority of the burden. He'd agreed with his sister at the time—why should *we* have to do more so she can do what she wants?—and it made his cheeks burn to think about it. Just two weeks ago he'd been watching Saturday morning cartoons, and his mother had come through with the vacuum cleaner, and he'd glared at her as he lifted his feet. Two weeks ago, and it felt like a lifetime. He couldn't remember the last time he had slept more than two hours in a shot.

His mother stood straighter as the Peanuts adult voice sound mumbled through the receiver.

"Mr. Johnston? Linda Ahern."

Could he get away with never attending school again? He could be like one of those homeschool kids he met in the bathroom a few years ago at Cascades on Ice, when his mom took him and Peggy to Sioux City for the day. She wrote it off as an educational experience, their last hurrah before she started her full-time job. That kid said his mother taught him science and math at the kitchen table and made him dress every day in trousers and a button-down.

"I'm sure tomorrow." She paused. "Friday? Oh, go ahead. My guess is Peggy will be home by then and embarrassed about the fuss and misunderstanding." How could she possibly think that? Milo wondered. It had been four days. Her mouth wobbled. "If they need to, they can pull a cheerleader from jv. Listen, Mr. Johnston, I have to go. Rolls in the oven." She hung up the phone, without saying goodbye!

"What was all that?" Aunt Sally asked, but Milo figured she knew as well as he did. Friday night was the annual basketball scrimmage between the dads and players, one of the three big fundraisers the boosters ran every year. This time it was for new uniforms before the season started in January, the old polyester home team tanks and shorts all aged to yellow. The dads played their own kids on opposing teams, the men usually out of shape and embarrassing, but they could choose one ringer to give them an edge, a younger guy in the community who could at least score in the double digits. This was the third year running they'd chosen Larry Burke. Most of Gunthrum would be there—students, their parents, oldsters with nothing better to do on a Friday night. They'd raise at least a few hundred. Milo's own dad had already said it was a shame they didn't do something similar for volleyball so at least he could get on a court, then looked pointedly at his unathletic son.

"Just the fundraiser scrimmage," his mom confirmed. "He's wondering if they should cancel."

"Nonsense," Aunt Sally said, and put a rubber band around the bag of chocolate chips. "She'll be grounded by then, mark my words, but back." She looked pointedly at Milo's mother. "She'll have the wrath of Grandma Ahern to deal with by then." Milo's paternal grandparents were coming Friday midday.

Since Sunday they'd been calling her disappearance a misunderstanding, and that still held some water on Monday, maybe Tuesday, but by Thursday morning even Milo knew it sounded more like denial, and the thought made him sick to his stomach. Would he still go to the game? It felt wrong somehow to miss it, the whole town together. He didn't want to go and have to deal with everyone; yesterday afternoon before the assembly, he'd gone to Gunthrum Foods with his mother for what she called the necessities but what he recognized as an hour to kill. Two separate old women he didn't know had pulled him toward their old-people bosoms and asked how he was holding up. Not well, you dumb ninnies, he thought, but he'd smiled and told them okay because that's what he was expected to do.

No, he didn't want to go to the scrimmage and get suffocated by people's pity and sadness; what he wanted was to hang under the bleachers with Scott and eat Peanut M&Ms and popcorn so salty his lips swelled up. He wanted to listen to the lame band at halftime and wonder if he could make first chair in trumpet next year as a freshman. To watch Peggy cheer for the high schoolers as the players' moms tried to keep rhythm with their pompoms, rooting for their husbands. That's what he wanted, and none of it was going to happen. Milo's life as he knew it was slipping away as well as the future he'd imagined.

Aunt Sally opened the oven door and slid in a tray of chocolate chip cookies. It was weird seeing her in his mother's oven mitt and apron. It was weird seeing anyone in them. Since his mom had gone back to work two years ago, the best he'd gotten was brownies out of a box and a paper plate full of cookies from a Christmas exchange, even though his mom didn't bring anything herself. "Those women don't understand how busy I am," she'd said, flopping the cookies on the table, the top Santa sugar cookie breaking at the waist. "I don't have time to stand around waiting for an oven timer to go off every eight minutes like they do."

Milo glanced at the clock. What was he going to do all day? Maybe it had been a mistake staying home from school. At some point he'd have to go back, and how would that look? Like he'd given up hope? Folks were still dropping off food and doing nightly chores for his father, but even Mr. McGee, who'd come every night, had sent a message with his wife and her slow cooker of hamburger soup that his back had given out that afternoon at the service station and he wouldn't be able to make it. It was one thing to be helpful when everyone was convinced it was a misunderstanding and Peggy would be walking through the door at any moment—maybe a couple of scratches and bruises but not much the worse for wear— but now? He hiccupped and felt vomit burn his throat. He made a gagging noise, certain he'd be sick.

"I want to go," Milo said suddenly, and his mother looked over. "To the scrimmage. I want to go." He needed that normalcy waiting for him the next day, something to hold onto.

"Sweetie, but your grandparents will be here. Won't you want to stay home?"

"You said yourself Peggy'll probably be back by then. So why not, why can't I go?"

"Might be good for him," Aunt Sally said as she rolled a ball of dough and set it on a cookie sheet. "Give us adults a chance to talk once Mother Alice arrives." It wasn't a big secret that Aunt Sally and Milo's mom weren't huge fans.

"I guess," his mom said. "If you really want to. We can make it happen."

A movement out the window caught his attention, and Milo watched Mrs. Costagan's yellow Vega turn down her lane with a plume of snow behind her. It was almost eight o'clock. Why wasn't she on her bus route?

14

Ten minutes earlier Alma had slammed into the kitchen, her hair every which way, flannel shirt unbuttoned and untucked. Clyle sat at the table with a cup of coffee and his morning peanut butter toast, surprise on his face. "Clyle Costagan, why didn't you wake me up?"

"I assumed you'd already left."

"You didn't see my car sitting in the garage? Didn't wonder why my purse and coat were still on the peg?"

"Alma, I'm sorry." Clyle shook his head and turned back to his paper.

She grabbed the half-drunk cup of coffee from the earlier pot and swigged it back. "Shit, shit, shit," she muttered. "Those Ahern men kept me up most of the night." Never mind that her sleep wasn't much worse than any other night, but she wanted someone to blame other than her menopausal body or Hal.

She snatched her coat, her right hand fishing frantically for the armhole. "Kids are going to be standing outside when it's colder than Billy-be-damned. Fourteen years, and I've never started a route late."

"Good—" he trailed after her, and the door slammed on *luck*.

Alma passed a blue Chevy Caprice on her way into town, the smug face of Lee Earl behind the wheel. Surely he was on his way to their house right now, but she would deal with that in a minute. Alma threw her car into park in a space adjacent to the school just before the first bell, kids pouring in from every direction, some with their mothers in tow, but most of them walking from home by themselves or trailing an older brother or sister.

As Alma ran through the halls, one of the stoner boys from her route held up his hand in a high-five, and without thinking, she slapped it. Birdie Langdon, Jill and Shelly's mother, shot Alma a dirty look as she hustled her kids to the third and fifth grade classrooms, her hair a flat mess on one side and a bird's nest on the other. Birdie in a bird's nest. Alma smirked, which didn't help Birdie's mood at all. "Glad to see you're okay," she said snidely to Alma. "We were worried when you didn't show up this morning."

"Overslept," she explained.

"Must be nice to get to sleep in. I haven't done that in eleven years." Birdie signaled to Jill, whom Alma assumed to be eleven.

"It is," Alma agreed. "I slept like a rock." It wasn't the thing to say, but she could not stand being needled.

In Irv Johnston's office Alma planned to make her apologies, something that didn't come easily but that she knew had to be done. He was standing next to the window, talking on the phone, and when he saw Alma, he pointed vehemently at one of the two empty upholstered chairs on the other side of his desk. A new picture of his wife and son faced the chairs. Bruce, now in high school, was at that awkward age where nothing about him fit—his feet and hands too big, his neck too skinny. In a way she found him endearing, and that Irv would display the photo she found endearing too. Still, Alma imagined that bit Bruce in the butt when his buddies had to stare at his picture as his father chewed them out for throwing wads of wet paper towels on the popcorn ceiling in the boys' bathroom.

"I'm sorry, Phyllis—" he said into the phone, then paused midsentence. "Excuse me, Mrs. Schroeder, but it's not going to happen again." Pause. "I know, and yes, of course she'll be excused for the first half of school today. If she can get here by lunch hour, great." Pause. "Yes, and that's fine too. We'll see Heidi tomorrow." He hung up the phone, ran a hand over his rubbery face, and sat back down. "You've put me in the eye of a shitstorm, Alma."

"I'm sorry, Irv. I don't know what happened. You set an alarm and hope for the best. Clyle must have turned it off without thinking."

"That's all well and good," he continued, "but we've got kids missing out on first through fifth period. Some I've excused for the whole day. These parents want some retribution."

Alma snorted. "Good Lord, it's not the Wild West. So kids miss one day. These parents overestimate how much we're teaching them."

"This isn't a laughing matter."

"I'm sorry, you're right. It was probably the one day teachers were going to cover all of the SAT."

"Alma, I need you to take this seriously."

Oh, she did, but as bad as she felt, she didn't know that she could behave herself. Irv sat there in his short-sleeved, button-down shirt and tie, his hoofy-goofy kid's picture on his desk, and took the world as seriously as a heart attack. "I'm sorry," she capitulated. "I am. But I've driven the bus fourteen years and never missed a route. That's got to count for something."

"It does—I'm just not sure how much."

Her mouth dropped open. "Are you serious?" She remembered all those years ago at one of the drinking parties, comparing Irv to a babysitter. She'd known at the time it was cruel, but four beers in, it seemed worth it to have everyone laughing at her jokes, just one of the gang.

He smoothed his tie through his first and second finger and rested the end in his lap. "I need to talk to the school board about this. Some of those kids were out there in the cold for up to an hour. Phyllis Schroeder is saying Heidi might have frostbite." Phyllis was the one who'd told Alma about Clyle's affair all those years ago. Heidi was her late-in-life surprise.

"It's not my fault that Phyllis raised a fool kid who doesn't know to come in from the cold."

"That is not the tack to take."

"What kid stays out there for an hour still thinking the bus is going to come?" She mimicked looking down an empty road, one direction and then the other, her eyes bulging. "Duh."

Irv leaned forward, tie dangling. "Listen, Alma, this town has had enough upset this week—Peggy missing, that assembly last night." He paused. "Hal and that business with Joe Ahern."

She narrowed her eyes. "What business?"

"Well, you heard Joe as clear as I did. He basically thinks Hal is responsible for Peggy going missing." He held his hands up as if at gunpoint. "Don't look at me like that, Alma. Most of the town thinks it, and you know it. Hal's never been right in the head."

"He's got nothing to do with Peggy's disappearance. You heard Peck—not a lick of evidence."

"Blood in his truck?"

"That was from a deer! And where'd you even hear about that?"

"Please, Alma. You know how this town operates. You've lived here long enough."

"Apparently not long enough to be cut any slack or to have my word count for diddly-squat." She grabbed her purse from the chair next to her, then flicked her wrist and sent the pic of Irv's wife and son clattering onto the desk. Irv pursed his lips, and she stared him down. "I'm going. I'll be damned if I'm going to stand here another second and listen to you slander an innocent man."

"You had to know there were going to be consequences, Alma," Irv said quietly, and she wasn't sure anymore if he was talking about Hal or was back to her missing her route.

Alma slung her purse over her shoulder. "I think I know a thing or two about consequences, Irv, don't you worry."

"I'm putting you on temporary leave, until the new year. I talked to the head of the school board this morning."

She glanced at the clock above his head—not even eight thirty. "You call and get him out of bed? Tell him you thought you had something that'd stick?" This wasn't about her being late—it was about her relationship with Hal and that comment she'd made a decade ago in one of the paneled basements.

Irv picked up his coffee cup and set it down without taking a drink. "Alma, don't act like—"

"No, you don't act like this isn't a witch hunt. You're going after Hal, and you're going after me." She grabbed the upended picture and threw it on the ground, and when the glass didn't break, she smashed it with the heel of her boot, a spiderweb of broken fragments spreading across his stupid, ugly family. "You can call the school board back and let them know I'm getting a lawyer."

Alma walked into the house to the telephone ringing, a migraine throbbing at the base of her skull, adrenaline still slick in her veins. She rubbed her chapped and pink hands against her jeans, then picked up the receiver and said hello. A stranger started speaking, a voice like an operator, a woman from the *Omaha World-Herald* saying she was doing a piece on Peggy Ahern's disappearance and would Alma have a moment? Alma hung up, her heart racing. The phone rang again.

"Mrs. Costagan?" the woman said. "I just want to talk."

"He didn't do anything. The police don't have anything."

"I know, or he'd be arrested. They don't even have a body. To me they're looking pretty incompetent if they're starting a murder investigation and they don't even have a body."

"Murder?" Alma repeated. "It's certainly not that. She's only missing. At worst if something's happened, it was an accident."

"What kind of accident, Mrs. Costagan?"

Alma hung up again, stared at the phone, then took the handset off the base. The incessant beeping was nearly intolerable, but she knew if she unplugged it, the second receiver in the living room would ring. My God, she thought. What if he did?

The full weight of speculation settled on her shoulders, and she sank to the kitchen floor. Kidnapping? An accident? Something more? Who knew, but she questioned in her bones if Hal could be involved. She tried to think it through—those blank hours between midnight and Sunday morning, when Hal and Peggy were both unaccounted for. But if he'd done something, where *was* she?

She thought about Clyle and his flat, honest face. Did he think the same? She imagined he must. He was a man who put two and two together, and unlike her, every time he got four. The real difference between them was probably not whether they thought Hal was guilty of something but whether or not it mattered. Clyle would walk Hal into Peck's office and visit him in prison twice a week for the rest of his days, but Alma knew Hal would never survive that life. When he beat that boy up in Wayne, he'd spent three hours in the county jail and looked like he'd aged three years overnight, even though he was the only one in the cell and a guard had given him a deck of cards so he could play solitaire. What would he do with a cellmate? That terrible, starchy food? And of course she'd seen much worse in the movies.

Alma got up and stumbled to the hall, where she couldn't hear the phone, her heart still pounding, then grabbed her purse and headed back to the car. In town she picked up double-A batteries at Pickett's Hardware, paid the electric bill, then stopped at Gunthrum Foods for their staples—milk, bread, peanut butter, the container of port wine cheese Clyle liked on crackers while he had his nightly drink. Anything but dwell on the call. Walking past the small array of produce, she picked up a cantaloupe and put it in the cart. It was her favorite fruit by far and well out of season, but despite everything, she wanted to have a little faith.

Lana rang her up, the tippy tap of her too-long nails skittering across the cash register. "I've always thought you were a saint for taking in that boy," Lana said, assuming every conversation was a continuance of an earlier one. She looked at Alma pointedly. "I know I couldn't do it." People said that all the time to her on the street—look at you, such an angel for taking in the special kid—but she knew that wasn't the case. They resented that she'd righted something that as a town they'd ignored, a reminder once again of their shortcomings. Was that it, she wondered now, or perhaps did they mean it?

"You don't know what you're capable of until you're put on the spot," she said neutrally.

Lana stopped bagging, the small cantaloupe palmed over the paper sack. "Tell me." Her eyes twitched for the truth. "You think he did it?"

"Of course not," Alma said instinctively, flashing to herself on the kitchen floor, the phone still beeping in her ear. She swiped the bag with one arm and the melon with another. "Although I guess it doesn't really matter. Everyone's decided he did."

"I guess. I heard about that reporter too."

"Which means everyone else has, thanks to that big mouth," Alma concluded. She pointed a finger at Lana. "You act like you're doing a public service, but it's just gossip, you know. You're a pot stirrer."

Lana laughed. "I am. But you know what I'm not? Wrong. Now it's just a missing girl, but you heard what Peck said at that meeting last night. Either way, Joe's got it in for Hal, that's for sure. And Joe's not the type to stop."

Leaving Gunthrum Foods, Alma glanced at the electric bank sign that rotated between time and temperature. Twenty-eight degrees. She folded her grocery bags into the back seat of her Vega, rubbed her hands together against the cold, and climbed onto the driver's seat. Lana's words rang in Alma's head: *Either way, Joe's got it in for Hal.* She was confident Lee Earl didn't have enough to arrest Hal, but God knew he could put the fear of Christ in him.

She looked up and down Main Street, a smattering of snow on the ground. In the bakery window fall-colored cookies shaped like leaves were resting against the pumpkin pies. It was a picturesque town in many ways but not the life she'd imagined and certainly not the one Hal would have imagined for himself. When Clyle's mother got sick, they were only supposed to come for six months. A few months out of a lifetime together, she'd reasoned with herself, while they moved into Clyle's childhood bedroom upstairs and his mother wasted away in the master on the main floor. The cancer had been swift, but then there'd been the farm documents to straighten out as everything transferred to Clyle's name, and he couldn't quite find a farm management that he trusted to rent the land. And what would another season be if he could just get the crops in himself, and then, of course, who would harvest them?

One day washing the dishes that weren't hers and looking out the kitchen window of her mother-in-law's house, she'd seen Clyle in the front lawn with one of the barn cats weaving in and out of his ankles. He bent to pet the cat, who scurried away, then sat down right in the middle of the gravel lane with his hand out and waited for the cat to slink back. My God, she didn't think she'd ever seen her husband so content. Every evening he came in and told her about the problems he'd solved on the farm—how to treat an illness with the hogs or keep the tomato plants alive or deal with the raccoons in the barn—and she loved that he was so satisfied. She convinced herself she could be happy here with him, that his happiness would be enough for the both of them until she was able to find work that fulfilled her and friends to alleviate the loneliness. And of course there was the corner of her mind that whispered what a nice place Gunthrum would be to raise a family.

Eventually, she had grown to resent Clyle for the move and convinced herself he had tricked her into suggesting they stay. The fifth baby, lost two years after they arrived, drove her further into her resentful shell, and eventually that happiness she'd seen in Clyle was pointed elsewhere. A year later he had the affair with Diane, and Hal had stomped onto her bus with his green underwear, another misfit no one seemed to understand. Hal.

She looked again at the bank sign; fifteen minutes had passed, and the temp had dropped another degree. When they arrived, she would have done anything for Clyle—a good man who saw the good in her—but now? Hal was the one who couldn't live without her, the one she'd do anything to protect.

She climbed out of the car and slammed the door, looking both ways as she crossed the street to the bank, never mind that there was never any traffic.

Standing in line, she twisted the strap of her purse back and forth. It was Thursday, nearly the weekend, one of the busiest days at the bank, so along with the yahoo tellers, she had every biddy in town here withdrawing just enough money for the weekend groceries so they could make Sunday dinner for the sons and daughters who visited once a week for a free meal.

Alma had two savings accounts: one for the farm they kept track of in a blue leatherette book in Clyle's tiny handwriting, the numbers neat and precise; and her personal savings account, where she deposited 20 percent of her paycheck every two weeks, a rainy-day account she never told Clyle about. She wouldn't have guessed, growing up in the thirties and forties, that she'd ever have this much money. Her father had deposited five dollars in the crock on top of the fridge every payday, knowing it wouldn't be enough for her mother to buy all the groceries, and eventually, hands wringing, her mother would have to approach him for more. He'd pull dollar bills out of his wallet and hand them over as if she were a child.

Before Alma married, she was making her own money as a social worker, and she could still remember her first extravagant purchases: a pair of navy, polka-dot rain boots and a novel she saw in a bookstore window and bought for no other reason than she could—*Peyton Place* by Grace Metalious. She'd read it cover to cover, twice, thinking there was no way such small-minded, salacious stuff went on in boring backward towns, but what do you know? Alma had never wanted a husband to keep control over her and insisted when she married Clyle that her name be on all the accounts. "Fine by me," he'd said, "you deal with it." And when they moved to Gunthrum, they went side by side to the bank to set up checking and savings accounts. The other savings account she set up a few months later, when she started working for the school.

Bev Barnes, a kind-faced woman married to Pastor Barnes, peeked around the woman who was still carefully placing her paper envelope in her purse. "Alma? You're next." She smiled as Alma approached her. "What can I do for you?" Alma wondered what it was like being married to a man of God, how difficult it would be not to swear in traffic with the windows down or to always have to smile at people you couldn't stand. She realized with a start that maybe it wasn't that hard for some people, that Bev smiled at everyone because she liked them.

The teller stalls were set up with foot-tall partitions between them so no one could spy on the transactions taking place, but everyone could still hear what was being said. Alma, head high, forced her voice to a normal register. "I need to make a withdrawal." The words didn't surprise her. She thought of Lana and those tacky nails: *Joe's not the type to stop.*

"Of course. Which account?"

"Both of them."

Bev nodded. "And how much?"

Alma looked Bev in the eyes. "All of it." She didn't know yet what she'd do with it, but who knew what had happened with Lee Earl that morning—his eyes blanked by mirror sunglasses when she passed him on the highway earlier. Alma believed she just wanted to hold the possibilities in her hands, to know she could help Hal if she needed to.

Bev was practiced in the art of financial discretion. "Of course." Money and sex: weren't they the two things people weren't supposed to talk about in polite conversation? Alma figured along with nurses, pastors' wives probably knew more about people's interior lives than anyone in the town. Bev's voice dropped to a whisper. "The entire balance from both your single and joint accounts?"

"Yep."

She nodded once. "I'll just need to get my manager."

Alma shook her head. "It's my money. No need to get a manager to give me what's mine." The last thing she wanted was another person nosing around in her business.

"It's bank policy," Bev explained. "Any withdrawal over a certain amount we need approval, and depending, we might need a few days to process. We don't keep as much money on hand as you might think."

One time, during a routine evacuation of the school for a fire drill, Bev was in the teacher's lounge after a conference with the choir director about the annual Christmas program. When the bell rang, Bev stood up with her purse in her hands, Alma in the chair next to her. The gym teacher had told her not to bother, it was just a routine drill, but she said, "If the kids have to evacuate, it's only fair that I do too." There was no way Bev Barnes was going to break the rules.

"Fine," Alma said, as Bev walked to the back of the bank, where there were two offices. The line was growing longer, and Alma saw Tonya Gary turn away rather than catch her eye.

"Alma?" Bev hadn't gone back around the teller desk yet but was out in the lobby with her. "Diane can see you now." Alma closed her eyes. Bev lowered her voice even further. "I'm sorry. Mr. Hall is out today." He was the manager, and Diane McGee was the assistant. Alma had always taken Bev for a fool—how could anyone that kind not be?—but she realized now that wasn't the case. Maybe all these years Alma had been taking the easy way out in assuming the worst about people, rather than being as perceptive as Bev. The pastor's wife had intuited Alma wouldn't want to deal with the woman who had slept with her husband for, what, a year?

Diane had her head bent over a ledger, an important-looking red pen in her hand, engaged in official bank business. Foolish, Alma thought. She knew damn well I was on my way back here, and Alma rapped her knuckles thrice against the door frame. Diane winced but didn't look up until her pen ticked to the end of the column. She had a picture of Lonnie and their two girls on the back credenza, all in buffalo plaid shirts.

"Alma." Diane crossed her hands over the ledger. "What can I do for you?"

Alma sat in the chair across from Diane's desk, feeling like a child at the principal's office for the second time that day. "Didn't Bev just come back here and tell you?"

Diane faltered. "She did, but I need to hear it from you." She had a smear of lipstick against her front teeth, and Alma wondered if Diane had hastily applied it when Bev told her Alma was on her way back.

Alma sighed. "Just give me my money."

"Fine." Diane stood up, smoothing the front of her wrinkled cotton skirt, a satin pink shirt with a bow for her top. "I'll need to get in the vault." She was back a minute later, a sheepish look on her face. "Alma, we're low on reserves today.

165

I'm afraid I can only give you five thousand." She handed the vinyl bag to Alma. "I hope it's nothing too urgent? That five thousand will do?" Alma opened her mouth, but Diane held up her hands. "Never mind. None of my business." Alma unzipped the bag and peered at the thicket of bills. It was much smaller than she would have guessed. "We should have the rest of it for you on Monday afternoon."

"I guess that'll do," Alma said, and zipped the bag and shoved it in her purse.

"I'm—" Diane cleared her throat. "I'm sorry, but I need the bag back. Bank property."

"Why'd you give it to me?"

"It was just to carry the money from the vault. So no one would see how much." Was this protocol or a kindness? "Listen," Diane continued. "I'm sorry about what's going on with Hal. He's always seemed like a nice guy to me. I don't think he's capable of what people are saying."

"Oh, he's capable. What man isn't?" His capability was what she and Clyle had been arguing with the county for all these years. He was capable of living on his own, cooking his own meals, driving his own truck and maintaining the payments. Clyle had taught him to shoot a gun, and he'd bagged his own deer. "But he didn't do anything. I bet my life on it." What was her life worth without family?

Even so, he'd come to the farm late Monday morning, the telltale marks of a hangover on his face—the puffy skin, the bloodshot eyes—and that was a full day later; how drunk had he been that Saturday night? When she and Clyle told Hal that Peggy was missing, he was confused, putting all the pieces together, but could it be he already knew? There were those doughnuts in their winter yard, how adamant Hal had been that he didn't know who had cut those grooves in the grass.

Diane smoothed her hands across the flat surface of her desk. "Listen, Alma. I know I'm not your favorite person"— Alma started to object but didn't—"but I'm a professional too. I won't mention the money."

"It's my money."

"I know, I know. I'm just saying."

Alma thought about Bev Barnes—an honest-to-goodness kind person, even if a dolt. "If that were true, you wouldn't have to tell me."

Dusk settled as she parked the Vega in the garage and came in through the kitchen. The shower turned on downstairs, Clyle in from chores. Hal's truck wasn't parked in the yard. She mixed her husband a Lord Calvert and Sprite, drank half with her mouth puckered, then refilled the glass.

He came up a few minutes later, his wet hair slicked back, the tooth marks from the comb still visible. It was the one time each day Clyle combed his hair, after a shower. He wore maroon sweatpants and a gray sweatshirt—school colors. She handed him the drink. He raised his eyebrows—*you never make my drinks*—and she took it back and had another gulp.

"How was your day?" she asked, and Clyle told her about heading to town for their feed order for January and a trip to Vandersloots to place an order for penicillin for another round of pneumonia on the rise with the hogs. "Also had a visit this morning from Lee Earl," he added.

"I'm guessing from what I saw of that man last night, he had lots to say but little to listen to."

"Pretty much," Clyle conceded. "Ran Hal through the ringer three or four times about Saturday night and whether he was at the OK or Castle Farm."

"He already admitted he was at the OK. No crime in that."

"Nope," Clyle agreed. "And no crime in being at Castle Farm, but looks mighty bad to have said he wasn't and now say he was." Alma opened her mouth, but Clyle shook his head. "Blackout drunk isn't much of an alibi. You know as well as me, if something new turns up, Hal is top of that list. They can't make any real charges yet without a, well, without a body, but if one turns up, Hal's as good as in cuffs." He lowered his voice, even though they were the only two in the house, on the farm, in this section of the world. "He's hiding something, Alma."

Reluctantly, she nodded. "I know." After Clyle went to bed, she would tuck the money in the pantry. She looked at his face; every line there she'd watched etch deeper with time. When they'd met he was in his early twenties—just a baby. Was she really willing to leave him?

"Alma?" he asked. She was still wearing her coat. "You okay?"

"What if he did do something?" she blurted out. "What then?"

Clyle paused a spell before saying, "We do what's best."

"But what's that? Do we turn him in and watch him rot? Does he deserve that?"

Clyle sighed. "We can't break the law, Alm. This is part of why I want Marta in on the conversation. It's not just up to us. He's her son."

"But maybe the right thing was to not drop him in a lake when he was a baby. To protect him."

"What are you saying?"

"I don't know," she admitted.

"Or maybe you do, but you don't want to tell me." Years ago, in one of their pillow talks, Clyle said to Alma that he felt there was a part of her that was unknowable, that she hid even from him. Rather than be insulted or defensive, she'd felt victorious. He was right. She wanted him to say what mattered was Hal, not the law. That by helping him, they'd be righting an injustice years in the making. What she wanted was for him to say that he'd stand by her no matter what.

"Jesus Christ," she said. "Just Jesus Christ." She drank down the rest of the glass and handed it to Clyle, her head a little slurry now. She grabbed his arm and turned him toward her. How often did they stand this close to each other—the only two people in an otherwise empty house, no more than six inches between them?

The whiskey rose in her throat. "I'm going to do whatever it takes," she said. "You hear me?" She dug her fingers into Clyle's arm until he winced.

"I do," he said.

"And you? Are you willing?"

"There's more at stake here than just Hal," Clyle started, and she turned away. That was her answer.

15

Friday morning the phone rang once, and as the caller hung up, Clyle sat down with a piece of toast and a cup of coffee. Alma had started toward the phone—"Who's calling at seven?" she muttered—and then it happened again: one ring and a hang-up before she could reach it. "What in the hell? You think we're getting prank calls?"

"Maybe." Clyle's hand shook slightly as he brought his coffee cup to his mouth.

Those two rings with a hang-up between were a signal from the past. Diane wanted to see him. She would have assumed Alma was on her route; her youngest had started college that fall, and with no kids in school, Diane might not know yet that Alma'd been fired, or "put on leave," as Irv called it. Normally, he'd call her back—two rings meant she was alone in the house—but that wasn't possible with Alma there.

He thought of seeing Diane earlier that week at the Aherns'. It certainly wasn't unusual to run into her in Gunthrum—at football games or the bank or on the rare nights when he made an appearance at the OK—but each time he wished the world would swallow him up, along with the mistakes he'd made.

Coming back to Gunthrum, he never expected he'd have an affair. That wasn't the type of person he was, but did anyone ever think they were? Some of the men—Lonnie, Diane's husband, among them—acted like it was their due, their reward for providing for the women they had pledged their lives to. Some happiness on the side, a relief from the ball and chain, as if the very idea of happiness in marriage was a foreign concept. But after a while Clyle began to believe it was. There was nothing but silence between him and Alma, those lost babies stacking up. She wasn't the only one who had wanted children. She wasn't the only one who had suffered. And more than anything, it was the baby with Diane that was the betrayal.

All those years ago Diane had shown up at Clyle's house at seven o'clock in the morning, tapping on the barn door, red rims around her eyes. His stomach had dropped, and his first thought had been, Did Alma see you? But no, Alma was on her bus route. Diane said she was probably ten or eleven weeks along, thirteen at the most. She wasn't a thin woman, so even when she was naked it wasn't noticeable yet. "What are we going to do?" she asked, like it was his decision, but how could he do that to Alma? All those failed babies with her—even the fifth, which he wasn't supposed to know about but had intuited. They'd been in Gunthrum for a few years by then, and he thought they were happy, but that last baby did them in. Alma had gone from assured and brash to mean, and not just with others but with him. Nothing he did seemed right, and a year later, when Diane sat rapt on a couch as he talked about the time he saw Dick Butkus of the Bears in line to see *Cool Hand Luke*—"Gosh, just like a regular person!"—he'd taken the first steps down the road of the biggest mistake of his life.

He and Diane thought the pregnancy over for a few days, her at home with Lonnie and he with Alma. He supposed that fact right there told them all they needed to know. It seemed so obvious suddenly, so blatantly clear to Clyle, that he did not want a life with Diane. Diane, who thought he could do no wrong and had the answers to life, despite the fact he was cheating on his wife. He was embarrassed for both of them that he acted like such a blowhard in her presence, blathering about how he felt bad about the affair while she nodded along, when Alma would have told him to get down from the cross, someone needed the wood. Diane, who in bed moaned at the same pitch every time, while Alma picked up his hand and put it where she wanted. Or at least she had, back in the day.

In the end Clyle left it up to Diane to figure out where to go, and he paid for it. He told Alma he had to travel to Lincoln to see about some farrowing hogs, then drove Diane to a clinic and stayed overnight at the Cornhusker. Lying in the king-size bed the night after the abortion, as chastely as brother and sister, not even holding Diane's hand to comfort her through the night, Clyle knew it was over. A year later the hotel was demolished, and he saw the pictures in the newspaper: the left side collapsed before the right, a plume of dust to the sky.

Out in the barn he checked that the feeders weren't jammed and the water not frozen, that the straw was still thick in the stalls. There was a wheezing noise behind him, a shuffling, wet sound, and he turned. A smaller pig was hacking, a thumping in his chest: another damn pig with pneumonia. He moved the hog to a private pen with the sorting panel and watched the shallow, quick beats of the pig's chest. It had been a short week ago when he'd helped Hal clean up his house after the deer. There had been blood in a thin path from the front door to the kitchen sink and halfway up the cabinet.

It wasn't the first time he or Alma had come through to clean up one of Hal's messes. There'd been that incident in high school with the boy he beat up, and Clyle, against his better judgment, had convinced the parents not to press charges, leaning heavily on the reason that Hal wasn't fully of his mind, that he couldn't be held responsible. It had been the wrong thing to do, and he'd done it anyway. Hal had been with them two years by then, and he had grown to love the boy. Partly because Hal was a good kid, partly because he seemed to be the only thing that made Alma happy. Shortly after Hal started on the farm, Clyle would find her in the kitchen humming over cookbooks, searching for a new cookie recipe to try. She would cut fresh flowers for the table because when she did, Hal would lean across and inhale like he'd caught the scent of heaven. For Mother's Day that second year, Hal gave Alma a painting he'd done of a deer—at least Clyle thought it was a deer—and Hal told Alma he knew she wasn't his mom, but was it okay anyway? Alma had stroked the painting and talked through a thick voice, saying, "Yes, Hal. It's fine. I love it."

Down the road a light was on in the kitchen of the Ahern house, along with the outside light that always blazed on a farm. In the pickup the night before, Joe had leaned his head against the window on his wobbly neck and was asleep before they were down the lane.

Clyle finished chores and headed to the basement to shower. The shower curtain clattered against the metal rod as Alma pulled it back, and he felt the cool air on his wet body. "What're you showering for?"

"I need to run to town."

"What for?"

"More antibiotics from Dan. Found another hog with pneumonia."

"Thought you got more yesterday."

He pushed his head under the stream of water to avoid her. "Not enough."

"You taking Hal? He just showed up."

Clyle squinted one eye closed against the shampoo burn. "We had a rough trip to the vet earlier this week." Had that only been Tuesday? Wednesday? "Can you keep him here?"

"Sure. Not like I'm going to work." She pulled the curtain closed.

Clyle finished getting ready and gave Hal a chore—clear out the hand tools in the shed and put them away—and ten minutes later parked in front of the bank. Inside, Diane talked to Bev Barnes, both women in plaid skirts and blouses with bows at the necks, an elbow tucked on top of a fist at their waists, coffee cups in their raised hands. Bev turned toward the street and raised her coffee cup. Diane met Clyle's eyes before turning away, her figure lost to the gleam of sunlight as she walked deeper into the building.

He backed his truck out of the parking spot on Main Street and drove two blocks north behind the feedstore, their old meeting place when they'd needed to meet during the day for a stolen moment. The logistics of an affair had always baffled him—the cloak and dagger of it all, the hidden rendezvous—but turned out it wasn't as romantic as he'd thought, the sweet and dusty smell of ground corn in the air.

A few minutes later Diane opened the passenger door and climbed in, her plaid skirt rising above her knee. "I see you still remembered the code," she said.

"Of course."

She smoothed her hands down her wool lap. "I wasn't sure you would." She leaned in and kissed his cheek. "It's been a while." She smoothed her hand to her knee one more time before rubbing her palms across her arms. It was only twenty-three degrees—he'd read it on the bank sign—but she'd snuck out without a coat.

"Here." He began to remove his coat, but she held up her hand.

"I'll only be a minute." She cleared her throat. "Listen, Clyle, there's something you should probably know. I'm putting my job at risk to tell you, so I hope you'll respect me enough not to repeat it, but Alma withdrew a good chunk of money yesterday."

An actual chunk flashed in his mind, a green block in his wife's hands. "Alma?" he asked, and she told him the amount.

"Who knows what she's planning to do with it," Diane continued. "And I certainly don't mean to be stirring up any ill will, but it's a lot of money, Clyle, and she's coming back Monday to get more. In my experience no good comes from all that money leaving the bank." She looked at him with her doe eyes—one of the first things that drew Clyle to her—and rather than a rush of affection, what Clyle felt was anger.

"What makes you think I didn't know about it? Not every wife keeps secrets, Diane."

That ruffled her up. "I'm trying to help you," she explained. "You're not really in a position to not take help right now, Clyle. That woman's robbing you blind, and we all know what Hal's been up to, so you should count your friends while you still can."

"So that's it? Hal's guilty? You think the same as anyone else?"

"Pretty hard not to, given the evidence."

Clyle tightened his grip on the steering wheel. "Evidence of what? Nothing. Could still be the girl just ran off."

Diane snorted, a sound so eerily like Alma that Clyle winced. "No one believes that. Certainly not her folks."

They sat in silence for a spell, their past still part of the space between them. "I'm sorry I said that about keeping secrets."

She reached over and patted his hand. "You're under a lot of pressure. I understand that." It had always been like that with Diane—the quickness with which she would forgive him was something he never got from Alma, who could carry a chip on her shoulder until the end of time. How long had she held those miscarriages between them? He would have made a good bachelor, he liked to think. Not one who went in for the rabble-rousing but one who could keep himself well enough occupied on a weeknight with one drink (maybe two) and a rerun of *M*A*S*H*. But sometimes, out on the farm all day, around three or four o'clock in the afternoon, he'd say something to one of the hogs—"Shoo" or maybe "Settle down now, there"—and the sound of his own voice in the silence would be like a stranger's, the croak unrecognizable. He wanted a partner to love.

He'd wondered for the year of the affair if he should have married someone like Diane—sweet, supportive, uncomplicated—but sitting in the truck with her now, he found the idea so repugnant he could hardly look at her. Every conversation an agreement, every fight repressed. It wouldn't be like living at all. He thought of Alma and her fiery grudges, the way she never backed down. Their first year on the farm, they'd fought about what kinds of clouds were in the sky and what they meant weather-wise, and he'd screamed, "You are literally fighting me about whether the sky is blue." That stopped Alma in her tracks. She looked at him, then let out a laugh like sunshine. They'd both dissolved in giggles, then went inside and made love, middle of the day on a Tuesday.

"Do you ever think about the baby?" he asked, and Diane turned to him, her eyebrows together, confusion on her face, until it dawned on her, and her eyes widened.

"I think about her every day and never at all." He understood what she meant. "You know Julie started college this year?" He nodded. "When she came home last weekend, she'd cut her hair, and I hardly recognized her. If I'd had the baby, she'd be seven by now."

"Or he."

She shook her head. "No. I'm sure that baby was a girl." She put her hand on the car door. "Don't trust Alma more than you should, Clyle. That's all I'm saying. A woman with a secret is a dangerous thing."

"I know my own wife," Clyle said, as Diane's high-heeled feet hit the gravel.

She turned around. "Do you?"

Later that morning, with Clyle driving the skid loader to haul away the wet bedding and Hal in the pens distributing the new straw, Hal pointed down the lane. "Look, it's Peggy's mom." Linda Ahern was halfway to the barn; the December air made her cheeks pink and healthy, though as she approached, Clyle could see her hands appeared brittle and chapped, her fingers curved in against the cold.

"Linda," Clyle said, a hand in the air. "Let's get you inside." He started walking toward the house, the two of them approaching it at a diagonal, meeting on the porch.

"I guess I didn't realize it was quite this cold." She was wearing a windbreaker and, when she unzipped it in the kitchen, revealed just a T-shirt underneath. Clyle hoped it was at least long-sleeved.

"When it gets this temperature in the spring," Clyle said, "everyone will be out in shorts." Hal leaned against the porch wall as he tugged his boots off, then came inside.

Linda smiled in a way that made Clyle think she had only half-heard, her eyes on Hal. Clyle couldn't imagine being in the room with the man people thought had taken your daughter. Did Linda believe it too? From the look of her, she didn't know what she believed.

"Can we have pancakes?" Hal asked, and Clyle shut his eyes.

"Not now, Hal."

"You must be getting ready for a late breakfast," Linda said, the moment broken. "I know Joe usually has one in the early morning and one in the late. Of course, not today. He's still in bed sleeping it off."

"Let me get you some coffee," Clyle said. "Warm you up." He got the canister of grounds out from the lazy Susan, along with a filter.

Linda sat at the table and rubbed her hands up and down her shoulders.

"Listen," Clyle began. "I'm so sorr—" and Hal interrupted. "I'm thirsty."

"Then get yourself a drink of water," Clyle said, his voice raised, and Hal's eyes widened. Clyle wasn't usually the voice raiser.

"Thank you," Linda said. "I appreciate that," and Clyle wasn't sure if she meant the admonition of Hal or the condolence. Hal stood up and filled a glass from the faucet, drank half, then filled another and placed it in front of Linda. He wasn't without his manners.

She wrapped her hands around the glass. "Thank you," she said, this time to Hal, then turned back to Clyle. "That's why I came. To say thanks for bringing Joe home the other night." She let go of the water as he passed her a cup of coffee, and she held the too-hot drink to her mouth and blew on it. "And now thanks for this," she said referring to the coffee.

"Wait," Hal asked. "Peggy's dad was here the other night? Why?"

"Because," Linda answered, "he got drunk like a fool and showed up here."

"But why?" Hal asked.

Linda glanced at Clyle. "Because he's a drunk. That's what they do." Her hands had started to shake, and she put the coffee down hard on the table, sloshing a bit. Clyle knew if Alma were here she'd be sitting on her own hands not to come over and wipe up the spill.

Linda shrugged. "I guess that's it. I wanted to say thank-you."

"Here," Clyle said and stood up. "Let me drive you home."

Linda stared at him blankly. "You don't need to do that."

"I'm heading out anyway," he said, although he wasn't. He imagined Joe looking out the kitchen window and seeing Clyle's truck bringing his wife back, but it was the right thing to do.

In the truck Clyle blasted the heat, then realized it was still cold air and turned it back down.

"I'm sorry he did that," Linda said, looking down the road at her own home.

"He's upset."

Underneath Lynda's nose, her skin glistened. "That's true."

"Listen," Clyle said, but then stopped.

He turned into the Aherns' driveway, the truck crunching to a stop on the gravel. "You need anything?" Linda shook her head. Their boy, Milo, was playing with his Rubik's Cube at the kitchen table while a houseful of people bustled around him. In the driveway, with a Cadillac, was the Aherns' newish pickup, a 1984 red Dodge Ram with the metal hood ornament in the shape of a ram's head. Last summer Clyle had driven by, and Milo was standing at the front of the truck bucking his head against the silver hood ornament—a miniature ram's head—rocking it back and forth.

"Maybe if I had—" Linda started, then stopped. She was a warm woman; he'd always thought that about Linda. He flipped his hand palm up and squeezed hers, and instantly her eyes filled with tears. He released his grip, worried he had hurt her, but she held on fiercely. "I just can't believe this is happening. I keep thinking I'll walk through that door and there she'll be."

Seven, Diane had said. What were seven-year-olds into? Fishing? Dolls? He had no idea. Alma wasn't the only one who missed out on those kids. At his most self-righteous he wondered if that was why he had had an affair. He thought he and Alma were going to have one kind of life, and they ended up with another. Didn't he deserve a little happiness? It made him sick to think he'd thought that the only way to find it was at the expense of his wife.

"I'm sorry," he croaked out. "It certainly isn't fair."

"Fair's got nothing to do with it." They both sat staring in the house. The warm glow gave nothing away, no sense that something was missing. Joe Ahern even threw back his head to laugh at something outside of their view as Milo clicked away on his cube.

"Actually," Linda said, "I do have a favor to ask."

16

Milo scooted across the pickup cab as George jumped to the street.

"I'll be here the whole game, okay?" Mr. Costagan said. "Anytime you want to go, I'll be ready." He held up an Edgar Rice Burroughs paperback, the spine threaded with white. Milo had learned about object permanence in human development class, and there was something comforting about knowing he could step outside at any time and find Mr. Costagan in his pickup, the radio dial tuned to the staticky voice of the news.

"Thanks," he said. "I appreciate the ride."

"Anytime."

Milo slammed the door and jogged to the school doors to catch up with George, already inside and rubbing his cold hands together.

The double doors to the gymnasium were propped open with their rubber stops, and Milo could smell the sour teenage sweat of the players mixed with the popcorn handed out by the boosters for fifty cents a bag. Milo shoved his hands in his pockets and took a deep breath. He was regretting now that he'd insisted the morning before that his life remain normal when there was nothing normal about it. He'd just wanted to see if he could get his mom to agree, and once she did, reality set in: he had to go to the scrimmage, and it would be nothing like what he wanted. Even standing outside the gymnasium doors, all he could think of was all the times he'd watched Peggy in the gym corner as her palm slapped the volleyball, an unladylike grunt accompanying the serve.

Milo wished now he'd thought to call Scott so they could walk in together, but instead, he was stuck with George at his side, a person so emotionally uncomplicated at least it made Milo's life easier just to follow his lead. He couldn't imagine George worrying what people thought or how he came off. He was the teenage equivalent of Tarzan. Me want, me do.

"Come on, numb nuts," George said. "Are we going to stand out here all night?"

"Fine," Milo said, and took one more look behind him at Clyle's pickup in the parking lot, exhaust fumes chugging from the back.

Milo took a step toward the gymnasium as the crowd roared at a play on the floor. He was just working up a headful of steam about where they'd sit and next to whom and would his boots catch on the rafters and send him sprawling and would everyone look and snicker when George just marched forward and sat in the first row. Players were already on the court, and the scoreboard read four minutes left in the second quarter. The high school boys were in their crappy faded uniforms, and the fathers were dressed in old Gunthrum Bulldog sweats and T-shirts, the few still in shape dressed in polyester shorts. Everyone's legs were a startling pale patched with red from exertion and the cool temp in the gym.

Milo unwrapped his scarf as Kerry Saunders faked left with the ball against Larry Burke, the adults' ringer so it wouldn't be an out-and-out embarrassment. This was Mr. Burke's third year in the role—he'd been picked over a month ago, the announcement made in the *Gunthrum Pioneer*—but it was hard to see why as Kerry rolled past him without a blink.

Kerry's layup went in, the old guys got the ball, and Mr. Pickett stepped out of bounds long enough to throw it to Mr. Burke as Kerry pawed it from the air, dribbled once, then turned toward the basket. His fingers were spread wide as he jumped up in slow motion, the ball leaving his fingers inch by inch in a perfect arc, the ball an extension of him as his feet landed in the exact spot they'd been, the muscles in his thighs flexing, then relaxing. *Like poetry*, Milo thought, then blushed as Mr. Burke put his palms on his knees and bent his head, taking deep breaths. The ball swished through the net.

"Come on, Lare!" someone yelled from the crowd. "Show 'em what you got!"

"You still got it, don't you?" another yelled, and the crowd laughed.

"You want out here?" Mr. Burke yelled back, and the heckler flinched. It was all supposed to be in good fun, but that was hard to tell from Mr. Burke's dark expression or the way Kerry rebounded with an elbow into one of the father's faces.

"Personal foul!" the ref yelled, and Kerry whipped around.

"Come on!" he said. "That was an accident!" But the ref had them line up for two free throws. Kerry seemed to be taking the game more seriously than a championship, and Milo caught him flipping off the ref behind his back. The ref was the man who ran the Pizza Ranch, someone from their town. Good fun, right?—but the mood had shifted. George went on, oblivious to the whole thing, yakking about the cheerleaders, the high school ones, not the moms in jeans and T-shirts too tight on their stomachs. Last year Mrs. Burke had been one of the cheerleaders and had cheered so fervently that Milo had had to look at his feet rather than watch her embarrass herself during the half-time jam, when the moms and daughters did a routine to "Eye of the Tiger." This year she sat next to Mr. Burke's mom in the bleachers, with Hattie on her lap and her usually big hair held back in a greasy ponytail. He was relieved to see she wasn't out there tonight, but then he remembered Peggy wasn't either and concentrated on the grommets on his Adidas to keep from crying.

Kerry jogged off the court and threw himself on the bench, shrugging off the shoulder pats from his teammates. Someone slid in next to Milo, with his hip bumping him into George, and he looked up, relieved to see Scott. "Kerry's in a shit mood," Scott said. "Laura dumped him before the game."

Milo tried to look surprised, but he remembered what Laura had said on Wednesday, how Kerry wasn't really boyfriend material now that she suspected him of doing something to Peggy. Although that wasn't really it. It was more that she suspected him of still liking Peggy. How could everyone go on with the same concerns they'd always had when his sister was gone, the very fabric of his world now cut from a different cloth? Even Scott, his best friend, sat next to him expectantly, awaiting Milo's response. What was he supposed to say?

He turned back to the game as Mr. Burke bounced his second free throw against the backboard—groans from the crowd—and one of his teammates, Mr. Pickett from the hardware store, rebounded and took a three-point shot, an air ball, as a long sharp whistle sounded: the end of the first half.

People streamed from the gym, and the steady clop of the bleachers emptying echoed in the cavernous room. Milo joined the crowd, still in his anonymous car coat and hat, with George by his side, a kid no one knew. Scott had taken off like a shot and was halfway across the court, leaning over and laughing as he approached the door, their classmate Jim Schneider next to him also bowled over. "Ah man, that's disgusting!" Scott said, and Milo instinctively took a step back as another gust of cold air came in and the smokers headed outside. It was like a ghost had passed, or maybe Milo was the ghost. He had the feeling if he reached out his hand, it would pass right through his friend.

"You got a dollar?" George asked, and Milo blinked himself back into existence. "I want some popcorn."

"Yeah," he said, and dug his nylon billfold out of his back pocket. He ripped open the Velcro and handed the dollar to George. "Get me one too," he said, then matched up the Velcro sides as precisely as if he were performing surgery. This had been a mistake. He didn't want to be here, surrounded by all these people. He leaned himself against the cement wall in hopes of blending in; when George returned, they'd leave.

Milo felt a hand on his shoulder and turned, surprised to see Pastor Barnes in a Gunthrum Bulldogs sweatshirt and jeans. He was one of those men who never looked normal in casual clothes, the jeans still creased from the store, or maybe his wife ironed them. Before Milo's mom went back to work, she used to press his father's jockeys.

"It's good to see you," Pastor Barnes said. "Your parents here?"

Milo shook his head. "Mr. Costagan brought me."

Pastor Barnes raised his eyebrows. Milo supposed it was weird: the employer of the man his father had accused brought him to the game, but that was Gunthrum. "Where is Clyle?" Milo thumbed toward the parking lot. "Guess he's not a basketball fan."

"I guess not."

Pastor Barnes lowered his knobby skull closer to Milo. "Any word?" he asked softly, and there was no need to elaborate. Milo shook his head. "Well, I'm praying for you and your family."

Milo felt a bleat of rage trumpet up his spine. All around him the people of his hometown were laughing, shoving popcorn in their mouths, stomping their boots against the slush outside. "It doesn't seem to be doing any good."

Pastor Barnes looked down at him, startled. "Milo, I understand you're angry—"

Milo lowered his voice. "Do you?"

"I do," Pastor Barnes said calmly. "Your sister is missing; your family is distraught. Of course you're angry and hurt and scared."

"Well, what can you do about it, huh?" Milo had to resist poking Barnes in his skinny chest, the end of his finger itching. He'd never spoken to an adult like this in his life. "Are you going to tell me something like God works in mysterious ways? Or that there's a master plan? You realize this happened on the day I was confirmed, right? What kind of master plan is that?"

Pastor Barnes rubbed a hand against his chin in a way that was familiar to Milo from their hours of confirmation classes. He was thinking his answer through and not dismissing him, and something about the frayed edges of Pastor Barnes's sweatshirt cuff made Milo look away, ashamed— whether of his behavior or his pastor's he wasn't sure. "I don't believe in a master plan," Pastor Barnes finally said. "I don't think it's like that."

"Well, what is it?" Milo demanded.

"Guidance, not a set plan." He shook his head slightly, and Milo looked over to see Mrs. Barnes approaching with two bags of popcorn in her hand. She stopped and smiled, then looked discreetly away. "The Lord's teachings instruct us how to behave, Milo, but there are plenty of people mucking that up, and the results are disastrous. You remember free will, don't you?"

"Yeah." It meant that Peggy could leave Gunthrum or a madman could kill her, but either way, Milo was helpless.

Pastor Barnes smiled again, kindly and sincerely. "Of course you do. You were a star pupil. I actually wondered for a bit if you might be a fit for the seminary. You're a smart boy, Milo, and you don't accept the easy answers."

For years kids in Milo's classes had teased him about just that thing. Teacher's pet, angel boy, straight-A nerd. He'd never been one for sports, and all his life in this stupid town his intelligence had been the butt of a joke. He thought of Kerry out on the basketball court, the way he'd ducked Mr. Burke's arm. *Poetry*, Milo had thought, but also just muscle and bone, tendons and organs. They were human beings, the same way a dog was a dog, and maybe that was all there was.

Milo's mouth fell open, and Pastor Barnes flinched. "I don't mean there's *no* plan," Barnes said.

"No," Milo said, and shook his head. "I know."

"God is with you," Pastor Barnes said, his frayed cuff scuttling against his closely shaved chin. "You're not alone, son."

"I know," Milo said, and he smiled shakily at his pastor—a man of God—and made up an excuse: he had to find his cousin.

"You're okay?"

"I am," Milo said, and felt a firm calm descend. He looked at Pastor Barnes's panicked face. "I get it, I do. God's got it all under control."

"Well, not everything, exactly."

He put a hand on Pastor Barnes's arm, an action he realized he was mimicking from Pastor Barnes himself, a man who knew how to comfort. Milo understood that the job Pastor Barnes had signed up for was shuffling old people to the great beyond, new babies and happiness, the wayward teen who found his way to Jesus. Not this. "Thank you, really. This helped."

Relief washed over Barnes's face. "I'm glad, Milo. If you need to talk, you call me anytime. At home or the church."

"Thanks, I might," he said, but Milo knew he'd never call him.

George lurched back, bouncing on his toes as he came to a stop.

"Where's the popcorn?" Milo asked, and George laughed, picking at the hair near his temples.

"I guess I forgot."

"Where've you been?"

George ignored Milo, and Mr. Barnes said he'd see them at church on Sunday. "God willing, Peggy as well," he said, and joined his wife as she made her way back to the gym. They followed the rest of the crowd in as someone blew the horn on the scoreboard, signaling the game was ready to resume.

Milo turned to George. His cousin's eyes looked wider, bigger somehow, and darker. "You look weird."

"You always look weird," George said, and laughed.

Scott headed toward the doors along with Lisa Rasmussen and another girl from their class; it was like he'd forgotten all about Milo.

"Let's just go," Milo said to George, and they headed toward the door. On second thought, he got the dollar back from George and turned toward the concession stand.

Mr. Costagan was waiting in the parking lot, as promised, and dog-eared the corner of his book before setting it on the seat. "Game over?"

"Not quite," Milo said.

George shoveled a handful of popcorn in his mouth, kernels falling on the cab floor. "It's still halftime. I don't know why we had to leave already."

"Is it okay if he eats in here?" Milo asked, and Mr. Costagan assured him it was. "Here," Milo said, and handed the second bag to Mr. Costagan. "I got you some popcorn."

"Thanks," he said, and shook a few kernels into his palm. "We'll share."

They sat for a moment in the parking lot, the few smokers still clustered by the door waiting for the game to resume, smoke and cold clouding from their mouths.

"Hal loves popcorn," Mr. Costagan said out of the blue. It reminded Milo of Peggy and how she'd bring up the name of the boy she liked no matter how tangentially related to a conversation. She'd watched Milo squirt mustard on a sandwich two years ago and told him that Kerry liked mustard too. He thought of Laura saying Peggy was seeing *someone*, but he couldn't remember her mentioning anyone. Was it that Laura was wrong or Peggy was purposefully hiding something?

"Did Hal stay home because of Peggy?" Milo asked. He thought of all the times he'd hung out with Hal at the track, how he was always at the games, how confused he'd looked on Wednesday night, how Lee Earl had called him "boy."

"He's home cleaning. His mom's coming tomorrow."

Milo turned to Mr. Costagan, who was fishing a kernel out of his teeth with his tongue as he put the truck in drive. "Hal has a mom?"

Mr. Costagan looked at him, amused. "Of course he does." One of the older women smokers paused at the school doors and held up a hand to wave at the pickup; Milo recognized her from the drive-thru at the bank and the drinking parties on the weekend. Mr. Costagan stiffened and turned away, and the woman walked in and let the door shut behind her.

"What does Hal's mom think about everything that's been going on?"

Mr. Costagan pulled the gearshift, and the pickup lurched out of the parking lot toward the stop sign they rolled out for games. "That's a good question."

It had been so easy to comfort Mr. Barnes, so easy to make him feel better. "I'm sure it's going to be fine," he said to Mr. Costagan.

Mr. Costagan smiled. "You might be right." He motioned to the radio and told them they could pick another station if they wanted, something on FM. Before Milo could say it was fine the way it was, George pushed the FM/AM button and torqued the dial. It landed on "The Power of Love," a song that had been a hit in the summer.

Mr. Costagan tapped his thumb against the steering wheel as he turned onto Highway 57. He really did seem to think things might be fine, and that had been all Milo, not God.

17

Saturday at noon they rode to Hal's in silence. Alma had struggled into a pair of too-tight pantyhose, the roll above her middle squeezed in half by the control top, her leg hair bristling against the nylon. Pantyhose on a Saturday. Why was it that all men had to do was slip on a pair of pants for every occasion?

"What do you want to bet she's late?" Alma finally said, breaking the thick silence in the truck. She was referring to Marta, Hal's mother, who was meeting them at his house for lunch.

"She's got farther to drive," Clyle pointed out, and Alma snorted.

"Probably going to get lost. She hasn't been here for three years."

Clyle swung the pickup into Hal's drive and parked in front of the dented garage. He kept his hand on the keys. "Now listen, Alma. I want you to at least be civil."

"Is that where we're setting the bar these days?"

"You know what I mean. She's his mother, and I do believe she's coming to help."

"What kind of help is she going to give? Get him institutionalized? Bring him to Jesus? Maybe set him up in a back room of her house and only take him out for walks?"

"Fine." Clyle opened his door. Behind the garage Peanut Butter and Jelly bleated. "I can tell you're going to do what you want."

"Damn straight," she said, but really what she wanted was for her and Clyle to be on the same side, her side.

At the door they rang the bell rather than walking in. Hal answered a moment later, a dish towel tucked in the front of his pants. "My mom's not here yet, but you can go sit at the kitchen table. I'm making supper for lunch. Spaghetti."

Hal had a limited repertoire of meals that he subsisted on—spaghetti, meatloaf, baked pork chops, fish sticks, macaroni and cheese—and frozen meals prepared and supplemented by Alma. For lunches it was always what Alma prepared and ham sandwiches on the weekend. When he'd moved out on his own, Alma had spent time making a menu schedule with him, along with a grocery list and a budget. She'd taken him shopping the first few times so he'd get a sense of how much to buy, how to pick a fresh pepper. Where was his mother then?

"One of my favorites," she said, taking in the dirty pans in the kitchen, the stove splattered with red sauce. The smell of bleach still hung in the air. Alma hadn't been able to help herself; as soon as Clyle left with Milo for the scrimmage, she'd driven to Hal's to help him clean. She would not let Marta show up and have reasons to doubt his competency.

"It's my mom's favorite too." He held on to these memories like trinkets.

"You need any help?" Alma asked, and Hal told her no; he wanted to make it all himself.

Alma held up her hands—*who am I to argue?*—then looked at the covered table, a vinyl Stars and Stripes tablecloth left over from summer. In the kitchen the night before, she'd bent her knees and made sure there were no spots of blood against the wallboards, no signs of evidence. Her heart flashed when she'd seen a clump of blonde hair in the corner by the pantry, but upon closer inspection she realized it was straw from his broom, the one she'd bought him at Pamida. She had to stop this. There wasn't a body; there was no evidence. She had to believe he was innocent.

In the living room the *TV Guide* was perpendicular to the coasters on the coffee table, the sofa pillows straight as soldiers. In his room he'd made his bed with care, although it was still messy, the edge of the quilt careening toward the floor.

She thought about the money behind the flour canister, how maybe it wasn't tucked as securely in the Crisco can as she thought and she and Clyle would arrive home to find it magically strewn across the kitchen and her with some explaining to do. Although Clyle had plenty of his own to explain. She'd followed him Friday morning after those hang-up calls, and sure enough, Diane had climbed into his truck. Did he think Alma was so stupid she hadn't figured out their signal all those years ago?

She'd found Clyle's truck on Main Street easy enough and parked a block away from the feedstore, sneaking up like she was the one with something to hide. She'd watched as Diane climbed into the truck and leaned over to kiss Clyle on the cheek. Had the affair been going on for the past seven years, or had it just started again? She was exhausted thinking how long she'd been played a fool. She'd spent years developing a carapace over that old betrayal, and here Clyle was, cracking it open. She breathed deeply. She was doing the right thing.

The gravel crunched underneath a car, and a rusted Plymouth Horizon pulled in behind Clyle's pickup, Hal's mother behind the wheel smoking a cigarette with the windows up.

"I'm nervous," Hal said from the kitchen.

"How long has it been since you've seen her?" Clyle asked.

"A year, maybe two?"

"Three years," Alma said, steeling her face. "Three years, and she only lives three hours away."

"We ran into her at the hardware store a while back," Hal said. "Remember that, Clyle?"

"I do." Clyle said. He'd told Alma about it, how awkward it had been to exchange pleasantries, then go on their way. They watched as Marta climbed out of the car, one slow foot on the gravel, then the other. It had probably been five years since Alma had seen her, but looking at Marta, it seemed much longer. She had gotten bigger in the way of some women, lumpier, and Alma recognized the effort it had taken for her body to unfold from the seat. Marta reached back in and pulled out a wooden cane with a rubber grip, then looked up with a sour squint on her face. As she started walking, she leaned her weight toward the cane.

"I guess I'll take the reins," Alma said, and heaved her own body toward the door and opened it.

Marta took another pained step. "Why, hello there. I thought I'd look up to see Hal."

"He's here." Alma moved to the side, and Hal waved shyly toward the door.

Marta stopped, a hand to her chest. She turned to Alma. "It's always such a shock. You think they're going to stay little boys." She turned back to Hal. "You're big as a horse."

"I am not," he said, and Marta laughed.

"A talking horse!"

"It's a saying," Alma said to Hal. "Big as a horse."

Hal looked at her, irritated. "I know that." How quickly his alliances could switch. He leaned over to hug his mother, engulfing her in his large arms, the top of her fluffy head to the top of his breastbone. "I made lunch. Spaghetti. I know you like that."

"I do." Marta came in and looked around her son's living room, then draped her coat on the sofa. "Nice place," she said, and then to Alma: "You help him keep it shipshape?"

"Nope. That's all Hal." It was for the most part, except on Sundays, when she'd stop by with a few meals for the freezer and maybe make sure he'd scrubbed the toilet and washed his sheets. And of course she'd been here the night before on her hands and knees with a rag.

"Well, it's very nice, Hally. Very nice." She canted toward the table and put her wobbly, empty hand on the back of a seat, settling in, and leaned her cane against the wall. She pointed toward the kitchen through the open ledge where Hal had placed two bar stools and always sat to eat his breakfast. Alma and Hal had shopped for the stools at Pamida. He had been perplexed that he should buy two when he could only sit in one at a time. It nearly broke Alma's heart that he hadn't been able to imagine another person there with a bowl of cereal.

"I see you got those towels I sent a while back," Marta said, and Hal told her how much he liked them, how good they were at mopping up when he made a mess, and Alma had to keep from rolling her eyes. They got through the rest of their pleasantries, and Hal put the noodles in the pot along with six shakes of salt, then stayed in the kitchen with the pot.

"So," Clyle said, and then silence.

"So," Alma repeated. She turned to Marta and asked her what she'd been up to the past *three* years. Marta went on about her husband's accounting practice, the hours she spent volunteering at the church where he was a deacon, the latest prognosis on her hip, which wasn't good. "Sometimes I'm not sure if doctors get paid by the hour or the word, the way they go on about a person's options when they're hardly options at all: just different variations on the bad news. I give it to God," she said wearily, and smiled.

"And how's that going for you?" Alma asked, but Marta ignored her.

The timer went off, and Hal drained the pasta in a colander out of earshot. "He looks tired," Marta said, and Alma straightened her spine.

"Of course he does. What adult in America doesn't look tired? Up by six for chores, work at eight. He keeps the same schedule as the rest of us."

"Any word yet on his arrest?" Marta shook her head. "I can hardly believe he's still a free man."

Clyle held up a hand to keep Alma from answering. "The girl is just missing, and they don't have any evidence Hal did anything. He's as innocent as you or me right now."

Marta pulled her pack of cigarettes from her purse. "You're sure?"

"Yes, we're sure." Clyle dropped his hand to Alma's shoulder, and the weight felt solid and familiar on her body yet also like a memory from the past. Had it been that long since they'd stood on the same side of an issue?

Marta stared at that hand a good bit, then lit her cigarette, leaning back. "Well, his dad, you know," she said, and exhaled a straight plume of smoke.

"That was him, not Hal," Alma said.

Marta leaned in close as Hal reached for plates from the kitchen cupboard. "I'm just saying, anyone who shares blood with Wayne Bullard has some genes to overcome."

Wayne Bullard had been a drinker—hardly a crime in itself in Gunthrum—but he was a rough one. Hal had stepped onto the bus more than once with a black eye or a wince as he strung his backpack over his shoulder. It was probably a few years after Alma and Clyle had moved back, a year after she'd lost that fifth baby, that Wayne was arrested for involuntary manslaughter. He'd upped his usual game from aggravated assault when he'd plowed down another drunk with his car one late afternoon with the sun in his eyes, smart enough at least to go home and sober up so they couldn't get him for drunk driving as well. He was sentenced to sixteen months and served twelve, let out to find his life was better than when he'd gone in: his wife had filed for divorce and kept their retard son, and he was a free man to do as he pleased.

The day Wayne was arrested, Marta had called Alma at home between bus routes and said there was a chance she might not be there when Hal got home, and could Alma maybe keep him for a bit after that last route? Alma explained that wasn't part of her job, and Marta said that was up to Alma, but if she didn't, he'd be left alone. Alma had brought Hal home with her, and they'd played Go Fish until dinner. She'd called and called the Bullard's house, but Marta hadn't answered, and Alma knew if it went on much longer, the only responsible action would be to call the police and let them know. Why hadn't she? But the answer was easy enough. She didn't want to do that to Hal. Marta came the next morning, a Saturday, Hal in a pair of too-short sweatpants he'd borrowed from Clyle.

Back in Hal's kitchen, Marta tapped her cigarette against the ashtray. Hal didn't smoke—one of the few vices he'd managed to avoid—and the smell of it in his house made Alma's stomach turn. "Clyle called you here for your support," Alma said. "Him, not me, but trust me, it was for Hal's sake so you could help, not so you could run your mouth off about how he's guilty."

"It's like I told that reporter yesterday," Marta continued, as if she hadn't heard. "I love my son dearly, but he is who he is."

Alma glanced at Clyle, his face pale. He'd fielded a call from the reporter as well while Alma was in town but stiff-armed her as Alma had. There'd been that much agreement. "You *talked* to her?"

"She called me up on Friday, said she'd heard my boy was under consideration and linked to the disappearance and wondered what I thought about it all. Said she was going to run an article about it on Sunday."

"What all did you say?"

Marta leaned back and took a drag on her cigarette, the divots in her cheeks deepening as she sucked. "She wanted to know what I thought about it, and I told her. I told her I thought Hal took after his dad more than me, always had. I didn't know if he'd had anything to do with that girl disappearing—he's not been very good about keeping in touch with me after he moved out, even though I've done my part—and I just had to hope not, although there were things that made me wonder."

"What kind of things?" Alma asked, ready to shoot down every excuse Marta offered.

"Well, his dad, that's for sure, and what a no-good he was, but also that incident in high school."

Alma held up a finger. "You know that wasn't his fault."

Hal stood in the doorway. "What wasn't whose fault?"

"That time in—" Marta started.

"Never mind." Alma felt her face strain into a smile. "All done? Need any help?"

The incident Marta was referring to was a fight in high school when Cheryl, Larry's then-girlfriend, said one of the Wayne guys came onto her after a basketball game and tried to stick his hand up her cheerleading skirt. Larry and Sam and a few other boys convinced Hal they needed to teach that guy a lesson. Hal had gone along, and when they needed someone to take the first punch, he ran ahead, caught up in the excitement. Alma had been furious, but Hal insisted they hadn't put him up to it, that he was just one of the guys. "He wanted to!" Larry said to her, but what did Hal know about what he wanted?

A day or two later it came out that Cheryl had made the whole thing up, but by then the damage was done. The cops had shown up at the hospital, and since Hal was almost twenty, they were ready to charge him as an adult; Hal had broken the other boy's collarbone. When the parents of the boy found out Hal was what he was, they dropped the charges, but that had been the final straw for Marta. She'd thrown in her lot with husband number two and left Hal in Alma and Clyle's care the summer after graduation. He'd been working for them on weekends for a while by then, his father now out of prison and on his way to the promised land out west. Alma and Clyle discussed it and figured, if they tightened their belts, they could afford him full-time.

"I got it." Hal set the bowl of steaming spaghetti on the table, the sauce already mixed in. He passed out the paper napkins and silverware—one knife each, one fork—and sat down.

Marta crinked her cigarette out in the ashtray next to her. "Looks delicious, sweetie," she said, and Hal beamed. Marta insisted on holding the table hostage as she said grace, certain to bless each and every one of them. After, she put a hand on Hal's. "You've always been a good boy. I know you've done the best you could."

"Thanks, Mom."

She gave his hand a squeeze. "But tell me the truth, Hally. Did you do something to that girl?"

"You don't have to answer that, Hal," Alma warned, worried suddenly what he might say.

Hal looked at his mother, confused, then over to Clyle and Alma. "No, ma'am. I don't think so."

Clyle folded his napkin and tucked it in his lap. "That's enough, Marta."

"What do you mean?" Marta pressed. "'You don't think so?'"

"What do you mean, what do I mean?" Hal's mouth started to quiver. "Do you think I would do something bad?" Alma wanted to stop them both, but she was frozen in the moment.

"You have before." Marta squeezed his hand again. "Remember high school?"

"That was an accident!"

"And maybe this was too."

Hal pushed back his chair. "That wasn't my fault!" He looked around the table. "You believe me, right?"

"Of course we do," Alma said, as if shaken from a trance. "Of course." My God, he was all she had if Clyle was back with Diane. All those years ago when Hal had stood on the bus steps with a macaroni necklace behind his back or a deck of cards with only three cards missing. "Here," he'd said. "We can be friends." He was the family she'd made.

"Hally, this is too much for you," Marta said. "I can see that. You need to get right with God and the police."

"You need to call back that reporter," Alma said. "Tell her you got the story wrong. Hal's not guilty of anything. Even Sheriff Randolph would say the same at this point."

"I don't have to do anything of the sort," Marta said. "I know what story I have to tell."

"What reporter?" Hal asked.

"Never mind," Clyle said.

"Hally," Marta said. "Honey, look at me." Hal turned toward his mother, a smear of spaghetti sauce on his chin and his eyes glassy. "Hal, I think it's too much for you, sweetie, being here on your own. I want you to know I'm looking into other options. Somewhere safer for you." Alma wondered briefly if she and Marta were on the same page after all—to get Hal away from Gunthrum and whatever mess was about to crack open. "There's a place in Lincoln, a regional center where you could live with like-minded folks and take care of yourself."

Alma slammed a hand on the table. "You want to lock your own kid up?" It took everything she had not to stab Marta's fleshy arm with a fork. "He's not crazy!"

"I'm just saying, I talked to the director about Hal, and they'd have the room. They know how to deal with people like him."

"Like what?" Hal asked.

"Special," Marta said, but Hal frowned, knowing that she didn't mean special-good.

"You going to pay for that?" Alma asked. "It costs a pretty penny, I'm guessing."

Marta raised her chin. "Eugene's got some money from a settlement." Eugene was her third husband.

Clyle put a hand on Alma's shoulder. "Marta, we're getting ahead of ourselves. You're talking about uprooting this boy—excuse me, this man—from the life he's built himself and knows and for a reason that might have nothing to do with him."

"Might," Marta said, and pointed her cigarette tip at him. "Even you have your doubts."

Clyle stood up. "I think we've accomplished all we're going to here today. Marta, I do appreciate you taking the time. Hal and I can walk you out."

Marta nodded once, dropped her fork on her plate, and stood up as she stabbed a fresh cigarette out in the ashtray.

Alma leaned over so Hal wouldn't hear and hissed to Marta. "You're a terrible mother."

Marta stuck her lighter in the front of her plaid cigarette case, tucked the soft pack of Merits in the main compartment, and snapped the metal closure shut. "How would you know what it takes to be a mom?"

Alma ran a sponge over the kitchen counter. There was spaghetti sauce on the fan over the stove, the underside of the saucepan, dried on the grease already coating the timer. She would clean that up, then finish the dishes, dry them, and put them away. She balled the dish towel—the one from Marta—and shoved it under the Ragú jar in the garbage as Clyle helped Marta to her car with a hand under her elbow. Jesus wept, he was a good man in so many ways, but that quickly, in her mind's eye, she saw Diane lean over and give Clyle a kiss on his weathered cheek.

As Clyle settled Marta into her car, Marta requested that her son come out, like he was being granted an audience with the queen. Clyle called Hal out, and Hal leaned down and stuck his head in the car window, both Marta's hands on his cheeks as she pulled him in farther for a kiss on the forehead.

As she drove away, Hal and Clyle continued to the sheep—the floater in the water trough needed replacing—and Alma watched Clyle kneel down in his good corduroy pants, pick up the floater, and blow in it, as Jelly nudged his shoulder. He stopped what he was doing to give the wether a good scratch, the wool so thick and matted you couldn't dig down to the skin. What amazed her was that she and Clyle had *kept* secrets, not that they had them. The last miscarriage, the affair, the money secured in a Crisco can. The keeping might be more painful than the secret itself.

One afternoon when they first moved to the farm, she and Clyle had made love in the hayloft. It had been romantic and spontaneous even with the straw scratching both their backs, causing welts, as they rolled around. Maybe it was romantic because of it. That night he'd traced the red lines on her skin, and for days he'd scratched his back against the kitchen doorframe like a boar and she'd laughed herself to tears. They'd always had secrets, but they used to have them together.

The men came in a few minutes later, after Alma had settled on the sofa with the TV *Guide*. Clyle went to the sink and tapped the faucet up with his forearm. "Look at you with your feet up," he said to Alma, and she snorted, threw the magazine back on the coffee table, then thought better of it and straightened it against the coasters.

"Rubbish. As if watching TV isn't bad enough, we've got to waste our time reading about it." She stood up. "You ready to go?"

Clyle bent his arms at the elbows with his hands up in the air as if he were prepped for surgery. He tore three paper towels off the roll on the counter and dried his hands. "Ready."

Hal came back from the bathroom still buckling his belt. "Toilet's clogged. Sorry."

Alma crossed her arms. "Why are you apologizing to me?"

He sat on the couch and put his feet on the coffee table, his boot sliding the TV *Guide* precariously to the edge. "Maybe my mom's right. Maybe I'd be better off somewhere else with someone to take care of me."

Alma felt a line of fire shoot up her back from adrenaline and anger. "Bullshit. You do just fine here, Hal. Just fine. She's not talking about someone to unclog a toilet; she's talking about someone to take away your independence." It occurred to her if she and Hal were to run, maybe she'd be doing that as well. No, she thought. *That* would be for his own good.

"It's not just that," Hal said.

"Then what is it?"

He shrugged. "I'm so dumb I don't even know."

"You're not dumb," Alma started to say, but that wasn't the truth. "Or maybe you are. But what matters is you're self-sufficient. Don't you let that woman fill your head with nonsense."

"That woman is my mom," Hal said defensively.

Alma reached for her purse and pulled it over her shoulder. "Don't I know it. Clyle?" She turned to her husband. "I'm ready to go."

"All right," he said, and they were out the front door. Settling in the pickup, Alma imagined Hal back in the bathroom, flushing and flushing, water rising over the bowl, turds on the floor. Could Hal make it on his own? She wanted so badly to believe she would do what was right by him, but was it really that she needed someone to need her?

"Maybe we should—" Alma started.

Clyle put a hand on her shoulder as he turned around to back out of the drive. "He has a plunger," he interrupted. "Let him be."

18

Milo sniffed the air, convinced he smelled smoke. He turned off late-night TV, hoping the silence would heighten his senses, and sure enough, the smell of smoke polluted the air.

He followed the scent out to the garage, where he found his mom, a lit cigarette in her hand and three butts on the ground. She'd quit about two years ago.

His mother held the cigarette up as if to say, *How'd that get there?* and took a drag. "I guess the cat's out of the bag. Doesn't seem like such a big deal now, does it?"

"I guess not."

She locked eyes with him as she inhaled, then exhaled. "You know why I quit?"

"Why?"

"I didn't want to smell like smoke at the hospital. It made me feel like a hypocrite telling all those patients to stop smoking when I was at a pack a day." She dropped the cigarette and crushed it under the toe of her tennis shoe, then sniffed her fingers, grimacing. "It doesn't even taste good anymore, but I light them one after the other." She smiled at Milo and reached out to ruffle his hair, the stink of smoke on her hand. "Don't tell your father. He'd have a conniption." His father wasn't home yet—he'd left around nine thirty in his pickup and was probably at the OK—and Milo liked the idea of having a secret with his mom.

"Can I ask you something?" he said as his mom pulled another cigarette out of the soft pack. It had been bugging him all week, how calm his folks had seemed until his dad lit on the idea that Hal had done something. "Did you really believe she just ran away?"

His mom winked against the flame and smoke as she lit the end of her cigarette. She inhaled deeply, held the smoke a long moment, and exhaled. "I thought about it. I know Gunthrum isn't exactly a thrill ride for you and your sister."

He looked at her, surprised. "You do?"

She smiled at him wanly. "I grew up here too, remember? I was a lot like Peggy back in my day. Popular, good at school, pretty—"

"You're still pretty," Milo said instinctually. Wouldn't that be what his mom wanted to hear?

She grimaced. "It's not the same. Back then, pretty was about all that mattered, but it was more of a liability than a perk."

"What do you mean?"

She leaned against the hood of the Buick. "I mean that's all that people saw. Boys would ask me out, and I'd try to talk during the dates, and they just wanted to put their hands up my sweater." Milo flinched, and she inhaled again. "You're old enough, Milo. You know what I'm talking about." He thought about Scott and the way he ogled Lisa Rasmussen, a collection of body parts like a mannequin disassembled. Had Scott ever even talked to her? Did he know she didn't know the difference between *you're* and *your*, and if so, would he care? Milo doubted it very much.

His mother tapped her cigarette against the Buick and ashed on the cement floor. "I hate to say it, but your dad was the same way. He liked me because I was a pretty girl and looked good on his arm. He didn't care that I didn't want to stay in Gunthrum or that I wanted to go to college. The only reason he even agreed for me to go to night school for my nursing degree was because I promised I'd have dinner warming in the oven at 200 before I left at six o'clock. And Jesus knows I'd come home at nine to not one dish washed." Milo was having trouble following all this—so was she mad at his dad about something that had happened a few years ago, or was this about Peggy? Should *he* have done the dishes?

She pointed her cigarette at him. "You know who was better than that? Your uncle Randall. Sometimes I think I married the wrong man."

Milo put a hand against the Buick hood, in danger of losing his balance. "You like Uncle Randall?" It weirded him out to have her talk to him like this. He'd always wanted people to stop treating him like a stupid kid, but now that she was, he wanted to cry out that he was only twelve years old.

His mom smiled. "No. Of course not. I'm just saying, I know Peggy probably wasn't as happy as people thought. That what looked like a perfect life might not have felt like one." She pulled the soft pack back out of her jeans pocket before recognizing the lit cigarette in her hand. "I knew about those parties at Castle Farm and how she'd sneak out at night—I'm not gullible like your father, Milo—and at first I thought she probably left on a lark, maybe with a boy. I just assumed she'd come home, but then after we lied at church, it was important to your dad we keep up appearances, and I guess I was scared not to. Scared to think what it would mean if she hadn't just run away." She turned to Milo. "I will never forgive myself for that. If we'd called sooner, if we'd taken it seriously, who knows where we'd be right now."

Milo sat down on the garage floor, his head reeling. So, his mother had known everything. All those times Peggy had shimmied down the drainpipe or come home drunk:

his mother had known every bit. He shivered on the cold cement, a shiver he didn't think would ever stop.

"So, what do you think happened?"

His mother stood with her fist balled under her elbow, the cigarette clenched between her fingers not an inch from her mouth. "Nothing good."

All his life his mother had painted a version of their family that had fooled the rest of the world—two shiny and bright kids; a husband who blew off steam with a couple of beers but nothing to worry about; a pretty wife with a slim waist and a brownie recipe envied by the town. Nothing bad could ever happen to them, that version said, and it had fooled him too. He thought about all the words he'd memorized for his confirmation, the oath he'd taken to God. Was that just another lie everyone told so they could get up in the morning? Were all these people who thought nothing bad could happen just fooling themselves? "But like, how bad?" he asked his mom.

"I think you know," she said.

Yes, he did.

The next morning Milo held open the church door for the family behind them. "How are you holding up, sugar?" the mom said, with the wide-open face of many of the women in town, everything about her a little puffy. His own mom was thin—not just by comparison, he figured, but thin by about any standard. She'd never been a big eater, and he could tell by the way she tucked blouses in her slacks that she was proud of her figure, although just a week into Peggy's disappearance, she looked sharp and frail, the tendons in her neck like knives.

Milo lay in bed last night after the garage talk with his mother, playing over what she'd said. For years he'd discounted her as just a parent, the person whose only job was to stand between him and endless glasses of Mountain Dew, but he realized now she was much sharper than he'd thought. She'd really seen them, both of them, and it made him want to cry to think someone had. He fell asleep in the milky light of dawn, his head heavy as a mallet.

Another family shuffled toward the entrance, so Milo continued holding the door, worried about not wanting to seem rude but also about how much cold air he was letting in the vestibule. The man of the family shook Milo's hand, his palm dry and callused, as he capped the other on Milo's shoulder. Milo marveled at how different each handshake could feel—some limp, others crushing—and with each one he just set his palm in theirs and followed their lead.

"Hey," someone said behind the man; it was Laura. He hadn't even realized it was her father's hand he'd shaken. Maybe he should apologize, but he had realized he could get away with about anything right now, as long as he didn't draw attention to it. He followed the Beckers into church, his parents already walking down the aisle toward their normal pew, not realizing he wasn't following.

"I can't believe they made you come to church," Laura said.

"I know. A missing sister should be good for something," he joked, and could see the horror on Laura's face. He couldn't help himself; if he made a joke, maybe people would believe things were okay, him included. Laura squeezed his hand, then slipped in next to her parents, a third of the way up on the left side of the church.

Milo turned around as if he'd been escorting her like an usher. People either made eye contact with a sympathetic grimace or quickly darted their eyes away. He raised a hand and waved at Scott, but even Scott studied his lap, his father's arm slung around him and resting on the back of the pew.

Milo felt a surge of energy, as if he'd further harnessed the superpower of invisibility. He headed back to the vestibule, and nobody said boo about it.

There he watched a family scuttle in late—a harried woman with a baby in her arms pulling a boy of three or four behind her, the husband checking his wallet, presumably for ones for the collection plate. At the entrance to the nave the woman passed the baby to her husband, smoothed her skirt, and walked inside.

Milo had noticed this about churches: they were the only place fathers took the lead on parenting, rushing temperamental babies to the lobby or fussy toddlers to the restroom. They acted like heroes, but Milo had it figured out: they just wanted to skip church. Sometimes two or three men would huddle in front of the kitchen, sneaking free doughnuts no one was supposed to touch until the service was over, their children running like little maniacs under the tables.

At the church kitchen Milo pushed open the swinging door. Eight large coffee filters filled with grounds were waiting next to the two-burner commercial coffeemaker, ten white carafes on the other side. Numerous plates and pans with rolls and pastries sat on a center island. Milo peeled back a corner of the plastic wrap on what looked to be cherry pie and swiped his finger clear through from the center to the edge and stuck it in his mouth. Yep, cherry, tart but sweet.

He left the wrap folded back and returned to the lobby to listen to the drone of Pastor Barnes's voice, the steady answer of the congregation. The first of the fathers came trundling down the aisle—Mr. Burke with a two-year-old girl in a pink dress in his arms struggling to get to the ground.

"Hey, Mr. Burke," Milo said.

Mr. Burke bent down to let the girl go, her arms irritated red from the too-tight elastic at the sleeves. He looked up and blanched. "Milo. Didn't see you there."

Of course you didn't; I'm invisible. He thought about what his mother had said about Peggy being pretty—how it was a liability and not a perk. For most of his life he'd lived in his sister's shadow, but maybe that had been for the best. "What's the Ahern boy's name again?" one of the people at his house had asked one Friday night. "Mick?"

He knew Mr. Burke from those parties. Mr. Burke was young for the crowd—Milo guessed late twenties—but everyone over twenty-five pretty much looked like any other adult to him. The little girl, Hattie, pushed her way through the swinging door into the kitchen, a nose for news.

"I should . . ." Mr. Burke trailed off and followed his daughter, Milo behind him.

"The pie's good." Milo pointed at the one he'd eaten from, his finger swipe like a backhoe through the top crust with a ditch of red filling.

"It looks good," Mr. Burke said, without a word about how Milo had ruined it. "Listen," Mr. Burke started again but closed his mouth, his eyes focused on Hattie reaching for a plate of cookies.

"Yeah?"

"I'm just." Mr. Burke stopped again. "I'm sorry to hear about your sister."

Milo nodded. Everyone was so damn awkward about it, and he couldn't blame them. He was awkward, too, but had discovered with his new superpower that really didn't matter. People were too focused on their own reactions to worry about his, and at least Mr. Burke hadn't added the fake sentiment that he was sure she was all right. "It's okay."

Mr. Burke's eyes locked on Milo's in a way Milo found disconcerting, and he felt his stomach drop.

"It's not okay." Tears formed in Mr. Burke's eyes. "None of it."

And that quickly Milo remembered Mr. Burke at one of the parties a few months ago, Peggy home on a Saturday night for no discernible reason. Milo had asked her when she got so lame, and she'd said her friends were babies and she had better things to do than hang out with them. She'd worn eyeliner, at home, another thing he pointed out as weird, and she finally told him to shut it. Scott had been there as well. Scott's parents weren't part of the drinkers, but sometimes he stayed over on the weekends.

Scott and Milo had been in the kitchen raiding the open bags of Doritos his mother now bought. Peggy flirt-whinnied from the stairway, a sound he recognized from the halls of school and the phone and basically anytime a guy talked to her at a football game. He and Scott had peered around the corner, expecting to find her on the phone, but there was Mr. Burke, a hand lifting up the back of her hair, Peggy's chin tucked toward her shoulder, her eyes peering up at him. "It's red, all right. Here." He blew on her neck. "Does that feel better?"

"That," Scott whispered, "is one lucky son of a bitch," and he'd shoved a handful of Doritos in his mouth, smashing the chips. As if on command, his mangy dog toddled over to hoover up the crumbs.

Peggy had lit up at the slobbering sounds of the dog. "What a cute puppy!" she said, even though she'd met Maury a hundred times and hadn't seemed all that impressed. She bent down to scratch the dog's neck. "Larry, look at this."

"Oh, I am," he said, and Milo followed Mr. Burke's eyes to his sister's butt.

The thing that had struck him at the time was the shock that Peggy hadn't pushed Maury away—she was allergic and didn't like dogs, which was why they didn't have one—and that she hadn't called Scott a Neanderthal for getting electric orange Dorito dust all over the palms and fingers of his hands. But what struck him now was the blowing of air on her neck. Mr. Burke's eyes on her butt. That she'd called him "Larry."

Mr. Burke patted his daughter on the back, avoiding Milo's eyes. Milo could feel the air shifting and reorganizing the molecules in the room, the temperature dropping along with his stomach. "You and Peggy." Mr. Burke turned around, rocking the girl in his arms as she gripped the collar of his shirt with both fists. "You guys were friends."

Another time at church Milo was sitting by Peggy, Mr. Burke and his family one pew up. Peggy had loudly opened the metal clasp on her purse, gotten out her lipstick, and twisted the tube. She smoothed the lipstick on her mouth, then smashed her lips together to blend the color across both. At the end she opened her mouth in a loud *pop!* and Mr. Burke twitched like he'd heard a shot. Their mother had leaned over and grasped Peggy's arm. *That's enough*, she said with that grip.

In the church kitchen Mr. Burke's face was ashen. "Like you and I are friends, Milo. I'm friends with everybody's kids. I see you guys nearly every week." But Milo knew that wasn't really true; Mr. Burke was one of the shadowy adults he knew by name whose appearance in the house marked a night of lax rules. Milo was as invisible to those adults as they were to him, yet Mr. Burke had seen Peggy. And Peggy usually wasn't home on the weekends, although she had been lately, hadn't she? Home with her eye makeup on, even going to other people's houses when the party was somewhere else. She'd told her mom she'd babysit the little ones for free—a selfless act! My God. How had he not put it together before now?

"It's not what you think, Milo. You've made some leaps here, buddy," but Milo didn't think so. Laura had said Peggy was seeing *someone*. Could it be Mr. Burke, a guy in his late twenties who had managed not to get fat yet, with those weathered good looks people went for in Robert Redford?

"I need to get back inside. My parents are going to come looking for me."

"Listen, buddy." Mr. Burke reached for the shoulder of Milo's argyle sweater, but Milo ducked.

"My mom hates when I miss the service."

"Milo—" he said, but Milo turned away, walking as quickly as he could toward the church entrance, past the vestibule with its large glass double doors. Idling in the parking lot was a police cruiser, Peck Randolph at the wheel, exhaust billowing behind the car. *What's he doing here?* Milo pushed open the second set of doors and was struck instantly by the icy air, a shock to his system. Peck looked up and said one word—it looked like a swear—and then turned off the ignition and clambered out.

Goose pimples formed on Milo's arms as Peck met him at the curb. "Let's get you inside, son." He put a hand on Milo's back, leading him to the foyer, now empty. What happened to Mr. Burke?

"Did you find her?" Milo asked Mr. Randolph.

"I need to speak with your folks, Milo."

"You did, though, didn't you?" A hymn started up, and Milo tried to discern each dour note to hear if he knew which one. Why did it matter? His head felt big as a balloon.

"They inside?" Peck asked.

"Yeah. You want me to go get them?" He imagined sneaking down the aisle like a ghost, no one even aware he was there other than the tickle of the air's disturbance as he floated past.

"Why don't we just wait." Peck looked at the large assembly. "Either way, it's going to be a mess," he muttered.

Milo nodded toward the common room with all the set-up chairs and tables for after-service snacks and coffee. He didn't know what church Peck Randolph went to but knew it wasn't the Lutheran, or he'd have seen him here, out of his uniform and in ill-fitting dress pants like the rest of the men wore. It occurred to him it was possible Mr. Randolph didn't go to church, that not everyone got up early on a Sunday to worship God. Some people might not believe and had even been given reasons not to.

In the church kitchen three women—Milo recognized one of them, Tonya Gary, Mr. Gary's wife, but the other two were old ladies—had skipped out on the end of the service to start organizing cups and creamer, slicing the donated coffee cakes into precise two-inch squares and setting them, piece by piece, on paper plates. Mrs. Gary slid the end of the butter knife through her thumb and forefinger and put her fingers in her mouth. "Where'd Cheryl go?" she asked. "Wasn't she on coffee duty this week?"

Milo thought about talking to Pastor Barnes at the basketball scrimmage, how he'd put his hand on his pastor's arm, how that had been enough to comfort him. Milo blanched. He didn't believe in God, not one bit. Not one little bit. He knew this as suddenly and cruelly as he knew something else and that these two facts would be forever linked together.

"She's dead, isn't she?" Milo said. Mr. Randolph turned toward him. "It's okay. I already know. I can tell."

"I'm sorry, son."

And like that, every fear Milo'd ever had came to fruition. "Where'd you find her?"

"I need to speak with your parents, Milo. I really do. Procedure and common decency. You don't need to hear this from a stranger."

"You're not a stranger."

"Well, yes and no."

Milo turned to Sheriff Randolph. "I don't believe in God," he said, and the words, for the first time in a long time, gave him a sense of power just as he burst into tears.

"Believing or not believing," Sheriff Randolph said, and pulled Milo into a hug. "They're different sides of the same coin."

19

Early morning, Alma tromped through the fresh snow to the end of the lane and retrieved the *Omaha World-Herald* from their mailbox, the Sunday edition thick as a log. It was wrapped in a plastic bag against the dampness, and she clutched it to her chest as she made her way home. Clyle was at the table waiting with two cups of coffee. He'd offered to go get the paper, but she said the fresh air would do her good; she could not sit at the table just waiting.

There it was on the front page: "Mother Tells Tale of Troubling Past," accompanied by a picture of Marta Bullard at her kitchen table, a cigarette in one hand and holding Hal's high school football picture in the other. Why hadn't they used his school picture, where he was smiling? In the football one the coach had encouraged all the boys to play tough and not show any teeth. Seen in context with the photos of the other boys, Hal's didn't look any different, but here, with just him, he seemed like a guy with a chip on his shoulder, one hoping to do some damage. Along with Marta's testimony, Larry Burke had been quoted as a friend of Hal, recounting when he had beaten up the child from Wayne, Hal by that point a legal adult. No mention of Cheryl having set the whole thing off to make Larry jealous. No mention they'd goaded Hal into it.

Alma stood over Clyle's shoulder, and they read in unison. Marta talked about Hal's father's past—the involuntary manslaughter that had landed him in jail in '75 and then the return in '78 for assault and battery. "It's in his genes, you see," she'd been quoted as saying. "That, plus he's simple. I never stood a chance."

She'd gone on to talk about Hal as a little boy—"always a bit off"—and how she'd had trouble controlling his temper when he was in junior high and high school, and as a result, he'd done everything he could to cut her out of his life. Only God had gotten her through. She'd painted herself a victim of genetics, fate, and society, ending with the line, "I don't know if he did something to that girl or not, but it wouldn't surprise me. Little about this world surprises me anymore."

No mention, of course, about that day at Fremont Lakes when she'd been sloshed on the beach while her son—two years old and a boy to boot, so without a lick of sense—had walked farther and farther into the water, eventually ending up back on the beach with a rescue squad and a mother who said it was his own fault. There were few things that made Alma as mad as a woman who got to be a mother and screwed it up.

"You were right," Clyle said. "I probably shouldn't have called her. You happy?"

In a rare concession Alma said, "She would have spoken to them one way or another. Not much we could have done about that. At least this way she had to look him in the face." She made a point of crushing the front page into a ball and shoving it deep in the garbage.

Clyle gave her a sweet look that could have melted metal—he seemed so thankful for her support. "Why don't you call him up. We'll go for a drive." It was what they did most Sundays—meandering roads for about an hour, both in their heads with the radio on—and it was a fifty-fifty shot if Hal came along based on his hangover, but Clyle was right: they needed to get him today before he saw the paper, perplexed by his own picture on the front page.

While Clyle was in the shower, Alma pulled the paper back out of the trash and smoothed it across the thigh of her jeans, her fingers grubbing black from the ink. She stared at the pantry—the five thousand dollars tucked behind the flour canister in an empty can of Crisco—and thought of Clyle's look just moments ago. She'd barely slept the last two nights and told herself that just because she was getting the money didn't mean she was going to use it. Her brain toggled between Hal out on his own, loading the Vega and following behind him, and just leaving the money tucked in the Crisco can. It was Sunday, and the bank was closed; no decisions to be made today.

They drove south down Highway 57 to Harington, turned around in the Trinity Lutheran parking lot, the white lines filled with pickups and sedans in varying conditions, and headed back home. Hal sat in the back seat, the fields barren, the harvested cornstalks fighting through the snow. As Clyle turned down their lane, Alma recognized the boxy shape of Lee Earl's blue car.

Clyle pulled in next to the Chevy Caprice and cut the engine. "Here we go." Mr. Earl was behind the wheel, the car still running and the heater, Alma guessed, full blast. She thought about Milo's quip about how Earl looked like he was on *Miami Vice* and felt smug to think he'd be soft against the cold, although in reality he lived in Omaha, which was every bit as miserable as Gunthrum in the winter.

Earl climbed out of the driver's seat in a wool, camel overcoat that hung past his knees; any man in something other than navy or black was unseemly. She got out and slammed her door shut but didn't speak.

"Mrs. Costagan." Earl doffed an imaginary hat. "You going to invite me in?"

"Isn't that where the problems start? Isn't it true if I don't invite you, you can't come in?"

"I'm not a vampire."

"Could have fooled me."

"They found the body," he said, his voice loud in the crisp air. Alma, Clyle, and Hal all stopped and turned toward Lee Earl. Alma fought against the urge to turn and look at Hal's face; that's where Earl's eyes were glued.

"I'm sorry to hear that," Clyle said.

"Lots of people are," Earl said. "How about you, Hal? Are you sorry?"

"What body?" he asked, and Alma flinched.

"Peggy Ahern."

Hal let out a breath, then stopped, the wheels turning behind his eyes. "Wait. What do you mean 'her body'? Is she dead?"

"Sure is," Earl said.

Clyle walked toward the porch and held open the front door. "Might as well come in. Alma'll put some coffee on."

Alma unwrapped her scarf and set her coat on the peg where two days before she'd hung five thousand dollars. That's the real cross against the vampire, she thought. She didn't offer to take Lee Earl's coat, and instead, he splayed it on the back of his chair. She started the coffee as the men settled in, Earl's boots melting snow on her wood floors.

"Well?" Clyle said. "What happened?"

Earl told them Peggy had been found off Highway 20 not far from O'Neill, "which, as everyone in this room certainly knows, is on the way to Valentine, where Hal and those other boys were camped." Her body was discovered by some hunters Saturday afternoon when they went in a few hundred yards to build a deer stand. "Took a while for the authorities to get in touch with the right county, but that article this morning helped. You see that, Hal? Lot of talk about what you might or might not have done, but that's all changed now that we have a body."

Alma felt a flare of anger but kept her face neutral; she would not give him the satisfaction of losing her cool. She'd dealt with men like Lee Earl most of her life—men who thought they had it all figured out because it never occurred to them they might be wrong about anything. One of the things she loved about Clyle was how he didn't fit that mold. Hal either. She cleared her throat, the words she had to speak ridiculous, like something from one of her evening shows. "And what was the cause of death?"

"Struck by a car." Lee looked meaningfully at Hal. "Or a truck, I'm guessing. Human being would make quite a dent if you're going at any kind of speed. Probably enough to look like you'd crashed into something as big as a garage." He reached into his pocket. "I've got a warrant right here to take your truck in and run some tests."

Alma pictured the truck on Monday morning, the clean sheen of the metal. Why had Hal washed his truck? She shook her head. "What's the warrant for? Just the truck? You got anything that's going to let you take Hal in?"

"Not yet, but that's coming. Mark my words. I've got a team in Omaha that can process whatever I bring them in no time at all. I get that back and there's even one speck of blood, I've got Hal behind bars."

"Go get it then," Alma said. "Get your damn sample, but for now, get out of my house."

Earl stood slowly and stretched his back before reaching for his camel coat. He looked like he was wearing a goddamned golden retriever. "I've got it. Already tagged and in my trunk. This here was a courtesy to let you know what's going on."

Alma snorted. "My courtesy is letting you leave without a boot in your ass."

Clyle held out a hand—how many times in their marriage had his hand swum up in her periphery? *Calm it down, Alma. Don't make a scene, Alma*—but this time he reached for the doorknob and held open the door, shutting it behind Lee before he was barely on the porch.

Lee tripped over a railroad tie hidden under the snow on his way to the car—oh, the joy Alma took in that stumble!—but regained his balance and climbed in. She kept her back to Hal and Clyle until the car rode out of sight halfway down the lane.

Hal broke the silence. "What does he mean, a warrant?"

Clyle set down his coffee cup. "Means he can look through your truck, see what he can find."

"What does he think he's going to find?"

Clyle explained, patiently as a saint, that Lee Earl's job was to figure out who killed Peggy. "What's that got to do with my truck?" Hal looked at Clyle, concerned. "Is he gonna look at that dent?"

Alma's heart stuttered into high gear.

"Why would you ask that, Hal?" Clyle said.

"No reason. I just. I told you I hit the garage. That's true. I hit that garage a hundred times."

Alma thought again about Hal's ability to stretch the truth. "Did you hit it that night? The night Peggy went missing?"

Hal's face crumpled. Oh, he broke so easily! He would never make it in prison, Alma knew. "I don't know. Maybe?"

"If not, how do you explain that dent in your truck, Hal?" Clyle asked. "Son, we need the truth."

Hal stood up, pushing back his chair with the backs of his knees. "I told the truth!"

"That's enough!" Alma said, and pointed to the stairs. "Hal, go lie down. Take a nap, and we can talk about this later. That's enough excitement for one morning." She could not hear the words he would say. It was one thing for her to suspect Hal as being capable of an accident, another for him to say something worse.

Hal hung his head but did what she said—God bless the bus driver voice.

When they heard the bedroom door slam shut upstairs, Clyle came to Alma at the kitchen sink and put his arms around her from behind. The hug was so unexpected, so unlike their affections in recent years, that she flinched.

"I'm sorr—" she started, but Clyle was backing up, his hands in the air.

"I've got some work to do outside," he said. "Farm never sleeps." It was what he always said when he wanted to get away from her, to make an excuse to not be in a sixteen hundred–square foot house with her.

"Clyle, listen, I—" She paused, and he stopped, his face open as rain. What even would she say? I'm sorry I flinched? There's money in the pantry; we can make our escape? I love you? The very thought of that seemed ridiculous, so long since she'd uttered those words.

Clyle shook his head and started for the basement stairs. "Work to do."

She listened to the hollow sound of his footsteps receding beneath her, followed by the door shutting softly behind him.

When Alma and Clyle were positive no children were coming, they'd turned the third bedroom into Alma's sewing room. When they'd do the Friday-night hosting back when they were in the drinking crowd, the wives would yabber about how lucky she was, a whole room to sew. Judy Cravens kept her sewing machine in a closet on top of her dresser, so she had to sew with her knees off to the side. Oh yes, Alma would say. I sure am lucky.

Alma was in the sewing room when Clyle answered the phone in the kitchen. She left the quilt block on the sewing machine and poked her head into the hallway as Clyle said, "Thanks for calling me back, Herb. I appreciate it." He paused again as their lawyer spoke. "Yep, afraid so. They found her last night."

Alma picked up the extension next to her Singer and held it to her ear, one hand over the mouthpiece. Herb was talking about the article in the *World-Herald*. "Not a very flattering portrayal, anyway," he continued. "Sorry to see that."

"So was I," Clyle said.

"Well, like Jelane said," Herb continued now, "this is a bit out of my purview, but I can tell you this: a bad mother running her mouth isn't enough to arrest a man. What else have they got?"

Clyle gave a quick rundown of Hal's interest in Peggy, how he'd come back early from the hunting trip, how he'd been down at the OK that night blackout drunk, the deer blood in the truck bed, the dent in his pickup grill, albeit with what appeared a matching one on his garage. "And," Clyle started but stopped.

"And what?" There was a pause. "I've got to know everything you can tell me, Clyle. I'm not saying I can represent him, but the more I know, the better I'm able to put you in touch with the right lawyer. Someone who can garner some sympathy or a shark." Alma bit her tongue.

"I get the sense Hal is covering something up."

"I don't mean any disrespect here, Clyle, but is Hal smart enough to mastermind a coverup?" Alma thought of how

Hal had lied about running doughnuts in the yard last winter and how he'd beaten the boy up in Wayne all those years ago. The boy had spent three days in the hospital, one of them unconscious. There were numerous witnesses to the beating, but Hal still had tried to lie and say it wasn't him. He certainly wasn't a mastermind, although the violence itself made her uneasy. In the hospital the injured boy's mother had screamed that Hal was a monster. Alma had sat stoically in her seat with her purse in her lap as Clyle apologized once again. Why the hell hadn't she defended Hal?

"Clyle?" Herb said.

Alma held her breath as long as she could then blurted, "A shark, Herb. We want a shark."

"All right then," Herb said, and she guessed he was nodding his head. "That's how we'll proceed. I'll look for a shark. Just in case."

She hung up the phone and came into the kitchen, Clyle at his usual chair with his forehead in his hand. "That's what I was going to say. You didn't need to police my call."

"You sure?" she asked.

"I want to do what's right. That's all I'm trying to do, Alm."

"That's well and good, but what I want is to protect Hal."

Clyle was shaking his head before the words were even out of her mouth. "Don't do that. Don't act like it's not what I want too. I'm willing to do what I need to do."

She thought of Diane leaning across the cab of Clyle's pickup just scant days ago. "Don't you worry. I know you'll do what you need to get what you want."

He squinted. "What's that supposed to mean?"

She willed the words to tumble out of her mouth—*I know about you and Diane*—but big, tough Alma, who everyone said didn't have a filter, couldn't get the words out. How was it she'd never said it aloud? How was it they'd kept the secret of the secret from each other? It was because deep down she knew he might leave her if it all came out, and the thought she wouldn't blame him if he did.

The air between them stayed charged an extra beat. She remembered Clyle all those years ago saying she held something back, something he couldn't access, and how it had felt like a superpower. Maybe that was the only power she had left.

In the end she acquiesced. "All I meant was that we need to do what's best for Hal. Hal needs to be the focus."

"You say so," Clyle said, and snapped off the radio. He took his slippers off by the door and, on the porch, slipped into his coat and pig boots.

Fine, she thought, just fine, and breathed in a deep gulp of air. Clyle would wait a few more days for the callback from Herb, then another day or two for the new lawyer to get in touch, and by then, who knew what might happen. Lee Earl with a blood sample result from the truck? Peck Randolph with a warrant for Hal's arrest? She had secrecy and a decisive mind and five thousand dollars. He could have Diane if that's what he wanted.

Alma watched Clyle from the warmth of the kitchen while he trudged through the snow to the barn, where she knew he'd snap on the radio and rather sit by himself, less lonely than he was with his wife.

With Clyle back out for evening chores, Alma tucked the money in her purse and drove the Vega to Hal's. He had left midafternoon, and she found him outside in Peanut Butter and Jelly's pen, a screwdriver in his hand as he messed with the waterer.

"Still giving you trouble?" she asked as she climbed out.

"Yeah. Clyle gave me a new floater, but it still don't work. I guess I'll just put out a bowl for now." He looked left to right as if one might appear. "Guess I'll get one from inside." Alma followed him as he scraped his boots off by the door and padded in his stocking feet to the kitchen, where he found a large plastic Tupperware Alma had sent him home with at some point full of bars. "What're you doing here?" Hal asked, as he filled the bowl at the sink.

"I want to talk to you about Peggy."

He peered at her over his shoulder as the water splashed over the edge onto his hands. "I can't believe it."

"I can't either, Hal."

"I didn't—" he started, but she raised her hand.

"I don't want to know one way or the other." She was beyond caring what had actually happened and had moved to problem-solving mode. She thought of her clients from all those years ago when she wore sensible pumps to work. They'd taken the drugs, beaten their children, or who knew what horrors. They'd sit in her office weeping, and she'd explain that was the past and this was the present. No changing that, but where do you go from here? She'd approached their lives as pragmatically as a math problem.

"Go," she said to Hal. "Get that water out so we can have a talk."

A few minutes later Hal came in brushing his hands against the hips of his pants. He sat next to her on the sofa and reached for the remote, but she put her hand over his.

"Let's just talk."

"About what?"

"Listen, Hal. I'm not sure you understand what's all happening here, but people think you had something to do with Peggy's death." He opened his mouth, and she held up her hand again. "They don't think it was an accident, and while

I know you well enough to know you'd never hurt anyone on purpose"—this was true, wasn't it? She brushed it away. Didn't matter—"other people don't know you that well, do you see?"

"See what?"

"Hal, you know how much Clyle and I love you, but—"

Hal brought his hand to his mouth, a surprised O behind his palm.

"What?" she asked.

"You never said that before." She looked at him quizzically.

She tumbled through the memories in her brain— Christmas mornings, days on the bus, her pride when he spent the first night in his apartment. Surely she had. "That's not true, Hal, you know—"

He shook his head vigorously in return. "Nope. Never. You never said it before."

My God, was he right? The macaroni necklace? When he tried to make her a coffee cake for her birthday, a charred lump in a nine-by-thirteen? Just a regular Tuesday when he came in from the cold and she handed him a cup of sweet coffee? Tears thickened her throat. "Well, I do, Hal. I do." She couldn't bring herself to say it again. "But you have to understand, we're your only friends. Your only family." She paused, wondering if Clyle even was or if he'd move on to a new family with Diane. He could adopt her pug-nosed daughters, already grown and in college, their brains intact. She reached for Hal's hands. "I want you to do something for me—can you do that, Hal?" He told her yes, and she explained about the money—five thousand, it would have to do—and how she wanted him to drive as far as he could. My God, she was losing another baby, pushing this one away.

"But I don't want to leave." She wrapped her arms around him, his solid shoulder to her chest.

She pulled back and looked him square in the face. There was the glimmer, of course, that he hadn't done anything, but she pushed it away. She had to act, not hope.

"Trust me, Hal. There's no other way."

20

Milo fiddled with the Rubik's Cube in his lap as the empty fields ticked past, only the edges visible at the outskirts of the headlights. Aunt Sally was talking about how she couldn't believe it was so dark already—only a spit past five thirty—and didn't it seem to happen earlier and earlier every night? Well, yeah, Milo thought. The earth's orbit and all. His mother was never so much of a talker, and he found Aunt Sally's yakking, no matter how well intentioned, exhausting.

They were heading into Gunthrum for a few groceries to fill in the gaps, but Milo knew an excuse when he heard one. His Aunt Sally was getting claustrophobic in all that sad silence, and now in the car she had the radio turned to Top Forty, George's favorite, even if the volume was low. She had shuttled George to the back seat, and he'd gone without comment. Had Milo ever been given the preferential seat of shotgun? No, and all he had to pay was one dead sister.

Since the police had found the body and he'd been informed that morning—Peggy's body, he reminded himself, not a corpse in one of his Chandler novels—he'd been skirting against darker and darker jokes about the situation. Shotgun: price of a dead sister. What a way to get the bigger bedroom back. There would be more dessert after supper. He thought these things to punish himself—the twisted-gut feeling of the wrong thought and validation that he was as awful as he felt.

Driving into the town with George and Aunt Sally, he had a good handle on the gruesome details of his sister's death: found in a field near O'Neill, hit by the ditch, then dragged into the field and covered in snow. Someone's hunting dog had found her. She'd been hit by a car and then—this was the kicker—run over. That's what did her in, George had said. Crushed her head like a grape. Only it was Milo who had said the thing about the head and the grape. Jesus. But what did Jesus have to do with any of it? Fuck Jesus, Milo thought, and didn't burst into flames, further proof He didn't exist. Not that he needed it; Milo knew what he knew.

Aunt Sally rotated the Caddy's large steering wheel to the left, turning onto Main Street. There were three high schoolers playing a pickup game of basketball on the plowed, outside half-court at the school, and she slowed down and veered to the curb. "Here. Why don't you boys blow off some stink while I go get the groceries."

Milo turned toward the back seat. George looked as enthusiastic about this idea as Milo felt. High schoolers didn't play basketball with junior high babies, much less uncoordinated ones they'd never met.

"Go on." She shooed them out. "I don't need you two nipping at my heels when they close in fifteen minutes. Go." It occurred to Milo she was as sick of them as he was of her, a thought he found somewhat soothing.

He and George reluctantly opened their car doors and climbed out, the double-quick slam of them shutting just short of unison.

"Now what?" George said as his mother drove away, the smooth purr of the Cadillac almost silent.

"Fuck if I know," Milo tried, and George laughed.

"Yeah," he repeated. "Fuck if we know."

234

Milo walked up to the chain-link fence in front of the basketball court and hung his fingers in the links, the cold metal sharp on his skin. He dropped his body lower like Hal used to do watching Peggy run around the track. He knew what all high schoolers loved was an audience, even if it was just two dumb kids, and sure enough, he saw one of them bop to the side in a fake-out and take the ball in for a showy layup.

One of his friends rebounded and held up his empty hand for a high-five, and the guy who'd made the shot stole a glance at Milo and George. "Hey," he said, stopping. "You're Peggy's little brother."

Milo felt his stomach sink. Everyone knew who he was now. Half the town knew before—old people knew everyone—but not older kids, athletes. The type who wouldn't deem him worthy of eye contact in the halls, the type now walking toward him and George, one of them—the tallest—lazily dribbling the basketball without looking down. How did he do that?

"Sorry to hear about that, man," the tall one said, an acne-ridden teen Milo recognized from the football and basketball teams. "That sucks."

The third guy guffawed and snuck the ball from the first while it was ascending back to his hand and dribbled it harder. "What a thing to say. 'That sucks.' No shit. His sister was fucking murdered."

"You don't have to say that," Acne Face said. "Jesus. Show a little class."

"What? I didn't kill her." Milo could tell the one with acne—or the one with the worst acne—didn't like the guy who'd stolen the ball, a towhead named Daryl Klaussen, who was one grade higher than Peggy. Small towns—you played pickup with whomever you could. He imagined what Daryl would say about his correct use of *whom*. Fairy? Faggot? What did it matter now?

"You don't have to act like an asshole," Milo said to Daryl, and cousin George looked over at him, surprise on his face like, *Welcome to the show, Milo. Way to man up.*

"What did you call me?" Daryl asked, walking closer.

"An asshole," Milo said, his voice shiny and bright. "A fucking asshole."

Daryl threw the basketball hard at the fence, clanging it quick against the metal, and Milo flinched, which made him madder.

"What?" Milo asked. "That wasn't an asshole move? Now you look like a *stupid* fucking asshole. A scared one. You going to just throw a ball at me or fight me like a man?"

George laughed nervously. "Okay, big shot," he said, but Daryl was already scurrying toward the edge of the court. Acne Face shot after him and grabbed the edge of his jacket as he rounded the corner ten feet from Milo, jerking the guy back.

"Come on," Acne said. "He just lost his sister."

"Yeah," Milo said, "show some class."

"They should have gone after you," Daryl said, spitting on the ground. "At least your sister was good for something."

Milo felt the words slither through his body, through every vessel with each beat of his heart. Yes, he thought. That's it. It should have been me. Daryl turned back toward the court, and Milo raced after him, jumping on his back and viciously clawing what he hoped was his face.

"Hey!" Daryl said. "What the fuck?" and his body toppled to the ground, Milo still on top and swinging, pummeling Daryl's back with his fists. *Ignore me now.* Daryl rolled over and gained his footing, slamming his fist into Milo's cheek and nose with a class ring the size of a walnut. The pain was righteous, shiny and bursting, like comets behind Milo's eyes.

"Yeah!" he heard George shout, and Milo knew it was because he had taken the hit, and with that he started swinging again, blindly, every few punches connecting with something meaty like a shoulder or bare skin, other times his fist skating past in the air. He wanted to open his eyes, but one was filling like a red balloon as Daryl hit him again in the same spot. Another burst.

"Come on," one of the older guys said. "Come on, man."

Milo kept swinging, but the weight on top of him lightened, then disappeared. He winked his good eye open and saw the other two had Daryl by the shoulder and elbow, pulling him back and twisting him around. "Come on," Milo said. "You gonna just walk away?"

Daryl kicked at him with a chunky white Adidas, and Acne Face gave him a tug. "Let it go, man."

"Let it go," Milo mimicked. Daryl turned around quick-like and swung his foot to kick Milo in the head, and this time Milo didn't flinch but smiled what he could tell was a crazy grin. Were his teeth bloodied?

"It's not worth it," Acne Face said, and glared at Milo like, *Can't you tell we're trying to help you?* "Let's go get a pizza." He and his friend tugged Daryl down the sidewalk, Daryl making a weak show of wanting to still fight, but eventually the dribble of the basketball started up and they were around the corner.

"See ya," Milo yelled in a singsong voice. "Wouldn't want to be ya!"

George started laughing, doubled over. "Holy. Fucking. Shit." He replanted his feet and held a hand down to pull Milo up. "Where'd you come from, little man?"

Milo touched the side of his face, the skin tender. He explored a cut above his right eye from the ring and could feel the tacky blood. "How bad does it look?"

"Fucking terrible." George laughed. "Hamburger meat."

Milo's stomach flipped as he pictured going home and facing his father and mother. The last thing they needed was to worry about him, but maybe that's why he'd done it.

Aunt Sally's Cadillac sailed down Main Street and swung into the parking spot in front of them. Sally turned her lights to bright, and Milo winced and held a hand above his eye.

"What in the Sam Hill." She slammed the door behind her. "Milo Ahern, what have you done to yourself?"

"He didn't do it to himself," George said. "He took on three high schoolers." Milo smiled at his exaggeration.

"And you!" She turned on George. "This has 'you' written all over it."

"I didn't do anything!" he said, an innocent hand to his chest like he was going to recite the pledge of allegiance.

"Oh, please," she muttered, and turned back to Milo, speaking loudly. "Milo? Are you okay?"

"I'm not deaf," he said, and George laughed.

"Shut it," Aunt Sally said to George, and walked Milo to the passenger seat. "Your parents are going to have a conniption. I just wanted to get you out of the house for a bit." She settled him in and slammed the door behind her, scurrying around to the driver's side.

She reached over his lap and opened the glovebox as he leaned his head against the cool window, smooth like a block of ice. "Here." She handed him a napkin. He lifted his head to take it.

"Oh, good Lord," she said, and he followed her eyes to the glass, smeared now with his blood. She handed him another napkin. "Here. Wipe that off, would you? I get blood in this car, and Randall's going to kill me." She gasped and put a hand to her mouth. "Oh, sweetie," she said to Milo. "I'm sorry. I shouldn't say things like that."

Back home Milo left the groceries in the back seat for George to bring in. Aunt Sally had cried about the dead comment, but Milo didn't feel bad about her tears. He'd steeled himself against them like he had against Daryl's kick and felt like nothing could make him flinch. His mother sat at the kitchen table with his father's mother, Grandma Alice, and as Milo came in, he squinted against the bright overhead lights, the skin around the right eye tightening and throbbing. "Milo!" his mother exclaimed, and sprang from her seat. "What happened?"

He started to tell her the truth but remembered the story George had spun in the car about the three guys, high schoolers, who had attacked them out of nowhere, unprovoked. *It makes no sense. Who's going to believe it?* He thought of his English teacher, Mrs. Toner, asking, What is this character's motivation? But you know what? Aunt Sally had bought it. It was that easy to make people believe what they wanted to believe.

George told it again, Aunt Sally even jumping in to tell the more gruesome parts, emphasizing her own innocence in taking them to town. Milo's mother got a bag of peas from the freezer and pressed it softly to his face, her own mouth grimacing at the imagined pain. "Kids can be so cruel," she said. "Animals."

Grandma Alice stayed at the table—she had a bad knee—but motioned Milo over so she could investigate his face. "You should put steak on it, Linda, not peas."

"It does the same thing," his mom said. "It's the cold that works, not the meat. That's an old wives' tale." She was a nurse, after all.

"All I know is it works, wives' tale or not," his grandmother said, and gave Milo a kiss on his bruised knuckles. "I'd hate to see the other guy," she said to Milo, and winked.

"Oh, he looks like hell," George said. "Hamburger meat."

His grandmother tsked. "Language."

"Sorry," he muttered. Everyone knew to obey Grandma Alice, even George.

"I wonder about you two," she continued. Milo assumed she was talking about him and George, but Grandma Alice was looking at his mom and Aunt Sally. "These boys running wild, no discipline. My boys never did any such thing."

His mother actually laughed, but another look shut her up in a hurry. "He's under a lot of pressure. Cut him some slack." Milo's heart warmed at the words.

"Laugh if you want, Linda, but none of this happened until you went back to work."

His mother flinched as if she'd been slapped.

"Wait now," Milo said, and his grandmother held up her hand.

"Milo, you know nothing about this," she said, but that wasn't true! He thought of his mother in the garage the night before and all those meals she'd left in the oven. He remembered with sparkling clarity all the mornings he'd grumbled his way down the stairs to find his mother hollow faced and tired at the kitchen table with a pencil stuck in her ponytail and her nursing books splayed in front of her. How much had she sacrificed for something her family should have made easier?

"Mother Alice," his mom began calmly. "I certainly don't think it's fair—" but she trailed off as the front door opened, his father on the porch wiping his boots, Randall behind him. Milo's dad stopped, assessing the situation. He'd joked one time that the Ahern family crest was four people fleeing the living room, Grandma Alice left by herself to preside over the silence. His eyes took in the room and settled on Milo, his beat-up face.

"What the hell happened to you?"

"I got in a fight."

"With who?"

Whom, Milo thought. "Some high schoolers."

His father tugged off his coat and slid the red-and-white MoorMan's stocking cap from his head. "Jesus Christ, Milo. We don't have enough to deal with?"

"I don't know," Milo mouthed back. "Maybe not."

His father stopped, the coat an inch from the hook he always hung it on, the one that stayed empty when his father was out; everyone knew not to junk it up with their backpacks or purses, umbrellas or jackets. "What's that?" His voice was low but recognizable.

"I said," Milo started, his voice clear, "that maybe you don't have enough to deal with."

Grandma Alice kept a sharp eye on her son and grandson. "What happened?" his dad insisted. "You tell me now." George started, but Milo's dad cut him off with a hand in the air. "Tell me, Milo."

"Some guys were talking about Peggy." He knew now he could make up any story he wanted. "Calling her names. Slut, things like that. Said she was dating some older guy in town. I said she might have been a slut but she was my sister."

His father crossed the kitchen floor in three long strides. "Don't you say it—"

"She was, Dad, that's what they're saying. She was a slut—"
And that did it, his father pulled his hand back and slapped
his son's cheek, the left one, mercifully not the right.

"Joe!" his mother exclaimed.

Randall stepped forward—"Joey"—and Milo felt the tears
pool in his eyes, begging them not to fall, the peas cold in
his hand.

"Enough!" Linda said. "That's enough. Stop it." She rushed
between Milo and his father. "That's *it*." She blocked Milo
with her thin arms. "You," she said, pointing to Joe. "Go in
the living room. Make a drink or something." She moved
her finger to point at Randall. "You go with him." The two
men left, and Milo was there with George and the women.

"He didn't say anything about—" Aunt Sally began, but
her voice trailed off. What did it matter now?

"Upstairs," his mother said to the boys. "Get ready for bed.
You're sleeping in the basement."

George read the clock. "It's barely past seven!"

"I don't care. Now."

As Milo left the kitchen, his grandmother said something about a little too little a little too late, but the rest
was drowned out by the pound of George's tennies on the
wooden stairs. At the top he turned around, a grin let loose
over the lower half of his face. "Ah, man," George said. "You're
a natural."

"I want the sofa," Milo said.

"What?"

"I want the sofa. To sleep. You get the sleeping bag tonight."
He would not sleep lower than his cousin and his plumb line
of spit. Never again.

George looked at him, puzzled. "Okay."

"And quit snoring so much."

"Fuck you, man. It's my sinuses."

Milo strode past him. "I'm brushing my teeth first. And spitting in the sink."

Fifteen minutes later Milo was settled on the couch with *The Long Goodbye* and a flashlight on his afghaned stomach. They could make him go to bed, but they couldn't make him sleep.

His mother tiptoed down the stairs and knelt next to him, her eyes red and skin splotchy. "You don't really have to go to sleep yet. I just needed you out of the line of sight." She didn't say a word about Milo on the couch and how he should let their guest have it. George was still upstairs pretending to brush his teeth, and Milo could imagine him leaning in toward the mirror, a blackhead squeezed between his two index fingers. Peggy used to do the same thing, a compulsion she couldn't stop even as she'd complain she was making it worse.

He poked a finger through the afghan and curled it around the yarn. "They didn't really say that. About Peggy."

His mother wiped at the damp on her cheek. "It doesn't matter one way or another." For the first time Milo felt a pang over his actions of the last few hours. "Do you think it's wrong?" his mother asked. "That I went back to work?"

Milo shook his head. "No. That's stupid."

She smiled. "Don't call your grandmother stupid."

"I didn't, technically. I just said her reasoning was stupid."

She smoothed his hair. "Well, you know what I mean."

Milo thought about it a moment. "I'm sorry we didn't help more. Peggy and I should have done stuff to help."

"You weren't the problem, Milo. Your dad should have stepped up." It was like last night, his mother confiding, but this time he felt more on her side. There were so many nights his dad would get in from chores, shower, and sit down with a drink in front of the TV while his mother, still in her nursing shoes, would stand at the stove stirring dinner. Were all marriages like that? For so long he'd thought about his powerful father—hand stuck under the belt of his jeans and leaned back in the recliner—and thought marriage seemed kind of great. It hadn't occurred to him to see it any differently. His father out there having his fun.

His mom smoothed the blanket over his chest, picked up the book, and pretended to read the back. "Do you know if it was true? About Peggy?"

"What?"

"You know."

Oh, man, if there was anyone in the world he'd like to tell that his mother was asking if his sister was a slut, it was Peggy. He felt the ache again, the squeezing of his chest like a heart attack, as he remembered Mr. Burke blowing on his sister's neck—the way she bent over Scott's dog, her arms contorted to push together her breasts, the elbows in, wearing a V-neck sweater and lipstick. He had meant to tell, he had, but then Peck showed up at the church and his family collapsed, and he didn't think he could bear to add one more truth. Instead, he pushed it down—just like his father had taught him—and started a fight in town, another one he couldn't win. Milo thought about his mother telling him that pretty girls attract trouble and that whatever had happened to Peggy, it was nothing good. If his own mother's feelings could be that inconsequential to his father, what would that mean for Mr. Burke and Peggy?

Milo took a deep breath. "Mom, I have something to tell you."

Milo pushed the buttons on his controller and missed the jump, Luigi doomed once again. George had brought his Nintendo with him this trip, the gray console tucked under his arm when he got out of the Cadillac, and after Milo told his mom about Mr. Burke and Peggy, she agreed to let them hook it up and had gone upstairs to talk to his father. He missed the joystick on Atari, which he could slam forward aggressively. Punching his thumb down hard didn't have the same satisfying effect. His face ached where Daryl Klaussen had gotten in his licks.

"I'm sick of this game," Milo said as Luigi fell off the screen and died.

"It's not like I can slow it down," George said. "There's no retard setting." And that of course reminded Milo of Hal.

The basement door burst open, and his father barreled downstairs in his farm clothes, tracking shit on the carpet. "What'd you hear?" he said, and grabbed Milo with a rough hand on his shoulder. "You tell me what you heard."

"Joe," his mother called, coming in behind him. "Joe, calm down!"

Milo cringed, frightened by his father. He wished the mark from his slap was as visible as the other marks on his face. His right eye was still swollen, the bruise moving to the deeper purple of an angry sky.

"What do you know about Larry Burke?" he screamed at Milo, spittle at the corner of his mouth.

Milo sat gape-faced as a dying fish until his father turned his wrath on his wife. "Did you know about this? Did you fucking know about this?"

"Of course not!"

"You were her fucking *mother*! How could you have not known?"

Her body collapsed just a millimeter, like a puppet with loosened strings. "I should have."

Milo's dad turned toward the stairs, taking them two at a time. "I'm calling Earl." From the basement they could hear the whiz of the rotary dial and then his father's voice again. "Larry Burke. He was on that goddamned hunting trip."

"What're you playing?" his mother asked, and it was so obvious she was trying to distract them Milo wanted to cry.

"Here," he said, and handed her the controller as George explained the rules, trying to make them sound more convoluted than they were, as if he were dedicating his life to something less lame than running and jumping and not falling in a hole.

"You basically just do this," Milo said, and showed her how to move his player in white overalls in four directions. For years he'd tried to get his mother interested in his hobbies, but she was always too busy—another load of laundry before she could sit down and take a break, which turned into an hour, then time to make dinner. Milo filled with shame again that it hadn't occurred to him to do something as simple as flip the clothes from the washer to the dryer.

"It's a little more complicated than that," George said crossly.

Milo's mom wiped her face, then moved down to the floor with them and sat cross-legged as she focused on the television. He thought of that blonde girl from *Poltergeist*. He hadn't watched the movie, even edited for television, but he'd seen the girl in the trailer and how when the mom held on to the door frame in a red football jersey, her white underpants flashed.

"Of course I didn't fucking know," his father said from upstairs. There was a longer pause as his mother clicked away on the controller.

"Here," George said. "You need to be quicker."

His father's voice went up a notch. "Goddamn it, Peck!"

Milo remembered his sister in lipstick and eyeliner, home on a Saturday night. "It wasn't like that," he said to his mom. "Peggy liked him."

"Even if it wasn't, it was," she said. "Mr. Burke's an adult." Milo ran a hand over his head, greasy from too many days without a shower. "You're too young to understand," she added, and Milo rolled his eyes. Wasn't he the one who had put it together? Weren't his parents the ones too blind to understand? "I'm sorry. You're right. If anyone's grown-up this week, it's you."

Grandma Ahern had told his mother she couldn't control her children, as if that's what they needed: to be controlled. "It's not your fault, you know," he said. She turned from the television. "It's good you went back to work."

Tears filled her eyes. "Thanks, sweetie. But I'm done with that now."

21

Alma awoke with a start to the ringing of the phone. She'd shot awake to that sound or a knock on the door more in the past week than she had in the past five years. Her mother had always said that no good news comes after nine o'clock, but then again, her mother, like her, could take about any news and turn it bad.

"You going to get it?" she asked Clyle, but his only answer was a long exhale. She grabbed the flannel shirt she'd flung over the armchair and lumbered to the kitchen, stubbing a toe against a table leg when she rounded the corner. "Goddamn it." She never slept all that deeply at the farm and was always tired. They'd stayed at a hotel a few years ago down near Sioux Falls for a wedding, and the steady hum of the interstate had lulled her into a deep sleep. Something in her brain recognized the sounds of her younger life. She wondered if still in her bones she was a city girl, if that was why the women here never accepted her. It was like they'd caught her city scent early on and recognized she wasn't one of them, no matter the costume she wore. Just a month ago, at the library, she checked out a book, and the volunteer said to her, "Alma, you're the only one who goes for these highfalutin books around here. It's nice to see a reader. Most of the ladies just tear through those Harlequins and dog-ear the good parts." For God's sake, she'd been checking out *Great Expectations*, not the *Iliad* in Greek.

She picked up the phone and said hello. "Mrs. Costagan? This is Deputy Ross down in Lincoln. We've got a man here says you're the one to call." Lincoln? That was only two hours away. She glanced at the clock; it was just past three in the morning. "A Hal Bullard?"

She sat heavily in Clyle's chair at the table. "Isn't he supposed to get to call me himself?"

"That's procedure, but we can't right let him out of his cell. He assaulted a man and a woman leaving an establishment." Alma's mind flashed with Peggy's broken body in a field, the teenager from Wayne with the concussion in the hospital bed. "When we showed up, he assaulted an officer."

Alma felt a pain in her chest. "Well, what did they do to him?"

"Ma'am?"

"Can I come get him?"

"In the morning we'll set bail, once he's had a chance to dry out."

"He's not just drunk," she said, although he was probably that too. She hated to say it, but she added, "He's simple."

"Ah," the man said, realization dawning as some missing pieces clicked into place, and then the final one. "He's that suspect in the Ahern case, ain't he? Well, that might change things."

"No one's been charged."

"Hal Bullard," the man said. "I knew I'd heard that name."

Back in the bedroom, Alma shook her husband awake. "Clyle, I need you. You've got to get up."

He peered through an open eye, squinting against the hall light. "Now what?"

She told him about the call as he hauled himself out of bed and slid on a pair of jeans, the belt still snaked through the loops. He ran a hand over his hair and down his face, the skin collapsing under the weight of his palm. *This is what he'll look like when he's old*, Alma thought. *Older.*

"Now what in the hell is he doing in Lincoln?"

"Beats me," she said, and turned toward the kitchen to make a thermos of coffee for the road. "I'll go," she said, when Clyle followed her down the hall. "You've got chores in a few hours. That trumps everything."

Clyle cleared his throat as she filled the carafe with water. "Did you give him all of it?"

She paused, a tablespoon of coffee grounds suspended above the filter. "All what?" She knew he meant the money.

She turned around to Clyle shaking his head, his eyes on the ground. "Don't do that, Alm. We know each other better than that."

"How did—"

He shook his head again. "We'll talk about that later. Did you?"

She nodded and slammed the lid shut on the top of the pot. "He needed a chance. I had to do what I could for him." She peered at his face. "Do you even understand that?"

The coffee began to drip, the smell sharp. "I do." The first cup was Alma's favorite—always the strongest and the most bitter, and for years she had to sit on her hands not to take it but let it dilute so Clyle could have a decent cup. She wondered if taking it early had even occurred to him. "What I don't understand is why you didn't tell me."

"Oh, please, I know what you would have said."

"What?"

"'Let's wait and see what happens. Have some faith in the system. Don't think the worst.'" It stunned her to realize that so much of it came down to him having faith in this town, faith she didn't have.

"I wouldn't have said any of that."

"How do you know?"

"Because I've known since Friday about the money, and all I've been wondering is when you were going to tell me or if I'd wake up and just find you and Hal gone."

Alma swallowed. Was that what he had hoped for? That she would go with Hal, that he'd be free of the both of them? The thought crushed her much harder than she would have guessed. She turned back to the cupboard and blinked several times as she reached for her traveler. "I have to go. Hal's waiting in jail."

"Is that what you want, Alma? To leave me?"

"Hal's wait—"

"Not now, I mean for good. Is that what you want?"

She slammed the mug on the Formica counter. "I didn't go, did I?"

Clyle barked once, a sound like an empty husk. "No, I guess you didn't." He reached for her traveler and poured in the coffee, then got another mug for himself. "But sometimes, Alma, I wonder why when it seems so clear you want to." He headed toward the basement, where he'd change into his pig clothes. No use going back to bed now.

For the past forty-five minutes, Alma was in an on-and-off-again battle of wills with the woman at the police desk. She had convinced herself the woman was the only thing standing between her and Hal, and whether or not it was true, Alma had begun to despise her. Clyle had said to her more times than she could count, "You don't trust authority," to which she had laughed and said, "Who does?" But you know who did? Clyle Costagan, again and again.

She had been playing his words over in her mind for the two-hour drive. He'd known about the money since Friday. Was that why he had been with Diane? She wanted to hope, but stuck in her mind was the image of Diane leaning over the pickup cab and kissing Clyle's cheek.

A man in uniform came out of the back and approached her, and just to be ornery, she stayed seated. She wasn't going to kowtow to this man and stand up when he entered a room. She'd make him look down at her and see how long it was until she got the upper hand. Not long, she guessed.

"Mrs. Bullard?" he asked, and she told him no, she was Mrs. Costagan.

"Mrs. Bullard is still on her way," the woman at the desk said, and gave Alma a smug look of satisfaction. Her left eyelid was droopy, and Alma thought, serves her right.

"Well," Alma said to the officer, "where is he?"

"In the back." He thumbed to the room he'd just exited. "We're still talking to him about the incident."

"No one will tell me a good fool thing about what that incident is." She shot the woman at the desk another dirty look and was satisfied when she rolled her fat butt away and faced the typewriter. "I'm sure whatever it is, it's a misunderstanding."

"No. No, it's not. He hit 'em, all right. Tried to leave without paying his tab at O'Rourke's downtown, and when the waitress tried to stop him at the door, he shoved her. Her husband's a barback there, and he jumped over the bar and got in the mix. The suspect turned on him then and punched Merle in the head."

Alma shook her head. "Like I said, a misunderstanding. Hal doesn't understand he has to pay. We live in a small town."

"I know where you live, ma'am."

"What I mean is, Hal's used to a tab." The OK didn't do that with everyone, but too often, Hal had forgotten his wallet at home or counted the bills wrong before he left, so they ended up keeping track, and he paid at the beginning of the month when the Costagans paid him. It was on his list of monthly bills along with rent, electricity, and water.

Had she really thought Hal could set up a life on his own? That he was going to find a bar that let him run a monthly tab? Or a cop that escorted him home rather than giving him a ticket for driving when he'd been drinking? Or a grocery store that didn't charge him for the fruit he dropped? Or a diner that didn't let him leave a twenty-dollar bill for a tip? It had taken a lifetime to establish all that, and she hated to admit it, but it was the good people of Gunthrum who made it possible.

"Used to it or not, you can't go around slugging people. Especially police officers. And women."

Alma stood up and looped her purse over her shoulder. "Oh, for Pete's sake, let me see him."

"He's still agitated."

"So am I. Let me see him."

"Ma'am—"

"Don't you *ma'am* me. Do you realize that boy has a mental problem? You let me talk to him."

The front door swung open, and Marta Bullard clunked in, leaning on her cane. It was morning by now, the sun rising in the pink sky behind the row of buildings across the street, lending a deceptively healthy-looking glow to Marta's skin. "Alma," she said, her left hand to her chest. "Thank you for coming."

"Of course I came. Hal called me."

"That's not technically true," the woman with the droopy eye said. "We wouldn't let him use the phone."

"He doesn't know how," Marta explained.

"Oh, bullshit," Alma said. "He might be slow, but he knows how to pick up a phone. They were denying him his civil rights."

"Now," the officer started. The door opened again, and Alma squinted. A tall, knobby man came in with a cowboy hat in his hands.

"This is Eugene," Marta said. "This is Alma. She looks after Hal."

"I'm his employer," she clarified. "He looks after himself."

"Not very well," Marta pointed out, then tried to laugh. She turned to the officer, sweeping Mrs. Droopy Eye up in her look as well. "I pray for that boy, I do."

Alma rolled her eyes. "Pray in one hand and shit in the other and see which fills up faster." It was something Clyle's dad used to say. She'd always liked that man.

Back in the cell, Hal slept with his mouth open, braying the snore-growl he got when he'd been drinking. "Hal," Alma said. "Front and center."

He opened his eyes slowly, and then they shot open. "Mom!"

Alma looked down at her feet. Oh, that hurt. All these years, and it was still his mother he wanted.

"Hi, Hally," Marta said, and put a hand through the bars.

"What are you doing here?"

"I came to see you. What are *you* doing here?"

"I hit someone. And pushed a lady."

"And you know that was wrong?"

Alma snorted again. "Of course he knows it's wrong."

"I didn't mean to," Hal said. When Alma was a child and had done something on accident like spill a jar of pickles, her own father used to say to her, *It's not enough to not mean to—you have to mean not to.* But then he'd smile, unlike her mother, who would purse her lips and hand Alma a rag. It would take two days before the kitchen didn't smell like vinegar.

"I'm going to get you out of here," Alma said.

"Well now," the officer interjected, "we've got charges against him, and even if Merle drops them—which he usually does after whoever has spent a night in the clink—I'm planning to keep him until your sheriff down there in Gunthrum's open for business hours." It was still only six in the morning.

"Can you do that?"

"We've got Merle's charge, and law says I can hold him for twenty-four hours on probable cause. That's what I'm planning to do until I can talk to the officer in Gunthrum."

"Why don't you just lock me up, too, then," Alma reasoned. "You've got as much evidence."

"You know what?" the officer said. He was all of twenty-five years old, with an Adam's apple the size of a baby's fist. "You're not very pleasant."

She held her two hands, palm up and cupped. "Pleasant in one and shit in the other."

Marta and Eugene sat across from Alma in a twenty-four-hour Perkins, passing time until the barback dropped the charges or word came back from Peck about whether to keep Hal locked up. In the meantime Marta pointed out that they probably would have been allowed to stay at the police station if Alma hadn't been so rude. When their eggs came, Marta and Eugene made a show of holding hands and bowing their heads, while Alma speared a big ol' sausage and shoved it in her mouth.

"We pray silently," Eugene said, "out of respect for others' beliefs."

"Then why hold hands and bow your heads? Isn't that just part of the show?" Alma hated self-righteous people like this, just hated them.

Marta put her hand over Eugene's again. "We won't be persecuted for our beliefs."

Alma laughed with her mouth wide open, the unswallowed sausage tucked in her cheek. "You're Christians in the middle of Nebraska. Who could be less persecuted than you?" The waitress came back and refilled their coffees without asking, and Alma bowed her head. "Bless you."

Marta leaned forward. "You don't have to make fun of everything. No wonder Hal's ended up where he is."

"Hal ended up where he is because you nearly let him drown as a boy."

Marta gasped. "That's just not true. I have done nothing but love that boy. He rejected *me*."

"And you're his mother, so you're not supposed to let him," Alma said. "That's the key. You just don't let him."

"We've been thinking," Eugene began, and Alma held up her hand.

"Don't even start."

"We've been *thinking*," Marta repeated. "Hal's best defense is mental incompetence. I talked to a lawyer who said we could probably get the charges dropped to manslaughter and Hal could spend his time in a facility rather than jail."

"He hasn't been formally accused!" Alma said, and their waitress paused with the coffeepot at the table next to them, clearly listening in.

Marta shook her head. "That's your defense? He hasn't been *formally* accused?"

Eugene rubbed her back. "Remember what we talked about."

Marta raised her chin. "We're Hal's family. We can get him the care he needs."

Eugene leaned forward. "The Lord says to provide for your own household."

"Well, the Lord says a lot of things," Alma pointed out. "You've got to take Him with a grain of salt."

"We only want what's best for Hal," Marta said.

"And what do you think Clyle and I have wanted all these years?"

"I don't know," Marta said. "He's ended up a drunk accused of murder. Is that it?"

"Well, Hal has some say in this matter, that's for damn sure, at least until you get him locked away."

"And don't try to tell me these shenanigans—Hal two hours away from home—were his idea. I know my boy better than that. This was you, Alma Costagan, and putting a boy on the run doesn't make you look like a very suitable guardian."

"He's over eighteen! He doesn't *have* a guardian." Alma took another gulp of her too-hot coffee, then slammed down the cup. She gathered her purse and swung it over her shoulder, leaving them to pay the check and wishing she'd ordered three of everything.

Back at the police station, she got Adam's Apple in her sights and told him she had talked to her lawyer and she had every right to meet with Hal in his absence—a blatant lie.

"That doesn't sound right," the boy said, but Alma had spent fourteen years getting children on the bus to put their butts in the seats and shut up, and it didn't take long for him to fold. "Ten minutes. That's it."

He opened the door to the room where Hal was—two chairs and a conference table—and Hal looked up at Alma but didn't stand. It was clear he'd been crying.

"You okay?" she asked, and he nodded. She looked back at the officer. "A little privacy, please?"

"Ten minutes. I'm setting a timer." He closed the door.

She took the chair across from Hal and reached for his hands. He gripped hers so hard she winced. "You know that day I came to work after I got the deer?" Hal said, and Alma tensed. It was the day this had all started—Peggy Ahern missing.

"Of course I do."

"Remember how I had that dent in my truck?"

She nodded slowly and hoped to God they weren't being recorded. Would it be permissible evidence? Did she trust they were alone?

"I—" Hal leaned his head down. "I didn't hit the garage." Snot started leaking from his nose.

"Hal, I don't—"

"It was an accident," Hal continued. "I didn't mean to hit her," and it was as if all the air was sucked out of the room. His face collapsed in a waterfall of tears, and Alma felt heat flicker its way up her back. She remembered how uncomfortable she had been at that picnic last summer, the sunburn on the back of her neck, how irritated Hal was when she told him Peggy wasn't interested. My God, he'd done it. He'd really done it.

"What happened?"

Hal sniffed wetly and wiped a hand under his nose. "I didn't see her. In the road. The sun was in my eyes, and I didn't see her before it was too late." It was winter now, daylight at a minimum and dark well before dinner. Peck had said the coroner had confirmed Peggy's time of death, at least within a few hours. How had the sun still been out?

"Hal?" Alma kept her voice calm. "What do you mean, the sun was in your eyes?"

"That day? When I shot the deer? I didn't shoot her. I hit her with my truck." He wiped his nose again, then his hand on his jeans. "It was an accident," he continued. "I didn't see her 'cause I was squinting. I didn't see her before it was too late." He put his face in his hands. "I hit her, but I wanted everyone to believe I shot her."

A great rush of air left Alma's lungs. "You hit her? You mean the deer?"

"With my truck. I got confused and had the sun in my eyes because I was going the wrong direction, and *wham!* out of nowhere it came up out of the ditch. I didn't mean to hit her, and I didn't want Clyle to know because he wants me to be a safe driver and safe with guns, and then I thought, I could just say I shot her, you know? So, I got out, and she wasn't dead yet, and I shot her, and then I put her in the back of my truck." So, that had been his big secret, what he'd been lying about. Alma felt relief she'd at least read that much right.

"What about that night, after the OK?"

"What do you mean?"

"Did you—" She paused. "Did you hit anything else?"

"I don't think so."

"Hal, 'I don't think so' isn't good enough."

"But I don't think I did!"

"'I don't think' and 'I didn't' aren't the same thing." She thought of her father again: *It's not enough you don't mean to—you have to mean not to.*

"I would remember hitting something. Why would I remember driving home from the OK? I do that all the time."

"Hal, we have to tell Peck all this."

Hal's eyes got big. "I don't want people to know. They think I shot that deer!"

"Hal, that doesn't matter. He knows as well as we did that you weren't telling the truth." A fresh sea of tears welled in Hal's eyes, and Alma felt them well in her own.

"Everyone thinks I shot it, that I got a deer like Sam and Larry. They're going to make me a joke."

She shook her head. "Hal, you don't understand."

"*You* don't understand. No one thought I could do it."

There were three quick knocks, and Droopy Eye opened the door and poked her head in. "We got a call from your guy Randolph. There's been a development."

22

Milo steered his bike on the gravel road, careful not to lose his balance. "How much farther?" George puffed. He was riding Peggy's old ten-speed with the seat as high as it would go, but his knees were still bent when he extended in a downward pedal. They were on their way to Castle Farm, the moon nearly full above them on a school night, a Monday no less. His mother, as an afterthought, had told him he could skip the week—the funeral was Wednesday—and go back after Thanksgiving if he thought he was ready. Maybe Christmas.

Usually his mother was done baking the Thanksgiving pies and coffee cakes by now and they'd sit tinfoiled on the screened-in back porch, which worked as a second freezer during the holidays. Every year, on the first Friday after Thanksgiving, the whole family would drive to Sioux City to buy cherry and apple fritters from Sunkist Bakery. No one had mentioned going this year, and he figured that was for the best.

Milo turned his head over his shoulder but held steady on the handlebars; George was about thirty yards behind him. "Two miles."

"Yeah, okay," George said, but it was obvious he was out of breath. He'd grown big but soft over the last year and was one of those boys Milo could imagine going to fat.

Laura had called Milo earlier in the day and said her friends were planning a eulogy, which Milo figured was code for drinking, but in honor of Peggy. Already she was becoming an excuse for people to get what they wanted: drunk on a Monday. "You can make it, right? It'd be nice to have, you know, a family member present." The phone sizzled. "Other than me."

And while it was true that for a long time Laura had felt like a part of the family, she didn't anymore. Only someone this close to tragedy, who had lived in the house, could claim that. "I don't know. It's pretty hard to get away. My folks really need me right now."

"*We* really need you," she'd said, and that had done it.

After dinner he and George had snuck out of the basement rec room through the back entrance his father used after chores, and Milo'd wished he'd been sleeping in his own room so he could have snuck out the window like Peggy used to do. It had been cold all day and afternoon, but now, with the sun down, the night felt almost warmer than the day, the air thicker, another round of snow imminent.

He thought of all the times he and Peggy had awoken in the morning to new snow and how they'd hunkered in front of their TV watching local news in their pajamas, hopeful as the school names scrolled across the bottom of the screen. Every time, he and Peggy sat with held breath, even though their county was a tough one on cancellations after the blizzard of 1975. That year they'd canceled so many times they had to run a week into summer. The buses couldn't get to the children, or more likely, the school realized that if the buses had arrived, there'd be no children to pick up. They'd been needed at home on the farms to help their dads defrost the water tanks and keep tabs on the livestock. Milo wasn't even in school when that happened, but every kid in the county knew the story.

Milo and George were about a half-mile away from Castle Farm now, and the bonfire blazed on the horizon. Milo slowed his pedaling as he got closer, giving George a chance to catch his breath in the cold. "Hey," George said when he rode up. "Let's stop here a sec." Milo broke and skidded on the thick gravel, his cousin pulling up next to him. "A little pre-party."

George tugged off his gloves and tucked them under his chin, then took a small manila envelope out of his inside coat pocket. It was no more than two inches, the size Grandpa Ahern had used for his coin collection. George pulled the flap back and tipped it carefully on its side, tapping the end with his flip-off finger into his hand cupped against the wind. The white powder landed on the thenar region—what a random word to remember right now from Mrs. Consolino's science class!—and George leaned over and snorted it up his nostril, then raised his head and pinched his nose, his eyes watering.

"What're you doing?" Milo asked.

"Pick-me-up."

"What the hell does that mean?"

"It's this stuff I get from the guys at my dad's feedstore. Here." He held out the envelope. "You're always talking about how dog-tired you are. This'll take care of that."

Milo remembered the week before, at the scrimmage, George and his wild, wired eyes. He imagined what it would be like to shake off the bone weariness he'd felt the last two weeks, the sense he'd never sleep deeply again. Maybe he wouldn't, but what if he didn't need to? He shook his head. "You're an idiot," he said to his cousin, and slung his leg over the bicycle bar.

"No, no. This stuff is the best. Two of the guys who work for my dad make it in their barn from shit my dad gets in bulk. He sells it to them on the cheap for a cut of the profits."

"What is it?"

"It's natural. Ammonia and shit. Like, stuff from the feed-store. It's how my dad's making so much money."

Milo thought of the Cadillac and Uncle Randall with his chest puffed up, talking about his success as a local business-man. "Is it legal?"

George scoffed. "Do you want some or not?"

He was on his way to a party to celebrate his sister's death, he hadn't slept in a hundred years, and the life he had planned was slipping away inch by inch, county line by county line. Maybe it wouldn't be so bad to have a pick-me-up. Maybe in addition to feeling better, he could feel nothing at all.

Milo hesitated, then took the envelope.

Inside the farm's drive, they let their bikes fall in the ditch next to a collection of others, cars and pickups parked in odd formations on the grass. About thirty people milled around, a huge crowd for Gunthrum. Most of Peggy's friends and classmates stood around with plastic cups in their hands.

Next to the open tailgate of a pickup, four or five foot-ball players milled around a keg in a trash barrel. Kerry was among them, along with Daryl Klaussen, and across the way Laura and a few of her friends roasted marshmallows at the bonfire. Scott had filled him in on the drama of Laura and Kerry's breakup and eventual reconciliation. Laura had told her girlfriends Kerry might be involved in Peggy's disappear-ance, and word made it to Lee Earl, who pulled Kerry out of Algebra II and questioned him so long he missed basketball practice. Supposedly, Kerry hadn't been given anything to drink or eat for six hours, which for a high school boy quali-fied as abuse. His parents were suing, either Lee Earl or the state, Scott wasn't sure, but then Larry Burke was the suspect being detained and the crime was jacked up to murder, and supposedly Kerry and Laura had talked about it and worked it all out since he wasn't a killer.

Milo had listened with one ear, shocked once again at how everyone could turn his sister's death into their own personal drama. Lee Earl and Sheriff Randolph had called Larry Burke in for questioning early Sunday—Milo learned this while eavesdropping on his folks—and he finally admitted that he'd been having an affair with Peggy and that, despite Sam Gary having vouched that Larry had stayed overnight at the cabin with him, he'd snuck out when Mr. Gary was dead drunk, then snuck back.

Regarding the niggling detail that he didn't have a truck, he said he'd borrowed his cousin's without asking, driven from Valentine to Gunthrum, then filled it back up when he returned. Something about the story still didn't make sense, his parents had said.

Laura waved at Milo, then handed her roasting stick to another girl and trotted over. "You made it!" She threw her arms around Milo.

"Yep," he confirmed.

"Hey, Laura," George said, but she ignored him. Girls like Laura always ignored boys like George.

She kept one arm slung across Milo's shoulders and pointed at the crowd. "Will you be able to say a few words?"

"About what?"

She rolled her eyes. "Peggy?"

Daryl Klaussen had spotted him by now, and rather than come over and further pummel Milo's face, he'd nodded his chin—*What's up?* "Well, think about it." She nodded toward the keg. "You want a beer?"

"I'll take one," George said, while Milo looked at her, somewhat surprised.

"Oh, come on." Laura swatted Milo's chest. "Peggy and I were planning on getting you drunk soon anyway. It's just a bummer she won't be here to see it. She would have taken bets you were a puker."

Milo didn't know what to say to that. It was true he'd always had a quick gag reflex. If milk was even a little wonky, he'd generally throw it back up, and if he ate too much sugar, that didn't turn out so hot either. He had thought a lot in the days since Peggy's disappearance about the things they'd no longer do together—brush their teeth at night (him spitting in the toilet, of course) or take the car over to Pamida to run errands for their mother, actually getting along—but he hadn't really considered all the things they'd miss out on in the future. Drinking together, buying their first cars, him raising a toast at her wedding, wearing a slim black suit with a pocket square. They'd joked that those trips to Pamida were test runs for the real road trips they'd take someday. One time at a stoplight in Wayne, Peggy sat with the sun streaming through the windshield and her hand on the wheel. She gunned the gas and asked, "Where we headed?" and they drove to Fremont an hour-plus away for Runzas and crinkle-cut fries. Someday Peggy was supposed to have a baby, and then another, and eventually some grandkids. He didn't know about all that for himself, but he was pretty sure that one day he'd get his own dog, and now Peggy would miss out on that too.

He felt the powder from George work its way through his body zip by zip, like an electric charge from a faulty wire. "Yeah, why not? I'll have a beer." He was a twelve-year-old boy in Nebraska; it's not like he'd never tasted beer. It was bitter and sour and both wet and dry, but he knew from nips of his dad's that it was a taste he could acquire if he worked at it.

Laura put her arm around his shoulder and hustled him over to the keg, plucking a red cup from its plastic sleeve. "Hey," said one of the guys—Bruce Johnston, Principal Irv's son. He was just a freshman, and Milo wondered how he'd gotten invited but figured he'd probably brought the keg. "Buck a cup."

"Seriously?" Laura pointed the cup at Milo.

"Oh, hey, man," Bruce said, taking the cup. "On the house." He nodded and opened the nozzle against the side.

"Thanks," Milo mumbled, and watched the beer foam.

"Free refills all night," Bruce said, as he handed Milo the cup. "Sorry about your sister."

Milo took a sip of the frothy beer, and Kerry came over and got another fill, leaning to kiss Laura as he did, the beer slopping on the ground. She reached a hand up to rub his cheek without turning to him and rested her back against his chest.

"Can you believe it?" Laura asked, and Milo just nodded, unsure what she meant. "I mean, I knew she was seeing someone—I told you that, right?—but to love her so much to kill her? Gawd. I mean."

Was Laura . . . jealous? He felt the beer rise back up his throat, but he kept it down. There was a stereo playing from one of the trucks—a Tanya Tucker hit about heartache—and some of the cheerleaders were singing along softly, swaying in front of the fire.

Everyone was subdued, keeping in mind that this was supposed to be a eulogy, but eventually one of the football players—not Daryl Klaussen but someone very much like him—said, "Hey, everybody, is this the kind of party Peggy would have wanted?" and that made it okay to switch from country to Huey Lewis and the News. Some of the girls started dancing, flinging their hair self-consciously in a way that was supposed to look uninhibited.

Milo guessed from nights watching his parents and their friends that eventually things would turn maudlin again, people crying in their keg cups about how young and beautiful Peggy was and how much they'd always miss her, but eventually that would swing, too, back to a reminder that they were still alive. But that was a few hours off. For now Laura linked her elbow through his and brought him closer to the bonfire, bending her knees to the beat and swaying her hip into his. "Peggy loved this song," she said, a big smile spread on her face.

It was an hour or two later—maybe three?—the party in full swing by now, everyone drunk and happy, a bottle of peach schnapps making the rounds. Milo took two long gulps, preferring it to the bitter afterbite of beer. The schnapps was followed by heat that spread through his stomach, although it was hard to say what was what at this point—the heat from the schnapps, the bite of the beer, the magical powder he'd snorted from George. Milo was fuzzy and cold and warm and sick and numb and on the verge of tears, his own body a betrayal of control he both loved and hated.

Adults had shown up by now; some he recognized from his parents' parties and the few times his dad had taken him to the o k. Mr. and Mrs. Gary were here—Mr. Gary, the one who must have lied about Mr. Burke being at the cabin all night—and about ten others who had graduated in the last decade, probably sniveling around the bonfire all those years ago that this was the end of it all. Hardly. People didn't let go that easily. Mr. Gary had handed Kerry a ten-dollar bill at the keg and told him he was ready to dig in deep, his wife behind him with her arms crossed, nursing the gold can of Miller High Life she'd arrived with.

Hal pulled in, slamming the brakes on his pickup a little too close to the ditch, one wheel not anchored on the ground, the battered front end pointed at the bonfire.

"Oh Jesus," Milo said. As much as he hated to admit it, he'd been enjoying himself. He and George had been adopted by the gang, on a mission to get them drunk, and while George had thrown up already, Milo was holding strong. Even Daryl Klaussen had filled his cup once, telling him bygones should be bygones. He pronounced it "by-goons," and that made Milo laugh, and next thing he knew Daryl was laughing too, his arm around Milo's shoulder. The guys had been treating him like a little brother, razzing him even, while the girls had likened him to a cuddly dog they could hug and press against their bosoms, tugging their cold hands through the mess of his hair.

The party turned its collective head toward Hal, shielding eyes against the truck's brights. Hal turned off the lights and engine and opened the door, one unsteady boot hitting the ground. It was apparent immediately, even to Milo, that he was drunk. Normally handsome, Hal's face was now slack and wet, his eyes set to dazed.

"No way," a girl near Milo said. "No freaking way."

People turned from one to another trying to figure out who was in charge, who was going to approach him. Laura set her face, and Milo wished he were closer to her, that he could tell her, *Hey, think about how much fun we're having for Peggy!* and *Hey, remember he didn't do anything?* but she was already stepping forward into the spotlight, her friends behind her.

She crossed her arms and jutted out her hip. "What are you doing here?" she asked Hal. Even with Larry behind bars, people weren't going to forget their suspicions that easily.

"Isn't this a party for Peggy?"

Mr. Gary stepped forward and pointed his beer. "You're not welcome here, Hal. I told you that." He must have run into him at the OK, Milo thought—it was pretty clear Mr. Gary had been drinking somewhere too—and that's how Hal had found out about the bonfire.

Kerry stepped forward and held a hand out to Hal in warning. "Get out of here, man. I'm serious. We don't want you here."

Hal's face looked like cold butter. "Why?"

Mr. Gary tucked his wife behind him. "Hal, now's not the time. You got to get out of here."

Mrs. Gary's face was splotchy, and Milo realized she was crying. "Sam?" she started, and he shook his head. "But—"

Hal took a step, and that's when Daryl Klaussen and another guy jumped forward and took Hal by the shoulders. Milo realized for the first time that he himself was also drunk, or at least that's what he figured must be going on. He lifted one foot and set it back down, but it wobbled like he'd set it on Jell-O. He felt an uncomfortable lurch in his stomach, like when his mother cooked liver in the pressure cooker and he imagined the taste.

"You've got to stop this!" Mrs. Gary yelled. "This is all Larry's fault!"

"It's bullshit!" Mr. Gary cried. "I know he didn't leave that cabin." He tried to maneuver his wife away from the fight, and she yanked her arm away.

"Don't you touch me," she yelled hysterically, and Mr. Gary held up his hands in the air. "It's all your fault! You men. Larry's just getting what he deserves."

Hal tried to shake his arm loose, but Daryl wrenched it, and with that, Hal landed the first punch.

"Don't," Milo said, but no one seemed to hear him. Had he said it out loud? Daryl took the hit to his jaw, and Kerry came in swinging, connecting with Hal's drunk face, the fist leaving a red scrape visible in the firelight.

"Hey!" Laura yelled. "Hey, now!" but more guys were moving toward the scuffle, Mr. Gary among them. "Fucking retard," he yelled.

"It's not his fault!" Mrs. Gary yelled, and Milo didn't know if she meant the fact that he was slow or what happened to Peggy. Hal was on the ground now, on his knees, swinging and trying to get his foot planted firmly enough to hurl his body up, but the other men wouldn't let him.

Milo shook his head, trying to clear out the slush. He had to help Hal. Hal didn't do it. He moved toward the pack and tried to tug one of them by the back of the jacket, hoping to get his attention, but the guy threw his arm forward, almost bringing Milo with him. George grabbed Milo's shoulder.

"We got to do something," Milo said, the words slurring so even to his own ear it sounded like *gosh*, not *got*. "I can't go home." Because even though his sister was dead and Hal was leaning toward unconsciousness, there was the twelve-year-old logic that you can't show up at your parents' house drunk, a blessedly normal thought.

"We gotta get out of here," George said. "I know which truck is Klaussen's, and everyone leaves keys in the cars."

Mrs. Costagan. Milo thought of the no-nonsense way she handled situations on the bus. He'd bet they could show up there drunk; he'd bet Hal had done it a hundred times. "Can you drive?" he asked George.

"I've been driving for years!"

"But are you too drunk?" Milo couldn't imagine the coordination it would take to alternate his foot from the gas to the break with the clutch just right, the steering wheel tight in his hands.

"No, dickbrain, I puked." George smiled proudly and flashed the peace sign. "Twice."

23

Alma folded the page down on her Larry McMurtry novel when she heard the truck in the drive. It was almost midnight, and they'd gotten a call an hour ago from Mick Langdon, Hal's neighbor, saying Hal's pickup was gone. "Damn near can't sleep an hour through the night in my own bed," Mick said, "but sack me out in the chair in front of *Airwolf*, the one damn show I like, and I'm a goner. I woke up, and his garage door was open."

"I appreciate you looking out for him, but you don't need to call us anytime he goes somewhere," Clyle had said. Mick had called them nearly every day since he'd found that deer head in his landfill. Alma suspected Mick would call every day until the end of time, suspicious of what trouble Hal Bullard was up to, never mind that he was innocent.

Mick barreled ahead. "I don't know how long he's been gone. Could be an hour, could be three."

When Clyle hung up, Alma admitted it made her uneasy. An hour or three was plenty of time to get a snootful and start making bad decisions.

Clyle had left for the OK, and Alma knew from the crunch of gravel that the truck driving up was a stranger's. Hal drove like the devil, but even Clyle drove faster than this truck was moving. She'd given up on sleeping some time ago. Ever since Peck turned down their road eight days ago, nighttime had brought nothing but bad news.

Alma rose from the living room chair, where she'd been reading the same paragraph over and over again, and put on her coat. She hadn't even bothered with a nightgown but was still in the flannel shirt and jeans she'd worn all day, the top button of her pants undone.

Outside, the truck tiptoed to a stop. Milo threw open the passenger door and was running to the porch as Alma, her heart flapping now, went out to meet him. He hugged her so fiercely he almost knocked her over, and she could smell the alcohol on his breath and smoke in his coat.

"It's Hal. He's at Castle Farm," Milo started, and Alma got the story piecemeal—drinking, beaten up, bad news, bonfire—as Milo's yahoo cousin fell from the high cab seat, righted himself, and kicked a tire. Milo pulled himself from the hug, Alma's arms suddenly empty. She brushed the snow out of her hair—when had that started?—and stomped her slippers by habit on the driveway, the first few flakes collecting on the ground.

She drove the pickup to Castle Farm, and they passed car after car, an unusual thing on their gravel road at any time, much less this late at night. Alma was sure that had she been able to peer into the cars, she'd have seen the frightened faces of stupid teenagers, some adults too, from what Milo had said. Sam Gary had been at the bonfire mad as a hornet now that Larry was under arrest, his confession given and signed. She turned the steering wheel, and the tires followed suit, moving the great machinery of it all into the abandoned driveway. Only Hal's truck was still parked at Castle Farm, even though Milo and George couldn't have left more than ten minutes ago. Smoke was still sizzling from the damp fire and, beyond that, what looked like a lump of bedding. Hal.

Clyle came into the waiting room carrying two cups of gas station coffee. He'd shown up at Castle Farm shortly after Alma, having figured from word at the OK that was where Hal was. Now they were at Providence Medical Center in Wayne, where Hal snored in an ER bed with a broken arm, bruised ribs, a broken nose, and a concussion.

On the way to the hospital, Hal had sat slumped against the passenger window not crying, and that's when Alma knew it was bad. Three miles from PMC, he'd finally fallen asleep— maybe they weren't supposed to let him?—with a hitch of a snore in the back of his dry throat. They'd dropped George and Milo off at the Ahern farm on the way to the hospital, not a light on in the house. She thought of all the nights the week before, when Peggy was still just missing, how the house had been lit in nearly every room.

Clyle handed Alma one of the Styrofoam cups and scrunched up his nose as he went to take a sip. As long as she'd known him, he'd done that in anticipation of the first hot gulp. There was another couple in the ER, a bit older, the woman with her hands wrapped around her stomach and a grimace like she was going to die. Every now and again she'd blast a noxious fart, a look of relief and embarrassment on her face. Across the way a young man who looked like a teenager but was probably in his twenties wore a nice pair of slacks and dress shoes, tear paths on his face. When he got up to talk to the nurse, Alma could tell by the way he walked that the stiff shoes pinched his feet. She'd bet he was here for his wife. She was sure of it. Maybe she was having a baby.

The doctor came out to tell them Hal was going to be okay in the long run, God willing on the head injury. "Might be just what he needs," the doctor said, and when Clyle and

Alma stared blankly at him, he added, "He's funny in the head, correct? He's the guy accused of murder?"

"No," Clyle said. "They've arrested another fella."

"Just goes to show," the doctor said, but didn't elaborate, handing them instructions for home care. "We'll release him tomorrow. In the meantime the nurse called his next of kin, and she said she's on her way." He pointed his pen at Alma. "Turns out you're not his mother." She'd lied when they admitted him so she could stay by his side.

"No," Alma admitted. "I guess I'm not." She'd been reminded of that more in the last week than she had since she'd taken Hal into their family and tried to convince herself she was.

Marta and Eugene showed up an hour or so later, Marta in a full face of makeup and leaning on her cane, the smell of cigarette smoke heavy around her. Alma imagined the steady hand it would take to run a mascara wand near your eye after hearing your son was at the hospital, and yet there wasn't a smudge on Marta's face. "Thank you for bringing him, Alma," Marta said, but Alma just crossed her arms and stared back. "Fine. Is that how it's going to be?"

Marta and Eugene were hustled back to Hal by a stick-thin nurse in Reeboks, while Alma and Clyle stayed slumped in their uncomfortable plastic chairs.

Alma opened her mouth, fully expecting to ask Clyle if he'd heard anything at the ok about Larry Burke, but what came out surprised even her. "I named them, you know."

"Who?" Clyle asked, and after a long pause, "What were their names?"

"Edward, Patrick, Nicholas, and Brett."

"So you wanted a boy."

Alma shook her head. "I don't know if I wanted one so much as I wouldn't know what to do with a girl. I was never one much for silly talk. And you know me, Clyle. I can get a meal on the table, but I'm not much of a cook."

"I like your lasagna."

At the nurses' station two women with crumbs from their doughnuts at the corners of their mouths scribbled their way through a stack of files. "There was a fifth," she said. "I lost that baby at about three months, two years after we moved to the farm."

Clyle nodded and took her hand. "I knew." She looked at him, surprised. "Or at least I suspected. I guess I didn't know how to ask."

Tears flooded Alma's eyes again. "Sometimes I figured maybe it's because I want them so badly that I couldn't have them. That maybe I just wasn't due that much happiness."

"That's not really how it works."

"Isn't it? Do you know anyone who really has what they want?"

He squeezed her hand hard enough she winced but then pulled her hand back. When they moved to Gunthrum and first started their Sunday drives, they would hold hands across the cab of the truck. Sometimes Clyle was so determined not to let go he'd turn the wheel with his left hand and a knee.

"I do," Clyle said. "You remember when we moved to the farm? In the beginning? You sewed us those centennial costumes and I grew a beard? We made that scarecrow out of those overalls we found in the barn? You *liked* it here." She looked at him, skeptical. "You did. I swear. The change was good for you after the city, after . . . after the miscarriages."

He reached a hand out and smoothed down her hair, which she always let loose at night after having it tied back in a ponytail all day, the telltale kink still visible. "When I was a teenager, my parents got a notice in the mail that the bank was foreclosing on the farm. They didn't get the mail until late on a Saturday and had all night and all Sunday up until Monday morning to fret about it, to try and figure out what went wrong. My God, they wanted to hold on to that little farm, even though up until that point they'd cursed it for not having the right soil or not enough acres or this or that. Turned out it was a mistake on the bank's part. They sent the notice to the wrong family. My folks had never been so happy to have what they didn't appreciate in the first place."

"You've told me that story, Clyle. Probably a hundred times."

"You know all my stories. Every one." He stroked her hair one more time. "I'm sorry about the babies. I am."

She reached for his hand this time and pulled it back into her lap. He rubbed the pad of his thumb over her palm, and she felt something inside her loosen. Alma cleared her throat. "Me too."

Peck showed up about an hour later in jeans, a flannel shirt, and a down vest with snow on the shoulders. "Still coming down. My guess is we're into it until spring." He sat down next to Clyle, pinched up the thigh of his Lees, and crossed his legs.

"You come to apologize?" Alma asked, and Peck gave her a half-smile.

"I don't apologize for doing my job. I'm sorry, of course, that Hal got dragged into all this, but that doesn't mean I have something to apologize for."

"What're you here for then? You got your killer."

"Well, what I got was a confession. Not the same thing."

Alma furrowed her brow. "What the hell is that supposed to mean?" Clyle put a hand on her arm.

"Means I'd bet dollars to doughnuts Larry Burke didn't kill Peggy Ahern."

"Well, Hal sure as hell—" Peck held up a hand to stop Alma.

"Not saying he did. But there are other parties to consider." He turned to Clyle. "Who's the one person you might confess murder to protect?"

Clyle glanced at Alma, and she believed for the first time in a long time that Clyle would do what he had to do to protect her.

"You don't really . . ." Alma started, and trailed off. "Well, doesn't that beat all. Cheryl Burke. A woman." The idea hadn't even occurred to her, but of course it made sense. Peck held up a hand and told her and Clyle it was just a theory, something he'd been wondering about after Sam Gary swore up and down Larry hadn't left the cabin. Alma knew a lot of drunks, and the unlucky of the lot were light sleepers, just like Sam swore he was.

At the nurses' station the young man with the pinched feet stood on one foot and leaned against the counter, talking to an older nurse. The woman, probably in her sixties, slipped a hand behind her hip and subtly pulled her underwear out of her behind, and with that Alma remembered what had been niggling at her brain about that picnic last year.

Why, it was the silliest thing. Alma had been standing next to the picnic table with the desserts, self-conscious and sweating in her too-tight shorts, the top button already undone and the thighs constricting to the point she couldn't sit down. She had to admit it: she needed a bigger pair. Each year she thought she'd take off a few pounds in the summer, weeding the garden and mowing the lawn, but come next summer, those shorts were two hairs tighter.

Cheryl Burke had stood nearby in a tight pair of her own, resigned already at the age of twenty-seven to the wild-patterned jam shorts you could sew yourself with a yard of fabric and a length of string. They looked good on nobody, which meant they couldn't look much worse on one body versus another. "Will you get a load of that," Cheryl had whispered to her friend, loud enough for Alma to hear, "Alma Costagan and her flabby white legs in a pair of shorts. I hope I have better sense when I'm that age."

Alma's face had reddened with shame. It was the kind of slight she felt nearly every day on the streets of Gunthrum, the sense of not belonging, of not doing things quite right, and the deeper shame that she cared. Her eyes burned, and while she told herself it was sweat and Coppertone in her eyes, she knew better. She'd tucked that moment away because it angered her how much she still wanted to belong, to be one of the women standing by the desserts with an iced tea in her hand and a smile on her lips. But now what she remembered was the cruelty of Cheryl's comment, that bite of hatred as she'd picked off the other women one by one.

On the way home, still fuming about the comment, she'd thought, what gives her the right? But she'd sat, waiting for the moment when Hal would tell her about Peggy, when he would recount that she had seemed interested and maybe he'd ask her out on a date. Alma had sat in the passenger seat with an empty casserole pan covering the tight crotch of her shorts, waiting for the moment when she could tell him he was a fool and pick off his stupid hopes one by one.

24

The older nurse spoke to Clyle rather than Hal as she gave the discharge instructions: plastic bag over the cast when he showers; PT starting in two weeks; change the bandages on his head after a shower in the morning. Clyle doubted in all the years he'd known Hal he'd ever sat on a bed with him. Even with another person in the room giving them medical instructions, it felt oddly intimate.

Clyle kept his legs crossed and his hands in his lap as he nodded to show he was paying attention. Marta and Eugene were in Wayne, at Pamida, picking up sheets and towels, so he'd have to relay the information to them. Marta said they were cleaning out the spare bedroom for Hal until they could get him set up through a facility in Axtell run by Lutherans. In the meantime they'd found some activities at the community center, group outings for people like Hal. One time, years ago, Clyle had been at a buddy's dairy operation to see his new milkers when a group of mongoloid adults came in wearing neon yellow T-shirts, their wrists all tied together by a rope. Clyle's friend had explained he was so proud of the new machinery that he'd opened the dairy up for educational tours. "Plus," he added, "a small fee."

This morning after chores, Clyle had stopped at the Standard on the way to the hospital for a cup of coffee and the scuttlebutt. Peck had been right. He'd called the Costagans at home that morning to let them know Cheryl had turned herself in and they'd sent Larry home. Clyle remembered Cheryl Burke at the Aherns' house with a bag of groceries in her arms when Peggy was still just missing. He hadn't thought twice about it; bringing food and helping out how you could was what you did. Already the counter regulars were jabbering about how Cheryl's lawyer—a guy from over in Omaha—was going to try to talk things down to vehicular manslaughter.

"Guess Larry got a taste of serving time and told Cheryl he was going to turn her in after all," Lonnie McGee, Larry's boss at the body shop, had said. "So much for cherish and protect. She was screaming and carrying on at the county jail last night about how it was all Larry's fault—how if he wasn't a no-good shit none of this would have happened— but eventually Peck made sense of it. Lare still says it was an accident, but with word out now about him and the Ahern girl, we'll see what comes of it." Clyle had had a yearlong affair with Diane. What would Alma have done in the same situation? Maybe Cheryl didn't hit Peggy on purpose, but maybe impulse and premeditation were two sides of the same coin. The action and reaction. The affair and the fallout. Either way, the outcome was the same.

For years after the affair ended, Clyle lay awake thinking about the easy way Diane had of smiling at the silliest things—a quarter she found in the pocket of her jacket or a candy bar, the one with coconut, that he brought her from the grocery.

And then there was Alma. One year for Christmas he'd bought her the complete set of the red *Encyclopedia Britannica Jr.* she'd had as a child. He'd found a set minus *I–J* at an estate sale, then after months of combing estate after estate, he'd found that volume too. She'd unwrapped the *Ready Reference Index* Christmas morning, and he'd grinned and said, "I've got the rest of the set hidden out in the barn."

She turned the heavy book over in her hands. "These must have cost a fortune."

Years ago she'd told him how much she loved the encyclopedias when she was a little girl, how she used to sit in her corduroy window seat with the sun streaming in and learn about Egyptian pharaohs, coal mining, the circumference of the Earth.

"You're worth it," he'd said, and winked at her—he'd winked!

She'd leaned over and kissed him loudly on the mouth as Hal laughed there next to the tree, a stack of presents a yard high.

That was Alma: work, but worth it.

Marta entered the room as the nurse finished up, Eugene behind her like an ever-present shadow. She carried a plastic bag full of Hal's belongings—his bloodied jeans and jacket along with his wallet and keys—pinched between her forefinger and thumb. That morning, when Clyle arrived at the hospital, the ends of his previously damp hair frozen crisp in the short walk from the truck, Alma had looped her purse over her shoulder and announced she was leaving. "I've said my goodbyes." She nodded toward Hal's room. "Don't need to say them again."

There were swollen bruises on Hal's cheek and near his eye; the scuff of scab looked like red drywall tape on his chin. His innocence wouldn't matter in the long run; people would only remember that Hal had been associated with the Ahern girl's death, not that he was a victim. His name would haunt Peggy's death like a fly circling stink. Maybe it was good he was leaving, or maybe that's what Clyle had to tell himself, same as Marta had to tell herself she was a good mother.

Clyle tuned back in and realized Marta was staring at him. "And we can, right, Clyle? Count on your help?"

"With what?"

She ticked the list off her fingers. "Landlord's name, electric bill, those sheep he's got out back."

He nodded.

"All right then. Glad to see you're the reasonable one of the troops."

At Hal's, Alma was waiting for Clyle in the living room, her feet up on the coffee table and the remote control in her lap. "You're calmer than I thought you'd be," Clyle said, and she pointed her thumb at the kitchen. Around the corner he saw the smashed plates and coffee cups on the linoleum floor. "Feel better?"

"Not really."

He sat on the couch next to her. "What're you watching?"

She pointed at the TV, where a good-looking couple was yelling at each other on mute, the woman with stiff black hair and streaks of makeup on her face. He couldn't tell one soap opera from another but knew from the large gold baubles and exaggerated shoulder pads this was one of them. "That woman with the black hair? That's Felicia Gallant. She's a troublemaker."

"You been watching these all along and I just didn't know?"

"Hardly."

In their pen Peanut Butter and Jelly gallivanted back and forth. They were in one of their playful moods—odd for early afternoon—galloping their front hooves through the air over each other's heads, then circling their bodies to escape. He was going to have to build a similar pen on their farm with a three-walled barn for winter. He needed to contact Mick Langdon and terminate Hal's lease and take care of the rest of the particulars. At least now there weren't many dishes to pack.

Alma leaned her head back. "I wasn't meant to be a farm wife."

"Why do you say that?"

"I've never fit here, Clyle. You know that. As long as we've been in Gunthrum—what, fifteen years?—"

"Fourteen."

"Fourteen years, and I still barely have a friend to call for a visit. No one whose house I can stop by unannounced and sit in their kitchen."

"Do you think you'd have had that in Chicago?"

"No, but maybe I wouldn't have needed it. I'd be working all day, for one thing. Keeping busy. Wouldn't need any fool friends to fill my days."

"Maybe that you call people fools is why you don't have any friends."

She smiled. "Well, that's a point." The woman on the TV—a real ballbuster, Clyle thought—was now shooting seductive glances at a man with a modern-day pompadour. "But I'd be busy there. I could go back to work doing what I love." Clyle didn't point out that most nights back then she'd come home talking about how her clients were messing up their lives with their bad decisions.

Outside, one of the sheep—he couldn't tell them apart from this distance—knocked the other to the ground and sat on its side, panting. "That quick, you'd just leave me?" He'd tried to say it in a joking tone but held his breath. That's what it came down to, he guessed: a yes or no. Was she willing to stay? Did she even want to?

Alma settled her hands in her lap. "Are you still seeing her?" The question took him off guard.

She looked at him pointedly, and Clyle felt a crack in his chest. They had never talked about Diane. All these years, outspoken as she was, they'd never said the words. "Alm . . . ." Clyle reached for her hands, but Alma clasped hers together, white at the knuckles.

"Are you?"

He thought of Diane in his truck, how the cloying smell of Love's Baby Soft had lingered. "No. I promise you that, Alma."

Alma shook her head. Was she crying? "I saw you with her. Friday."

"She called to tell me about the money. That's why. I . . . I haven't seen her for years."

Alma picked the TV *Guide* up off the coffee table and fanned herself with the magazine: another hot flash. "I knew she couldn't keep that secret."

"You really think you could go to withdraw our life savings and me not hear about it? You've been in Gunthrum long enough to know better."

"It wasn't our life savings."

"Close enough."

They sat in silence through the end of the commercial break—Tide detergent, Velamints, and quick and easy Tyson Chick'n Chunks. Clyle had never stared so raptly at a TV and seen so little. He had screwed up his life, his mistakes ricocheting and piercing Alma with the shrapnel, along with Diane and he supposed Lonnie and who knew who else. "I'm sorry, Alma. I am. By the time I wised up, you were gone somehow, and there was nothing I could say to make it right."

She turned to him, and yes, she was crying. He felt he could count the times on his two hands. "You know what bothers me about it? You're the kindest man I know, Clyle. The kindest by far, and if you're capable of that, what hope is there for the rest of us?" There was nothing he could say.

"I thought you'd be glad for me to go, but then I couldn't go through with it." She looked away. "I guess it doesn't matter why."

He put his thumb under her chin and pulled her face toward him until she looked back at him—her eyes a dull blue and lined now with age. "I would have come with you and Hal. I would have left Gunthrum in a heartbeat."

"But you love this town."

It was true. Despite those years in college and at IBM, that he'd promised Alma the move home was temporary, he'd ended up just where he wanted to be: Gunthrum, Nebraska. "It doesn't matter."

Alma held on a beat, then leaned against him, his hand stroking her cheek. "I'm an old bear, Clyle. People say you're a saint to put up with me."

Clyle's throat thickened. "It's been an honor. Every second."

She tucked her feet underneath her on the sofa. "You really would have come with me?"

"Yes," he said, and it was as true as the color of the sky that they'd fought about all those years ago. It wasn't out of a sense of responsibility or a fear of loneliness; he really did love the woman next to him. "All you had to do was ask."

25

Alma sat in the waiting room with her purse in her lap and her mittens still on. It was two days before Christmas and cold as February. She'd told Clyle at breakfast that morning they were in for a brutal year, but then stopped and added, "Good thing I'm not driving the bus. Mrs. Dunn'll end up more in the ditch than on the road, I'm guessing." She was trying to find the positive in things. Trying to make an effort.

Peck came out through the back room and shut the door behind him. "She's all ready for you," he said, taking a seat. They were at the jail in Thurston County where they housed women awaiting trial. The rumor mill had it that Cheryl's mother-in-law was taking unofficial custody of Hattie until then, saying it wasn't right that Larry should have to care for her on his own. Wasn't that the way? Men making babies when they acted like impetuous kids themselves. Peck had called the day before to say Cheryl had requested a meeting with Alma. "You up for it?" he asked.

Why not? Alma had thought. She was curious what Cheryl had to say for herself and even more curious why she wanted to say it to Alma. Peck stood up, and Alma followed him to the door.

"You okay meeting with her uncuffed in the conference room?" he asked. "Protocol says we can restrain her."

Alma shook her head. "Uncuffed is fine." In the light of day, even with all that had happened, it was hard to imagine Cheryl Burke as dangerous.

He took Alma through the door and then through another, to a blank room with a six-foot folding table and four chairs, a mildew smell that reminded Alma of the old tackle box Clyle kept in the basement. Cheryl sat at the far end, her foot drawn up on the chair she was sitting on, her chin resting on her knee. She was wearing blue prison pants and a gray sweatshirt, and free of makeup, she appeared younger than she normally did at the football games, where she'd have mascara clumping her eyes and lipstick smoothed on her mouth, just so she could stand out in the cold and clap like her boyfriend was still on the team.

"Hi, Alma. Thanks for coming."

Peck stood at the door. "I'm going to leave this open and the outer one too. You ladies need anything, just let me know."

Cheryl nodded, her chin still on her knee. Alma sat down, took off her mittens, and put them on top of her purse on the floor.

"Thanks for coming," Cheryl said again.

"I was curious when I got the request. Couldn't quite imagine what you had to say to me."

Cheryl twisted her mouth. "Sorry, I guess."

Alma wasn't going to let her off the hook that easily. "Sorry for what?"

"Hal? You know, him being accused?"

Alma sniffed. "Well, isn't that big of you."

Cheryl flashed her a look of irritation. "I am trying to apologize."

"So, now you want me to make it easy on you?"

"No, it's just—" Cheryl stopped and cleared her throat. "I didn't mean for it to happen. I know that doesn't count for much, but it's true."

"So, it was an accident?"

Cheryl twisted her mouth again. Alma knew that look from when Cheryl had ridden the bus, torn by who she should sit with. "Yes, an accident. More of an impulse, I guess. A mistake. I mean, I did it, but I guess I wasn't in my right mind? That's what my lawyer is saying. Larry got me a guy from Omaha, a real tough guy. He's going to get the charges reduced. I'll still go to jail but not for near as long."

"You think that's fair?"

She shrugged. "I've got a daughter. I need to be there for her."

"Maybe you should have considered that earlier."

Cheryl put her foot on the ground and leaned in. "I knew about the affair, you know." For a brief moment Alma thought she meant Clyle and Diane. "I'd just figured it out about a week before, finally pieced it all together, and was deciding what to do." Alma wondered if someone had tipped Cheryl off about Larry and Peggy, like Phyllis all those years ago when Alma sat in her salon chair, a wet comb in Phyllis's hand. "That idiot. I knew something was up; I just didn't know with who. Then the Friday before—at a football game—I was wrestling Hattie out from under the bleachers when he was supposed to be watching her, and I saw him run his finger up the crack of Peggy's butt at the concession stand." She ran her forefinger up like a zipper. "Zzzp, just like that. Then a day or two later he's talking about this hunting trip, saying it's with Hal Bullard, and I figured it was really a weekend with his girlie on the side. No way anyone'd let Hal shoot a gun. When I saw Hal that night at the ok, I knew for sure, you know?—that Larry had lied to me."

"But he hadn't," Alma pointed out.

"Oh, he had. Plenty. When I saw Peggy at Castle Farm that night—Tonya and I went there after the ok—I figured

I'd double-check if she was there since Hal was in town yakking it up about that deer. Anyway, I cornered Peggy out in the field where she was peeing and said, You'd better stay away from Larry. We've got a daughter and all. I told her she couldn't just try to snatch my life away from me." Her jaw tightened, and she locked eyes with Alma. "You know what she said to me?"

"I haven't a clue."

"She said she didn't want my shitty life. Said that wasn't what she was after. She was going to UNL when she graduated to study education. She wasn't planning on staying in a crap town like this, getting trapped in a life like mine." Cheryl hiccupped, trying to get enough air in her lungs. "Looked me right in the face and said that. Why not, right? I do have a shitty life in a shitty town."

"You haven't improved your prospects much," Alma pointed out, and Cheryl laughed, a hysterical sound.

"No, I guess I haven't."

"So, what happened?" Alma asked. There'd been rumors a plenty—Cheryl hit Peggy by accident, ran her down on purpose, thought she hit a deer, and so on. You name it, people had speculated it. For once Alma wanted something from the horse's mouth.

Cheryl shook her head. "I can hardly remember, you know? Like, I've remembered it so many times I'm not sure how it really happened? I left the party with Tonya and took her home, but I couldn't, like, stop hearing that comment. I decided to go back—half in the bag, you know?—and she's walking the side of the road, and. . . . I hit her, down on that gravel road over by your house. It really was an accident. I didn't mean to. I mean, I saw her, but it was dark and like—" She paused. "I don't know. I didn't mean to."

Alma wondered how that could be, but one time she'd run into Diane at Gunthrum Foods a few weeks after she'd figured out the affair with Clyle and had to grip the handle on her grocery cart to keep from slapping the woman. Alma hadn't moved her hand so much as an inch yet felt the itch so deeply she would not have been surprised to look down and see her palm was red—it would have happened that fast.

"Larry figured it out almost immediately, what happened, or that I'd done something. I had to drive to Valentine to get them—took Larry's truck since, you know—and tried to pull myself together. I didn't know what I was going to do. He took one look at me and knew something was wrong. Just knew it. He thought at first I'd figured out about his fling, that I was going to confront him about it right then and there, but by the time it all came out, we were way past that. He washed my car and replaced the fender and headlight at the shop. He became—what do you call it? An accessory? We figured, even if I was found out, they couldn't make him confess because we were married. I'm pretty sure that's how it works."

Cheryl grimaced, highlighting the faint lines around her eyes and mouth, the first signs of a woman's age. She leaned in. "Can I tell you something else?" Alma shrugged. God help her tough-guy lawyer if he put her on the stand. She'd say whatever popped into her head. "That week before he came forward to Peck and told him he'd done it, well, I hate to say it, but that was the best week of our marriage in a long time. We were scared and all, but still. We were in it together."

Alma picked up her purse and fumbled through for some Sucrets. Anything to avoid Cheryl's naked face. After the first miscarriage she'd fallen asleep with her head in Clyle's lap, his hand stroking her hair. When she woke up an hour later, his hand was still moving at the same rhythm, and her first thought was how glorious it felt. She took a Sucrets and held the tin out to Cheryl.

"Then all that started up around Hal," Cheryl continued, as she popped the cough drop in her mouth. "How people were saying he'd done it and had to be guilty, and we kind of figured, maybe that wouldn't be so bad, you know? They'd put him in some kind of home for people with problems and he'd be taken care of. He's done other stuff too, like beat people up when he's drunk, so maybe it was just a matter of time before he'd end up somewhere like that anyway. We thought he'd go somewhere and be okay."

Alma snapped the Sucrets tin shut. "Hal had a life in Gunthrum. And despite what it might have looked like to you, it was a good one. He had friends, family. People who love him." She thought back to a second ago—the empathy she'd had for Cheryl and her broken marriage—but that was gone. You couldn't just ride over people's lives without consequences.

Cheryl stood up, her hands on both sides of the table. "I have a child!"

Alma felt a fire ignite on her face and down her shoulders: another hot flash, or maybe this one was anger through and through. "They hand them out like candy, don't they? We'll see how much she wants to spend time with Mom when she hears what you've done or how well that marriage of yours is going to last once you go to prison. Best week of your marriage. Jesus."

"Listen—" Cheryl said.

"No, you listen!" Alma squinted. "Wait. You said that people were talking about Hal, and that gave you the idea to make him the suspect, but her body was found by O'Neill." Cheryl bit her lip and looked down at her hands. "You had to have moved the body. You and Larry. You had to have done that almost right away. *You* started the rumors."

"I didn't mean to do it!" Cheryl said, but Alma had her purse in her hand and was moving toward the door.

"Wait," Cheryl said. "I don't—"

"Oh, good Lord." Alma left the room, slamming the door behind her. How quickly people were willing to ruin other people's lives, like it was all a big game. Had she done the same, nag by nag and grudge by grudge? Alma breathed deeply, then headed down the hallway.

Peck was sitting in the waiting room, shuffling through paperwork on his lap in a way that made Alma guess he'd just picked it up after eavesdropping. "How'd it go?"

"About how you'd expect. All the reasons it wasn't her fault."

Peck nodded and scratched his chin. "Have to say, I was a bit more sympathetic before that."

"I can't feel an ounce of sympathy," Alma said. "She killed that girl and tried to blame someone else, an innocent man."

"How did you feel when you thought it might be Hal?" Alma conceded with a nod. He was right—she hadn't really cared what happened to Peggy, only about him. "People don't think emotions should be a part of policing, but they are. It's a lot like parenting—you try to use them for the good and do what's right while staying within the laws you've laid down." He chuckled. "Pretty funny, me comparing this to parenting. An old bachelor like me." He looked at Alma. "You ever wish you had kids?"

In a flash a child grew through her mind: swaddled in a blanket, bronzed shoes on the mantel, running after a hog in short pants, a square hat with a tassel tickling his nose at graduation.

Peck held up a hand. "None of my business. I just regret it myself sometimes, not settling down. 'Specially here around the holidays."

"I did," she said, her voice thick. "I wanted a child more than I've wanted anything in my life."

Peck nodded thoughtfully, then looked her in the eye. It was rare, that close kind of eye contact. "Sorry that didn't happen for you."

Alma gulped. "Thank you." She allowed herself to stay there for a moment, her eyes locked with Peck's, before she slipped on her mittens. "You want to come to our house for Christmas?" She was surprised as the words came out. "I make a ham, and Clyle spikes the eggnog with Lord Calvert so when I burn the dinner you won't even care."

"Not much of a drinker."

"No," she agreed. "We're really not anymore either. Clyle usually has two glasses and falls asleep. You could stay up and play gin rummy with me."

Peck shrugged. "What the hell."

"All right then."

He nodded as she slung her purse over her shoulder, the holidays settled. "All right then."

Out in her car Alma held her mittened hands in front of the heater vent, the air still warm; she'd been in with Cheryl only fifteen minutes, hardly enough time for the car to cool down.

An accident. That might have been true about killing Peggy, but it wasn't true about blaming Hal. Alma had wondered at times if Hal had done it. They all had, even Clyle. Hell, even Hal had, she supposed, as he tried to remember that Saturday night through a head soaked in alcohol. Cheryl would be waiting in her cell every week for visiting hours, waiting for Larry to comb their young daughter's curls into submission so she could visit her mother.

Alma had to make an effort. Mad as she was about Hal moving in with Marta and that fool Eugene, she was going to have to make an effort. Write him letters every other day;

visit him once a week. She'd take him packages of Oreos, which she doubted Marta would let him have. She'd bring him Southern Comfort too, let him turn his drunk self on Mommy Dearest and see what she thought of her decision to leverage the family ties then.

Oh, she would have to try.

Alma pulled the gearshift to DRIVE and decided she'd swing by Pickett's and get some garland and lights. She bet they hadn't decorated the porch in a decade. Every year the Aherns' house was lit—colored, dancing lights from stem to stern— but this year it was illuminated only by the halo of the farm light. She'd go for white lights that didn't blink, in case the Aherns looked over—she didn't want to be ostentatious—but then chided herself for thinking the Aherns had nothing better to do than critique her tacky decorations or that her tacky decorations might remind them of what they'd lost. Everything, she supposed, would remind them of that. She thought of Milo on the bus, how he'd tried so hard to act normal, back when Peggy just was missing. Maybe he would appreciate the lights. Milo, who had shown up at her house in the middle of the night, knowing she was a woman who would help him.

Pulling into the parking space in front of Pickett's, she figured she'd ask whoever was behind the counter what they recommended she use to hang the whole mess, then sneak home and do it herself. What the hell, she thought, maybe I'll even bake Christmas cookies, and felt a sharp pang that Hal wouldn't be there to tell her Oreos were better. She would write him a letter tomorrow, and added stationery to her mental list, Pickett's right next to the drugstore. As for today, Clyle was at a machinery auction for the rest of the afternoon—a lot of farmers retired in December—and she'd surprise him. He wasn't too run-down yet without Hal's help on the farm, but come spring would be another story.

She imagined him coming home at dusk, the lights twinkling as the snow fell. "Why, look at that," he'd say, stepping out of his truck. "Looks like Santa's coming after all."

She imagined she'd have come out onto the porch to see his surprise, wiping her hands on a dish towel. Her first instinct would be to tell him he was a fool for getting excited over some plain white lights, but maybe she'd bite that back. Maybe she'd walk out to the driveway and snuggle into his arms—maybe she wouldn't be wearing a coat, not having thought she'd be out in the cold more than a second—then lean herself against his chest and say, "They're pretty, aren't they? I just put them up today."

26

Milo lugged his backpack onto his shoulder as he climbed the bus steps, his winter coat tied to one of the straps. He'd have to put it on before he got off the bus or his mother would have a shit fit. The weather had cracked fifty and was expected to get almost to sixty by the weekend, only to plunge back to the thirties early next week. But still, it was nice while it lasted.

Scott caught Milo's eye and scooted from the aisle to the window. "You see Lisa bend over for the chalk in fifth period?" he asked, before Milo had even sat down. "My heart about stopped."

"Pervert," Milo said, and Scott waggled his eyebrows. They'd managed, as best friends do, to find their old tongue and groove, to get past the weirdness of Milo as the Boy Whose Sister Was Murdered, although murder wasn't what it was officially called. The woman had pled down, so Milo was really more like the Boy Whose Sister Was Vehicularly Manslaughtered. Peggy used to razz him about being so particular, and he wondered if she would have thought that was funny. She was the same sister who used to wipe her boogers on his leg, so he guessed there was a pretty good chance.

He didn't want to admit it, but his memory of her was diminishing the tiniest bit. Last summer his mom had decided it was time to clean the carpets, and they'd moved the sofa away from the wall. He never would have guessed that the carpet had faded that much, but the patch underneath was a different shade altogether.

When he first came back to school after Christmas break, everyone had given him a wide berth, an invisible force field following him down the hall. Teachers put their hands on his shoulders; the lunch ladies gave him extra pickle slices for his sloppy joes, even though the rule was two. His aunt and uncle had sent George down for a weekend a few weeks earlier under the guise of lifting Milo's spirits, and George had left a small envelope of that white stuff "in case of emergency." Milo thought about it but eventually flushed it down the toilet, knowing even if he never got out of Gunthrum, that was no way to stay.

By mid-February, on his way to band practice, Milo passed Daryl Klaussen, who smacked an elbow into Milo's shoulder, then glared at him like it was his fault. For the next few days Milo had touched the tips of his fingers to the bruise to feel the dull pain. After that Scott had him over one Saturday for a sleepover, and they ate so many Little Debbie Oatmeal Creme Pies that Scott had thrown up in the toilet, and things were pretty much back to normal, at least on the surface.

"You get your algebra test back?" Milo asked, and Scott yanked a hand up and cocked his neck like he was hanging himself. "Yeah, me too," Milo said even though he'd gotten a B+. Junior high was so different from grade school, where they spent the whole day together in the same room. Now, after algebra, Milo headed to English and Scott to shop.

"You talk to your mom yet?" Scott asked, and Milo shook his head.

"I'll do it tonight." He'd spent the last three Saturdays at the Rosses', while Scott whined about wanting to be at Milo's playing Nintendo. Milo had gotten it for Christmas along with Super Mario Bros. and Duck Hunt and a TV for his room. It was quite a haul, although his family had celebrated the holiday a week late, and no gifts were worth his having to sit under the eagle eye of his grandmother, the only child opening presents as his father put bourbon in his coffee. His mom hadn't returned to her job at the hospital. She stayed home baking cookies and smoking cigarettes in the garage, her face hollow under her cheekbones.

He was anxious about asking his mom if Scott could stay the night. He imagined the sound of two kids upstairs making their kid noises—thumping, laughing, and the rising *blew blew, blew blew, blew blew!* of time running out on a game. It was amazing the decibel difference between two kids in a house and one. Milo alone kept the volume so low on his TV he had to sit two feet away. His father spent evenings at the OK, while Milo and his mother ate microwaved lasagna; then Dad came home and skipped dinner, blowing chunks sometimes in the middle of the night. None of them slept.

What was it like for his parents? Both up in the middle of the night with nothing to say, him hiding in his room because he didn't have anything to say either. After Cheryl Burke had come forward, Pastor Barnes told Milo this would be the closure his family needed in order to move on, but it wasn't like that at all. Nothing had closed. If anything, doors kept opening to other doors to other doors and other ways of thinking. That day Sheriff Randolph showed up at the church to tell Milo his sister was dead, he said believing and not believing were different sides of the same coin. Milo had puzzled on that a lot and thought he knew what it meant: not believing was still a form of believing, just in something else.

Scott got off the bus at his house with his little sister, a dull-faced girl with braces. He turned around as the bus pulled back toward the center of the gravel road, kissed his middle finger, and saluted Milo. Milo waved back. Since he'd started grade school, since his father first had him do chores on the farm, all Milo had thought about was the day he would leave Gunthrum. He'd graduate high school, go on to college, and finally move to a big city where no one knew who he was. Up and out. Upward and onward. He'd imagined his whole trajectory based on what he'd leave behind, but could he do that now? Had his parents lost too much? He'd ask his mom when he got home if Scott could stay the night. He had to.

Something sailed past his head—a jock strap or a sock, he couldn't tell—and Mrs. Dunn's burbly voice came from the front of the bus. "You stop that, you hear me? None of that." It never did any good. Scott told him that one of the first days she had driven, she'd cried because a fourth grader wouldn't stop running up and down the aisles and she didn't know what to do, and if a fourth grader could break you, you were screwed.

The bus turned onto Milo's road. Mrs. Costagan stood at the end of her lane, pulling the newspaper and a stack of mail from her mailbox, then slipping in a letter and flipping up the red flag. She had a smug look on her face as the bus came trundling forward. Milo wondered if she missed driving the bus or if the other students had noticed by comparison what a good job she'd done at keeping them in line and all the wheels on the road. The fifth-seat aisle had tally marks for the number of times Mrs. Dunn had stalled out the bus, not managing the switch from clutch to gas.

"Hey," Milo said, and picked up his backpack. "Can you let me out here?"

Mrs. Dunn caught his eyes in the rearview mirror. "I'm supposed to take you straight home unless I have a note from your mom."

"She forgot to write one, really. I'm supposed to stop at the Costagans'."

"All right, I guess." She slowed down, curving the wheel to the right. Milo clomped down the large stairs—"Have a good afternoon"—and Milo waved in return.

He walked over to Mrs. Costagan, who tucked the mail under her arm. "You have a note?" she asked, and he shook his head. "Figures. I'm surprised anyone's making it home anymore with that fool woman at the wheel." Her face was chapped red from the cold even though the temperature was higher today. How long had she been standing outside?

"How you been?" she asked, and he shrugged.

"Okay, I guess."

"Your parents?" He shrugged again. "I suppose that's about right." She made a show of flipping through the letters in her hand. Did Hal ever write her? Milo didn't guess letter writing was one of Hal's strong points. Milo knew that Hal had moved away, his farmhouse now rented to a young couple who had married in a shotgun wedding, two seniors a grade ahead of Peggy.

"You have any plans for the weekend?" Mrs. Costagan asked.

"I'm going to ask if my friend Scott can stay over Saturday night, but that's it." He was going to ask as soon as he got home, even if his mother was in the garage with her cigarettes.

"Nothing on Sunday?" He shook his head. "How about you ride your bike down to our place and Clyle can put you to work."

"Doing what?"

"It's a farm. We'll figure something out."

When he was little, Milo had loved nothing more than spending time in the garden, shelling a pea pod with his thumbnail and popping the peas in his mouth. At some point, though, it turned into work: pulling the weeds, emptying the slop bucket, eventually cleaning pens with a skid loader. Somehow Peggy had gotten out of all that; she'd sat in the kitchen drinking iced tea with their mother, learning how to bake bread. He didn't know if it was the work he hadn't liked or working next to his father. Maybe he'd get to feed those cute sheep the Costagans had now, the fat ones who hadn't been shorn all winter.

"Five bucks an hour," Mrs. Costagan added, and Milo's eyebrows shot up. That was his allowance for a week.

"Sure. Yeah, I'll do it. It'll have to be after church, though." Even though he no longer believed, it was an appearance he had to keep up. Living in Gunthrum had taught him that much.

"That'll be fine."

"Maybe you can tell me about living in Chicago," he said. Her face softened, and he wondered if she'd ever regretted leaving. He couldn't imagine why someone would choose to leave Chicago for a town like Gunthrum. What possible reason could someone have? "I want to live there when I grow up."

"Expensive city," Mrs. Costagan said. "This'll give you a leg up."

"I want to get an apartment with wall-to-wall carpeting. Even in the bathroom."

She shuddered. "You've never lived with Clyle." She smacked the short edge of the envelopes against the top of the mailbox to even them out. "Eleven o'clock work?"

"Yes, ma'am."

"For fool's sake, call me Alma."

"Alma."

"What?" she replied, and he furrowed his brows. "It was a joke. You said my name to test it out, and I acted like you were going to ask me a question. People assume I don't have a sense of humor, but they're wrong."

"I don't know. No offense, Alma, but that wasn't that funny."

She grinned and turned toward her farm, a hitch in her giddyup. "Damn cold," she said, and started walking. He was sure now that she'd been waiting for him down by the mailbox. Mrs. Dunn didn't drop kids off at a consistent time like Mrs. Costagan had, whom you could have set a watch by; who knew how long she'd been out there. Milo watched her walk away. He doubted she was a person who would turn around and give him a final wave; she wasn't what he'd call the friendly, sentimental type. Milo could still envision Peggy sitting in the kitchen, their mother swatting Peggy's arms to get her elbows off the table. Or Peggy with her legs flipped over the armrest of their father's recliner, a string of gum wrapped around her finger. Peggy on the volleyball court. Peggy popping a zit while leaning close to the bathroom mirror. All of these things had happened; all of these moments had existed. She would stop at seventeen, and in five short years he'd be older than she ever was.

His stomach dropped when, to his complete surprise, Mrs. Costagan did stop and turn around after all. He felt like he'd been caught spying on a personal moment, but she was just an old woman walking down her lane. She yelled something to him—*Be safe? You're great?*—and he pointed a finger to his ear. She cupped a hand at her mouth and raised her voice: "I said, don't be late!"

He nodded, and she turned back toward her farmhouse. There was no way he'd be late. He probably wouldn't even be able to sleep Saturday night he'd be so excited. Or maybe, just maybe, he'd finally sleep through the night.

Lamb Bright Saviors	*Skin*
Robert Vivian	Kellie Wells
The Mover of Bones	*The Leave-Takers: A Novel*
Robert Vivian	Steven Wingate
Water and Abandon	*Of Fathers and Fire: A Novel*
Robert Vivian	Steven Wingate
The Sacred White Turkey	
Frances Washburn	

To order or obtain more information on these or other University of Nebraska Press titles, visit nebraskapress.unl.edu.